10/09/12

This book should be returned/renewed by
the latest date shown above. Overdue items
incur charges which prevent self-service
renewals. Please contact the library.

Wandsworth Libraries
24 hour Renewal Hotline
01159 293388
www.wandsworth.gov.uk Wandsworth

L.749A (rev.11.2004)

SOPHIA BLACKWELL was born in Newcastle in 1982, read English at Oxford and now lives in London. She has performed her poetry at some of the UK's biggest venues and festivals and her first collection, *Into Temptation*, was published in 2009 by Tollington Press. Her short stories have been included in the Limehouse anthologies *Boys & Girls* and *Men & Women*. This is her first novel.

AFTER MY OWN HEART

Evie Day has never wanted a boyfriend – she's gay, out and proud, and as far as she's concerned, her life is perfect that way. But when her girlfriend leaves her for a leggy blonde, everything changes – her flat, her friends, her future – and she finds herself having feelings for an old friend, who just happens to be a man. To say that things aren't turning out the way she planned is an understatement.

With her best friend Jamie's Big Fat Gay Wedding looming on the horizon, Evie struggles to choose between her ex, her old friend, a new best friend in the form of a beautiful, chaotic burlesque artist, and a grumpy but distracting new flatmate.

All she wants is to find The One, but for Evie, thinking straight never did come naturally …

After My Own Heart

SOPHIA BLACKWELL

LIMEHOUSE
BOOKS

For Ella and Helen,
The Girls

Part One: Heartsick

Counting the Thunder

There are some people you feel sorry for. Not just the ones who've always had it bad. Not the earthquake victims and abuse survivors and anyone who happened to be in the wrong country at the wrong time, but the ones whose lives just don't go right. The ones who leave school trailing Girl-or-Boy-Most-Likely clouds but never figure out what they want to do, whose wedding photos are shamefacedly shoved in a drawer within two years of the ceremony, who never quite hit rock bottom but still don't manage to do what they came to do.

When I turned twenty-nine, I started wondering if I was one of them. Now here I am, sitting in a horseshoe of fold-out chairs full of people who woke up one day and decided something was wrong.

I'd like to say that I chose to be here, but I didn't. I'm here because Jamie, my best friend and ex-girlfriend, recently had her life overhauled by this mildly worrying group called The Path and asked me and my girlfriend Kate along with her tonight, 'just to check it out.' The Path encourages you to ask your mates to do this, but we're still horrified that Jamie asked us and traumatised that we're here.

Jamie is smiling like an aid worker and keeping an eye on us to check we don't bolt into the nearest pub. Kate's hardly said anything all night, but that's nothing new; she's hardly said anything for weeks. She gets depressed sometimes, I know, and this is one of those times. She gets up and goes to work every day, but still some days, especially on weekends, I come home and it feels like she's hardly moved. She can sit for hours when she's like this, staring at the walls.

I try not to worry. I tell myself we've got through this before – we can do it again. Winter makes people sad sometimes and this has been a long one. It's January, the sluggish, coal-scented early days of the year, and I know I can't be the only person on earth who feels relieved that Christmas is over, that all that enforced happiness, is behind us. Next year, I tell myself, will be better.

I'm over-compensating like the bargain-basement singer I am. It's hard to turn it off. I smile encouragingly as people with nametags spill the details of their lives, like I can't think of anything better to do with my Thursday night.

Our group leader is young, sharp-suited and so clean he looks like he's been laminated. Surely no one looks like this in London. His level of happiness is bordering on offensive; I consider it a victory if I leave the house without being mugged or forgetting my keys.

'I always thought I knew how to live, how to listen,' he tells us. 'I was a success at my job, popular, had plenty of money... but something was missing.' He pauses for effect. 'There were so many possibilities that I was missing out on. Now I've completed the course, I know what I'm committed to... being the best version of me I can possibly be. And now everything is amazing. *Amazing*.'

He looks like he's on the verge of orgasm. I could do without this, frankly.

I give him my best contemptuous stare but he beams back, unaware that he's being scorned. My world does not admit these squeaky-clean young men with their sleek hair and city pinstripes. I like dark, quirky things. East End pubs that look like they were burnt out in the Blitz and never redecorated, gay clubs with sweaty go-go-dancers' poles and posters for Porn Idol.

He passes out pieces of paper and tells us to start looking at the areas of our lives we could improve. Everything's neatly compartmentalised; health, career, relationships. The tick-boxes remind me of the forms I used to file back in my temping days in medical records. The ones for the children always upset me; they had little cartoons they could tick or circle to indicate their level of pain. Smiley face, frowning face, clenched face exploding with tears. I'm glad I don't have one of those forms; there isn't a face bad enough for my state of mind tonight.

Defiantly, I give myself decent marks; I can do that, I'm an adult now. Kate hasn't written anything. Our leader looks around and politely asks the red-haired Australian girl on my left to tell him what she's written. She starts talking about how she's never got on with her mother. I relax slightly. Maybe he'll never get to me. Mothers take up a lot of time.

I'll admit it, I'm not good at dealing with people's pain. One of our friends, Cathy, had just split up with her girlfriend after ten years, and while Kate was spending a lot of time with Cathy, I avoided her, like her sorrow was catching and my resistance was low. At my birthday party last September, Cathy had strode in, pale and drawn, declared her intention of getting completely plastered and sat in a corner gulping wine so relentlessly the air around her seemed to evaporate. She ended the evening hanging over our toilet while the guests made nervous jokes about peeing in the empty bottles. In a flat as small as ours, it's hard to avoid something that toxic. Pathetically, I tell myself that things might not be perfect, but at least I'm not Cathy Holmes.

Kate, Cathy, her ex-girlfriend Zoe and I used to be a foursome. We'd go to each other's houses for dinner and play at being grown-ups. Pub quizzes, Sunday roasts, endless games of Pictionary. Cathy and Zoe's breakup affected Kate and me like a virus, as if, once we'd seen it was possible, it seemed suddenly, horribly likely.

After another strained night out with Cathy, Kate had turned to me and said, 'You know, even if that happens to us, I still want you in my life.'

I panicked and blurted, 'You can't have me. Not like that. If we broke up, that would be it.'

It may have been naïve, but at the time, I hadn't known it was a choice.

Kate and I weren't getting on. She hated her city law firm job. She hated everything about it; the pressure, always watching her back about her sexuality, her creative leanings, the poetry she wrote and everything else that she couldn't talk about at the water cooler. She told me I was her real life, but something about the look on her face when she said that made me feel like she'd rather I wasn't, that she wanted something of her own.

She should have had something of her own. After all, I was always out singing, chasing my dreams in the back rooms of pubs with sulky boys and doll-dressed girls. Everything in my world's ironic. None of it's like this room, this stew of grievances and revelations. The idea that people can work on themselves makes me nervous; if I start admitting to myself my life might be better, it might fall apart, and so I keep telling myself to accept the imperfections in our relationship, to make a virtue of constriction and compromise, like most of the girls I know.

The red-haired girl with the mother issues finishes her story and hints that she'll sign up for the course. Our little preacher turns away, satisfied. Don't pick me, I think, for once in my life.

'And how about you?' He squints at me. Of course.

I wonder what he sees when he looks at me; unwashed hair, dyed black and bundled Rosie the Riveter style into a polka-dot scarf, the Camden girl's uniform. Skin-tight, straining cherry-print dress, bubblegum pearls and heels that could have your eye out.

'I'm fine.' I show him my score-sheet, like it means something.

He looks scandalised. 'Really? Fine? Everything's completely perfect?'

'Pretty much.' Jamie's looking at me like I'm not playing right. 'I'm only here with my friend. Because she asked me to. We both are.'

Look at me, Kate, I think. Back me up. Laugh at this with me.

Jesus, didn't I deserve to be happy? I'd never approached the world thinking it owed me anything; I was too much of a girl for that. I was grateful, a tad complacent maybe, bordering on the kind of smug-bastard cheerfulness usually only seen on celebrities and toddlers. On good days, I told myself that this, my happiness, was my contribution to the universe. On bad days, I knew that was basically crap.

'Everything's fine,' I say. It is, damn it. I've got the lot – a plushy PR job in publishing, a feisty, successful girlfriend, a flat – and outside the nine-to-five, my singing career's going pretty well. Even on the days when I suspect it's not, at least I'm not old enough to have outgrown my 'up-and-coming' tag. Not quite. I just have to keep slapping on the pancake makeup and playing in darkened rooms.

'Tell us a bit about yourself,' the boy in the suit says. Usually, people don't have to encourage me to perform. It seems ironic that it should be happening now.

'Look, I … I'm sorry, but I'm not really into this.' The Australian girl looks mutinous. God, she only sold her soul a minute ago. 'I'm just happy with what I've got. OK, it's not always been easy, I've probably got a few things that need working out, but …'

He pounces. 'Like what?'

'Well … my dad left when I was sixteen.'

'That must have been hard,' he says. 'What happened after that?'

'Well, I'm gay, so that wasn't always easy, though I think my mum might have been even more pissed off if I liked boys. Definitely the ones who got you knocked up at nineteen – like her. She was very beautiful. Still is. Used to be a model and general girl-about-town and she was way wilder than I'll ever be. She's not one of those creepy I-could-be-your-sister women, though. She knows she's my mum and she makes sure I know it too. She always had men beating the door down …' Suddenly, I feel as tired as I am. 'I don't see the point of this. I'm happy now. I grew up, got a job, got a girlfriend …' I indicate Kate, branding her, forcing her briefly into my life. 'I'm fine.' Then a moment of madness overtakes me and I hear myself say, 'The only thing that's not working is my relationship.'

I'll always remember how I said that. My problem. Well, it is now.

Kate gets up. 'I'm sorry,' she says, her voice cracking. 'I can't.'

I watch, disbelieving, as she walks out, leaving me with my ex and a room full of earnest strangers. One of the group leaders follows her out, a mumsy blonde who's presumably on hand to help anyone who cracks. I imagine people do, but it takes more than a temporarily mad girlfriend and a man who looks like the lead singer of a Mormon boy-band to break me.

'You see?' I spread my hands, vindicated, and get up to follow her.

Jamie puts her hand on mine. 'Let her,' she says. 'If you want to stay, stay.'

I don't want to stay. I didn't want to be here in the first place. But as the door swings shut behind Kate, I realise something scarier, given that I have nowhere else to go.

I don't want to be with her either.

I sit down, ignoring the stench of pity. I'm fine. Haughty, feisty, string of gritted pearls for a backbone, still my mother's free spirit, my father's Princess Eve. I just took my eye off things for a moment – that was all. I never was the kind of person you felt sorry for. But now, apparently, I am.

I stand in the street outside our flat, phone in hand. I don't know what's waiting for me but I don't think it's good. I just want a moment's silence first. It's cold enough for snow. Lyrics for a new song have been bumping around in my head since I got off the bus. Kate usually writes my lyrics – she's the poet – so it's odd that they should be springing into my head now. To calm them down, I'd taken out my work diary and scribbled them in the back: *Perhaps I should shut my face and just let some kind of grace unfold / but there's no coat, no leather, no fur / no joy, no glory, no her / it's the coldest day of the year / and nothing can make it any less cold.*

Freezing rain is coming down. The thunder's started, the sky rupturing above our street. Where will I go, if I don't go in? If I can't go home?

I count the beats between the thunderclaps, the way my mother taught me when I was small and scared. *One one thousand. Two one thousand. Three one thousand* – and then it comes.

I open the door, walk through the tiny hallway and turn into our bedroom.

She's sitting on the bed, knees hunched up, head bowed.

One one thousand. Two one thousand.
When did I stop paying attention? How can I take it all back?
She looks up at me, and I know this is it.
She says my name. 'Evie.'

Story of My Life

If I'd been directing the movie of my life, I wouldn't have chosen this rain; way too obvious.

Also, if I'd been in charge of casting, I'd have been the mistress, not the spurned woman. I'm in in the wrong story. I'm not dressed for it. My cherry-print dress is bright as a painted egg, black hair a forties crown of pin-curls that makes drag queens wince and smart-arses in the street shout, 'Oy, oy, love! Air raid!' as I stumble past in my four-inch heels. I might look like a very short, hungover transvestite, in fact it's a distinct possibility, but I don't look like anyone's wife. Never have. Perhaps that's the problem.

'You're going to hate me,' she says.

Standing beside our bed, I feel Amazonian, even though I barely scrape five feet without my precious red heels.

It's Cathy. I know it is. We'd talked about it. We'd tried. We'd argued for nights on end, but even as I'd tried to ban Cathy Holmes from our lives I knew it was too little, too late. Besides, I didn't want to fight for Kate. I wanted not to have to.

Being right for a change is strangely liberating. I'm high, already imagining what I'll do next what I'll drink, smoke, smash if I get really decadent. I've been scared of my own shadow for weeks, but now she won't even be able to tell me off for smoking. Strange, the consolations we give ourselves. I feel relieved, but not just that. I feel pretty, powerful, capable of wringing her neck, like the girl she fell in love with in the first place.

'I slept with Cathy', she says.

In my experience of melodramas, the mistress usually gets the best outfit. Furs, lacy negligees, heels named after weapons. Cathy does not dress like this; she dresses like an outdoor-clothing commercial. If you had to imagine the opposite of me, she'd be it; tall, blonde, pretty without a lick of makeup. That girl-next-door look, which I could no more pull off than I could fly.

'Evie, say something.'

'How many times?'

'I don't ... I don't know.'

'Yes you do. How many times?'

She pauses for a painfully long time. 'More than once. I don't know what it is, we just ... I didn't even think I wanted her.'

'Well,' I say evenly, 'you can have her now.'

And that's it. Our tiny, beloved flat, the mismatched collections of plates and cups, my books rubbing up to hers on the shelves, our space, our history, our future.

This is strangely boring. Maybe I'll break a few plates. This spurned woman stuff must have some perks and I've never liked those ones of Kate's mum's anyway.

I sit on the front step, smoking, drinking room-temperature gin. Mother's ruin, napalm for women, like I need that. How am I supposed to act now? Slash up her suits, fill the curtain rails with prawns? How do women behave in these situations?

I think back to long Sunday afternoons on the couch with my Dad watching old movies. That was how I got into singing, the old razzle-dazzle; you didn't need talent if you had style. You could be plain, you could be batshit crazy, so long as you could arch an eyebrow and pull off mink. It's a safe world, and I long to be back there with him. Snuggled into him, I'd breathe his scent; fresh wool, bergamot aftershave made just for him at an Oxford Street perfumier's. He was a bit of a dandy like that. Beneath the cologne was a sweet, fuggy undertone of vanilla tobacco. Even his cigarettes smelled clean.

My mother, Pina, wasn't interested in our matinee afternoons; these were the movies that she'd been brought up with in a stifling North

London suburb. She preferred painting angry, splattery paintings, trying to overthrow the government, flirting at dinner parties and losing me at Glastonbury for seven consecutive years.

'Look at you two,' she'd mutter despairingly, sticking her rusty punk-striped head round the door, 'Right pair of Judy Garlands. Evie, when are you going to start staying out all night and telling me how much you hate me? I'm sure I was doing that at your age.'

We'd flap our hands at her, and she'd huff like a stuck bull and lurch off up the stairs, muttering. We loved her though; Dad to the point of distraction in those days, me because I had no choice, and we never needed to say it. She knew. 'Dinner's in the ... supermarket,' she'd murmur, tripping over something – a cat, usually – on her way to somewhere else, and I'd lean back into Dad's chest, memorising the folds of an actress's gown, the way she held her highball glass, her smile.

I light my fourth cigarette. Inside, Kate's still crying. I'll have to go back in, but not right now. If this was a movie, if I was directing, if I was the star, what would I do?

Friday dawns, a glaring, shallow white. A blank canvas. Sleepless and sandy-eyed, my stomach in knots, I'm grateful to have a gig in another town tonight. My dissolute existence has its perks.

Kate follows me around, when she isn't crying in the bathroom. I'd never really known how small this place was until now, when we're bumping into each other at every turn. We lived here for years. What's wrong with us? It's like there's a dance and we've forgotten the steps.

I stand by the front door, knowing I've probably left something crucial, like underwear, but I can't spend another minute here.

'Where are you off to?' she asks, her voice subdued. She looks stunned.

'York. Took the day off and everything. I'm sleeping over at the organiser's house.' Another small comfort. 'You know how I'm, like, never here?' Bitterness creeps into my voice and I realise I'm mimicking her.

Jesus, who are we? Didn't we used to be friends?

'Do you have …' she says hesitantly, 'do you have everything you need?'

I stare at her incredulously and snarl, 'What are you *talking* about?'

Kate's face crumples and she retreats to the bathroom. I stand in the hall, wondering whether to go, but when it's clear that she's not coming out any time soon, I knock on the door. 'I'm going now.' I'm going to have an audience for this if it kills us both.

The door opens on her blank, red-eyed stare. 'Let me know when you get there?'

'Why do you care?'

'I still love you, Evie.'

'Clearly.' I move back towards the door with its raft of takeaway leaflets we haven't thrown out, my keys in the lock.

'I might have known last night was a bad idea,' she says. 'Can't believe I signed up.'

'You what?'

'Yeah. Fifty quid deposit. She kept talking till I gave in.' I wonder if that's roughly what happened with Cathy.

'You knobhead,' I say, almost fondly. 'You're going to get lectured by that twat again.'

'He is a twat, isn't he?' She gives me a watery smile.

'Yeah.' I open the door, step out. 'He is.'

I look back at her. If I'd have known this was our last moment of connection, I would have framed it, like my dad told me to frame the first money I got from singing. In true rock and roll style, the first money I got from singing was spent on petrol and a curry, but I remember that night just as well as I remember every night with Kate.

I'd had five years of her, from the night we met at that black tie party, the only two dykes in dresses. We fancied each other so much all we could do was laugh, frightened by our own good fortune.

If I close my eyes I can see her, not the shellshocked girl in the suit standing in the hallway with her eyes full of tears, but the glowing girl I'd met at Heathrow after her year in America. She was twenty-three and, Christ, she was beautiful then, even if she didn't know it, her face flooding with light as she walked towards me, gathering speed with every step that led me to this.

The Mothership

'I want to kill her,' Pina says again.

'You're not helping, Mum.'

It's Sunday morning. I'm staring at a laptop, which is showing us a selection of London 'studio apartments'. Their grimness is off the scale. I've been here before, flying from one fraught house-share to another. This time I'm just desperately trying to find somewhere I can afford which doesn't involve strangers who might have reasonable objections to me howling all night, every night, for the foreseeable future.

After the gig in York, where I'd spent Friday night sleeping on the floor of the loved-up lesbian couple who'd invited me, I'd arranged to visit Pina. She'd met me in her local, a dingy, cavernous pub where the old boys seemed to worship her, and ordered champagne, 'Darling, I believe in celebrating disasters.' She's still a fine-looking woman, with dark, grey-swirled hair and Apache cheekbones. Imagine Cher without the surgery. Back at her place, we drank some cheap red Bulgarian paint-stripper, accompanied by one of her usual semi-raw, garlicky casseroles, and a neat little spliff. It's always a bit disturbing to see your mother smoke dope, but that night I relished the distance it put between me and the world. We finished the night by dancing to the songs of other wronged women, belting their blues into the night as we jumped around her kitchen. Today we're both hungover and awkward, eating breakfast at a table strewn with Sunday supplements and cat hair. Two single ladies.

My mother told me that, when my dad left, the fact that I needed her was the only thing that kept her sane. She wasn't always easy to live with, though, from the first precious moments we shared, Pina staggering around with a dead leg from the epidural, alternately cooing to me and hissing not-so-sweet nothings at my father. She was naturally an insular person, an artist, who could have kept herself amused in a Thai jail (something she'd narrowly avoided in her druggy teens). Sure, she could be the life of the party, wreathed in cigarette smoke and men. I remember sitting at the top of the stairs, watching her with envy and satisfaction, knowing that this was one of the reasons she was on earth, what she came for. Pina needed an audience, but she needed, more than anything, to be alone. Even if she'd had a perfect, gravy-advert family, she'd still have been watching the clock, smoking on the back step, packing me off to bed when it was still light. Of course, we had our sociable times too; hours working together on murals, Pina teaching me to use a glue-gun or make a non-lumpy white sauce – but there were still times when I'd look up at her blanched, taut face and think, 'This won't do. We're going to need another person.'

I like my mother's new house. The rooms are a patchwork of different-coloured walls; one painted in a thick, warm raspberry pink, one covered in black wallpaper with white tulips, a couple collaged with the things she loves and dreams of. There are flyers for hundreds of gigs, pictures of me – vacant and hungover in a graduate's gown, twelve and doughy in one of Pina's old jumpsuits, in a strapless prom dress dancing with Kate – she hasn't taken that one down yet, but she will. A photo of Pina at my age stares at me, her wild dark hair bundled in a big polka-dot scarf, a cheeky, up-for-it look in her eyes that belongs to a more innocent time.

The house is chaotic, but homely. I shouldn't even have been in that featureless flat with its cardboard carpets and one-size-fits-all kitchen. I should have been somewhere like this, with soul. I should have been with my family, which pretty much consists of Pina. I know how much she means to me, and it scares me so much that I try to see her as little as possible.

'This one looks OK,' I say, hating the brittleness in my voice.

She peers nearsightedly at it. 'Too expensive. I mean, darling, for what it is? You could make a sandwich and have a wee without getting out of bed.'

I don't want to tell her they're all like that. The photos are half-hearted illusions, shot so a corner of striped mattress protrudes into the shot of the oven or sink. Everything seems so insubstantial, and still insultingly out of my price range. My salary would barely cover the rent, leaving me with nothing for essentials like caffeine, sparkly dresses and maybe anti-depressants.

'You shouldn't have to be worrying about this now.' Pina, looking as defeated as I feel, puts her hand on mine. It feels weird; for all her hippy-dippy trappings, we aren't very tactile, but I welcome it. 'Let her bugger off with her other woman for a while. I don't care if she owns the flat. Something'll come up, and she might as well stay out of your hair till it does.' She pauses. 'Or I can always have her killed.'

'Try not to have her killed, Mum.'

'What I don't get,' she says, pouring more mud-thick coffee, 'is that you were friends with this other girl, weren't you? The one she's messing around with?'

'Cathy. Yes, I was. I knew her first, actually. She used to live with Jamie back when we were still dating.'

'Ah yes, Jamie. Nice girl, I always thought. Pity you couldn't have stayed with her.'

'Yes, not a good time to get into that, really, Mum.'

'And so this … what is it, Cathy? Has she got anything to say for herself?'

'Yeah, she sent me a text.'

'What, that's it? Christ. You kids, really. What did it say?'

'Oh … I don't expect you to forgive me, I know what this is like, especially as it happened to me too, you don't have to reply … so I didn't. Can we talk about something else now?'

'What do you mean, it happened to her too?'

'Her girlfriend cheated on her. Bit ironic, isn't it? She started hanging out with us more after that. Well, with Kate, really. I thought we were doing her a favour. I was grateful, even. I was so busy. Lots of gigs and stuff …' the box-rooms on the screen blur in front of me and I swallow tears with another slug of coffee. 'I mean, I know it's bullshit, Mum, I know it might never get me anywhere, but it's still my life. She said I was never around, but I would have been, if I'd known. Hindsight's great, isn't it?'

'Bollocks to hindsight. You don't want to be looking over your shoulder the rest of your life. That's how it was with your dad.' She doesn't talk about him much, but all our usual rules are suspended today. 'I was like you in these last couple of months, except for me, it was a couple of years. Always trying to fit round him, hardly breathing, knowing something was going to set him off because he was feeling guilty about some groupie, another Simone de Beauvoir wannabe who wanted a piece of the famous poet. I was so young, so bloody young I can't believe it. I look back and I just want to smack him. I had really bad hair, too.' She looks me up and down. 'You don't. Bloody weird, that Goth black. Wish you'd let it get back to normal, but at least it's interesting. Your dad had me looking like a sodding newsreader.'

'It was the eighties. Everyone did.'

'Well, I wanted to look sophisticated, Left Bank, that sort of thing. I should have known better. It wasn't like he was some City whiz-kid, either. He was just a boy, thinking he was a big literary rock star …'

'Like me.'

'No, not like you. You are a star, Evie, and don't you forget it. Of course, you're a star whatever you do. Even if it's, I don't know, knitting or something.'

Apart from Pina, gigging is the one thing that's never let me down. Even though I've had some truly awful gigs in my life, even if it rarely fattened my wallet, I've always found purity in seeking something outside the ordinary world of re-runs and meal deals and other people's weddings. I couldn't tell Pina that, at the York gig, no one had really wanted to hear my bluesy angry-girl songs. They wanted to get off their pierced tits on poppers and dance to YMCA and I couldn't entirely blame them. As it was my first gay day out as a single girl, I'd been desperate to pull to know I still could, but I'd forgotten that quick, casual sex with a lesbian was as likely as cracking cold fusion. The scene hadn't changed much since my dismal teenage years. The gig had just reminded me of being young, horny and hopeful, heading off night after night and looking for love among the ruined.

I scroll down the webpage. 'Check this one out, Mum, too good to be true?'

She cranes over and nods. 'Yeah … scam written all over it, right down to the spelling. Aren't any of your friends looking for flatmates?'

'They're all shacked up themselves. Most people my age are. God, what if I never have that again?'

'Don't worry about that now, Evie.' She gets up and kisses me on the top of my head. 'You'll find somebody.'

Hungover and exhausted, I feel that vertigo tilt; I thought I already had. I've done my time, put the work in, but have nothing to show for it.

As Pina escapes to feed her half-Siamese, fully-mad cats who think they're guard dogs and hiss when I get between them and their mistress, I open one of the Sunday supplements and read an article about women having babies in their early twenties, saving their careers for later. The journalist lives in a world where this is an option.

The journalist's asking if this is some sort of trend. I don't think so. I know these girls. There's one in every class at every school, girls who excel at cooking and tennis and bargain label-hunting, with shiny hair and expensive smiles. They aren't a phenomenon, just creatures who found a place to shelter. Pina wanted autonomy for her only child, not Ugg boots and Princess on Board car stickers. I've never been encouraged to envy these fresh-faced girls, costumed for the shoot in bright dresses, babies slung on their hips like designer bags.

Suddenly, it seems as though every choice I've ever made – the gayness, the gigs, the big city, the job for an intern-filled company of fresh-faced, double-barrelled kids – all of it's temporary, flimsy. All of it's brought the wolf worryingly close to my door.

Pina's back, wearing a cat like a moth-eaten stole. 'I don't want you to go back today, but I know you're going to.'

'I don't even know if she's at home. Anyway, I've got an interview later.'

'What kind of interview would you have on a Sunday?'

'Just some groovy wanker's magazine that makes no sense to anyone outside the Hammersmith Flyover. Probably going to last two issues, but it's something to do.'

Pina looks unimpressed. While she's proud of my singing, she isn't bothered by things like this – celebrities glimpsed in basement clubs, dresses stolen from photo-shoots, or articles like this on 'My favourite places in London' for a new magazine called Old China that will no doubt make everyone throw it in a skip in disgust.

'Can't you put them off? Not as if it's urgent, is it? There's got to be more important things right now.'

'It'll just take an hour.' More than that, once I've slogged across town, but who cares? 'I don't want to change things around, Mum. Besides, today I'm just about capable of something like this. Probably be good for me.'

'OK, if that's what you want. But why don't you call her and tell her to be out when you get back?'

I stay quiet. I'm afraid to think where else she would go. Cathy's is the only place I can think of.

'I don't care where she goes,' Pina says, reading my mind. 'The damage is already done, isn't it? Tell her to sling her bloody hook.' Slang always sounds strange in her fruity boarding-school tones. 'You'll do that for me, won't you? Evie. You're not looking at me.'

I look down at the magazine again, then back from the young mothers to the thumbnail bedsit pictures with their fatal-looking gas rings. I don't trust myself to speak.

I'm not young any more. I'd thought I was in control, or at least that I'd made the right choices. I'd thought I had time.

The Memory of Hunger

I head towards Chalk Farm and Andra's Ice Cream, where we're having the photo-shoot. Sunday transport carnage means the Tubes are barely running. A litany of closures greets me as I stand sweating on the platform, followed by the coda, 'Apart from planned engineering works, a good service is operating on all other London Underground lines.' Good to know.

On the rail replacement bus, I text the journalist, Jean, to tell her I'll be late. It turns out that she's running late too, so much so that, as I sit at the counter and start on my sundae, I wonder whether she's actually going to show up. Still, I'm content for the first time in days, weeks . . . a long time before Thursday, anyway.

I can't remember when I last felt this relaxed. It's almost a relief to be able to give the rottenness in my relationship a name. I know I'll have to go back to Kate later, but for now, the long afternoon is mine. It feels like a reprieve to be sitting at the counter where I perched as a child, green feather butterflies from Pina's craft stash pinned in my piled-up hair. I could easily eat another sundae if the journalist and photographer need one for the shot. I could eat several. As my stomach slowly unclenches, I realise I could go on a real binge right now; I haven't done that in years.

Andra's Ice Cream, with its long smoked-amber windows, is the place my mother took me when she'd get nostalgic about her modelling days in Soho and Chelsea. It's where I went after I had my ears pierced at thirteen, after weeks of battling with Pina, defiant and scared at once, knowing I'd have to go home and show her.

Andra's was the place I treated myself after getting into University, shopping for leather-bound books I never read. It was the place I returned after graduation, unsure what lay ahead, the world spread out in front of me as I dawdled through my usual coffee and pistachio sundae, which the owners, remembering me from ten years before, garnished with a teddy-shaped wafer.

I met Kate a year later, when I was twenty-three, in the no-man's land between college and compromise. We were living in Brighton, where we'd both gone to University, but if we'd ever seen each other at a student party or drum and bass night, we couldn't remember. We met at a party for one of our friends, who was convinced he'd screwed up his Masters so badly that he'd better have a party before leaving town. He'd booked out one of my favourite haunts, the Boudoir Café, a tiny room with walls the colour of green tea and mirrors strategically placed to make the rooms look larger, confusing drunken undergraduates as they mistakenly tried to pull their own reflections.

Kate and I had already been in the working world for a year; torn between journalism and a law conversion course, she was knocking out articles for the local paper on small claims court cases and road rage. I was a filing clerk who spent every night singing and every weekend lost. The night ended with the two of us wrestling on my single bed, heaped with the dingy silks of saris and parade flags, kissing until our lips were smudged and swollen. Her dark, curly brown hair was short in those days, her body all hipbones and ribs. I straddled her knees and watched her in the half-light, waiting, as she laid her fingers between my thighs.

'Trust us to get it all backwards,' Kate said later, in bed. She was about to leave for an internship in America, writing articles for one of the papers. 'Three years in the same town and we meet three days before the end.' We were intoxicated with each other, going hungry day after day, our histories rising from our mouths and bobbing like balloons against the ceiling.

Once she left, I thought I'd go right back to my old bachelor-girl freedom, but I knew I wasn't the same. Part of me would be waiting. It still was.

The day after she left, I'd gone to Andra's and, later, sent her an email describing my sundae, bear-shaped wafer and all. Later she told me how she'd read it and smiled. 'I'd thought you were kind of a diva,' she explained, 'you know, with that glamour-puss thing of yours. But something about that teddy bear wafer made me think of you as a little girl. I realised you were human.'

Of course, she'd forget that when it suited her, but it makes me feel better that someone once knew there was more to me. I pick up the wafer and bite the bear's head off.

Jean eventually texts me. 'So sorry, running late. Family stuff. Any chance you can make it over to Maida Vale? Buy you a drink.' I'm tempted to tell her no – after all, I don't get paid for pretending to be famous and I could do it at home – but it's not as if I've got anything better to do. Kate's waiting, and I'm in no rush.

The second stage of my journey is a jerky, staggered mixture of rail replacement buses, Tubes, and walking, which is not a great idea in these green, pinching shoes. The butterflies in my hair are wilting, I'm sweating and I'm sure I stink; all last night's wine-and-weed excess is bubbling to the surface.

By the time I make it to the pub I'm exhausted and convinced that despite having taken up most of my afternoon this interview is still going to start: 'Evie Day is an hour late. What an arsehole.' As I power-walk down the street having an emergency fag, a gaggle of posh-voiced children shout at me, 'Excuse me, do you have a spare cigarette?' I'd smile, if I wasn't down an emotional mineshaft.

When I finally arrive, Jean's sitting at a table near the window with a bottle of red wine. 'Sorry,' she says. 'Hell of a day. My grandad's ill and I had to help my mum out. Anyway, not your problem. Drink?' She pours me a glass without waiting for a reply, not that my arm really needs twisting. 'The photographer's late too, the shoot he's doing for one of the other bands ran over because the frontman thinks he's fat and keeps sucking his cheeks in like David Bowie or something. Mind you, he's right. How are you?'

'Yeah, good, thanks.'

At least I'm unlikely to put on weight in my current state, but then, I no longer have anyone who's promised foolishly to love me if I gain ten pounds. Jean gets out her digital recorder while I sip the wine. It hits my tender stomach like battery acid.

'So, Evie,' she says. 'Any favourite places in London? I'd just like to know about a few of them. Stuff to recommend to our readers, you know…'

I tell this almost-stranger about my favourite parts of town. As I talk, I think about Selfridges Food Hall, Kate and me laughing at the prices and snatching up free samples on our way to the bagel counter. I tell her about our specialist bookstores full of unloved theatre histories, anarchist tracts and Afro-Caribbean romances; we'd battle to find the most obscure title and whoever lost had to buy the other a beer. I think of Soho boutiques, dresses patterned with cowgirls and rose-twined skulls, me rummaging through the rack and Kate checking her watch and smiling by the door. Kate-and-Evie. We discovered this town together, and now I'm regretting it.

'I think that'll do,' says Jean, cutting gently into my ramblings about the vintage crockery in Miss Molly's Cupcake Shop. 'Let's have a bit about you.'

I'd prefer to stick with cake stands for now, but I know the drill. 'Right, well, I've been gigging for about eight years, since I was twenty-one. I started playing at a night called Mighty Wonder in Brighton. Lots of musicians, hippies, DJs, guys in lumpy knitwear. I met this bloke from London on my second gig, he gave me my first ever paid show. He was my agent for a couple of years and then we parted ways, but he got me most of my connections, so it all worked out pretty well one way or another. Since then, it's been a fairly steady sort of thing, you know? I've done the stages at most of the major festivals and some pretty obscure ones too … and there's an album, finally. It came out about two years ago, and now people want to know when the next one's out ... I don't know, to be honest, I think I want to do something a bit different, but frankly I think I'd stick to just getting twelve tracks together.' It seems like quite an ambition, especially when I'm having trouble remembering to eat and breathe.

'There's something I want to know,' says Jean. 'I'm tone-deaf myself. How did you know, I mean, when did you realise you could sing?'

I find myself smiling. 'My parents always said I could, like when I was a kid. It wasn't something I thought about but I knew I could carry a tune. I got the lead in a lot of school shows on account of my voice, and I decided that what I really wanted to be was an actress. I couldn't imagine anything else, you know? I thought my life was going to be all backstage mirrors and flowers and lights and beautiful girls with lots of eyeliner.

Anyway, I was desperate to act, I'd spend hours watching old movies, musicals, that kind of thing ... my mother thought I was insane. Four-hour stretches every Sunday staring at some Technicolour nightmare. It was, I don't know, comforting. It was a weird time for me, being twelve, thirteen ... I knew I looked weird, for a start. Puberty was not particularly kind to me, and the puppy fat ... Jesus. I looked like a potato with eyebrows. All the actresses I used to worship seemed so thin and pretty, and so were most of the girls in my school. My mother also used to put me in these weird lumpy hand-knitted things that she could pull off, but I couldn't, and when I did try to dress like the other girls, I just looked like a middle-aged hooker.' I take another gulp of wine, steeling myself. Should I talk about Dad? No. Probably not.

'It was also about that time that I realised I was gay. So you could hardly blame me for wanting to spend my weekends eating chocolate and watching Judy Garland in a shiny dress. It made me feel like there was something else, something bigger, outside my life. But the moment I realised I could sing ... yeah, I know when that was.'

***

Girls' voices break too. I never knew before it happened, but they do. The voice I knew, high as a flute, capable of switching smoothly between one register and another, left me by the time I was twelve. Instead, what I had was something heavier and harder to predict, a foreshadowing of the deep, bluesy voice I'd end up with. I'd learn to love it, but at the time, it just felt like everything else. Uncontrollable.

I wasn't a looker in those days. I had dull, tangled hair, tender new breasts pushing against my thin school sweaters and a tendency to trip in the hallways while dreaming of another life. I was a mess. My thighs rubbed, sweat circles bloomed under my arms, and I bitterly resented all the girls around me who'd managed to hold onto their childhood bodies a little longer. I was still proud that I was the first girl in my class to get my period, though Pina had wept. 'You're so bloody young,' she kept repeating, before pulling it together and going to the corner shop for chocolate and nappy-thick sanitary pads. I could sense her confusion when she presented them to me – the chocolate was what she'd soothed me with when I was much younger than this. She was floundering, and so was I.

I had friends, other studious, slightly uncool girls, but my place in the school hierarchy was painfully low. My arch-enemy was a girl called Gina Lemmon. As 'lemon' was playground slang for 'lesbian' at the time, I took a lot of pleasure in her name, but I couldn't think of anything else about her that was flawed. Gina was skinny, flat as a board, mousy hair pulled back toffee-smooth, narrow-thighed in her designer-labelled jeans. In the trailing skirts I stole from my mother, mirrored hippy blouses and knuckleduster earrings, I scared the hell out of this anaemic girl, and she frightened me too. She was a junior version of Cathy Holmes, with her pinched lips and pale eyes that never missed a trick.

Gina decided that I was a lezzer, which at least meant she was smarter than she looked. After she shared this insight with my class, they treated me like I had a communicable disease. We didn't really know what gayness was; I certainly didn't. All I knew was that I was already indefensibly

Other, with my woman's hips, 'foreign,' features courtesy of Mum's Eastern European and Dad's Irish blood, my flannel shirts and velvet Goth gowns. When I think about that girl, I know how frightened she was. I know she was much braver than I am now.

I did have crushes on girls, but it wasn't a wildly sexual thing. I dreamed about closeness, soft skin against mine, a wisp of perfume in the air. I lived every day in a haze of longing that I channelled into sneaking cookies out of the tin downstairs as I watched another snow-flecked video. I had a crush on my drama teacher – odd when I think about it, she must have been younger than I am now. One evening after school, she took us into the music hall, so we'd all get a chance to sing. The other girls chose songs from the musicals – you'd think I would have, too, but instead I chose a song from one of my mother's blues albums, one we sang together in the car with the windows down. I wanted to make a statement.

On the first verse, I could barely hear myself. On the second, something happened; another kind of break, but a good one. Some people say they've been touched by angels. My angel was a fat, laughing black-winged one with whisky for perfume and grease on her chin. I had a voice big enough for cathedrals, dirty enough for brothels, and above all, loud. Within five minutes, I went from being a dumpy girl to a small goddess. It wasn't about me any more – my hair, my sweat, my temper, my dreams. It was something bigger than me. It was the closest to religion I'd ever get.

'Wow,' said the music teacher, when I was done. I felt wrung out, like I'd just run a marathon or eaten an eighteen-ounce steak. Or had an orgasm.

The class was silent, all of them wearing the same surprised expression. I looked at Gina Lemmon, saw the naked dislike on her face and grinned. Usually, she just ignored me. If she hated me, I figured I must be somebody.

Butterflies

Jean smiles and refills my glass. Something over my shoulder catches her eye. 'Hey,' she says, suddenly. 'Mate, you took your time – how fat *is* he, for God's sake?'

I turn around, and when I do, I'm glad she can't see my face.

I know him. Better than most people do.

Roshan Iyer. Long limbs, messy hair, skin the colour of strong tea, dressed in black from head to toe like a tortured artist should be. His shoulders seem broader than when I last saw him, and there are a few more scribbles of grey in his black hair, but otherwise, he hasn't changed.

I know I have. Trying to stay afloat and alive in this town, I've become more cartoonish. More tits, more hair, more makeup, as though I'm painting over the person beneath. I thank God that at least I had a reason to put on makeup today. I'm pathetically grateful for the green butterflies in my hair.

'Evie,' he says. I'd forgotten how deep his voice was, like it rumbles straight from his chest, bypassing his throat entirely. 'I didn't know it was you.'

'No, me neither. I mean, I didn't know you were doing this.'

'You two know each other?' Jean asks.

He smiles and ducks his head, a curtain of hair shielding his face. I'd forgotten he could be shy.

'Yeah,' I say, oddly aware that she's still recording. I think of my own voice speaking back through Jean's earphones and wonder if I'll sound shaky. 'We go way back.'

'Way, way, way back.' He folds himself into the chair next to her. 'We were at school together. I just can't believe this. Evie. Jesus, it's been forever, hasn't it?'

'A year.'

He nods, unsurprised. If I've been counting, so has he.

'Small world,' says Jean.

She's right. Between him and Kate, I can't think of a safe, untouched corner of this town. My only consolation is something that this man sitting opposite me once said, that London renews itself so often that if you set out to explore it, what you left would be different by the time you returned. He said it was like a body that way. Or a relationship.

I wonder how long it'll be before things stop reminding me of Kate. I'm sure they will, but at the same time I know that even years from now she'll be brought back to me by one small, stupid thing; a name, a T-shirt, a turn of phrase. I know, because that's what happened with him.

'Get yourself a drink, babe,' Jean says, handing him some money. 'And another for Evie. We're pretty much done here, so you can just take the shots and then we can chill.'

He nods and points to the bottle. 'More of this?' We make agreeable noises, and he gets up and goes to the bar.

'Big, isn't he?' Jean says. 'I keep forgetting. What do you reckon he is, six foot three?'

'Four,' I say too quickly. 'Six foot four.'

'Wow. Was he like that at school?'

I smile, distracted, rooting in my bag for my mirror and makeup, my armour. God, I wish this was a couple of weeks earlier, when I had that sheen of denial. Now is not a good time. 'Yeah, he's always been a big guy. Ten pounds when he was born. No wonder his mum didn't have any more.'

'Christ. That's stopped my biological clock for a few more years.'

He comes back with the wine, sits down and takes a few shots of us to warm up as we chat; I'd forgotten how the camera becomes an extension of him and you stop posing. Then, snap, he gets you, a stealth paparazzo, moving with surprising speed and economy for someone so big. He's more comfortable behind the camera than anywhere else, and more focused – his calmness, his need for perfection, are contagious.

'We need to move the bottles off the table. This was meant to be cheesecake stuff,' Jean frets. 'Now we've got her looking like a pisshead.' Appropriate, given that since Thursday I've been drinking at least a bottle of wine a night.

'Not here,' he says, meditatively, 'I'm going to perch her up on the windowsill. With that stained glass behind her, it'll be lovely.'

Lovely. I've missed it, that old-fashioned, slightly effeminate English of his.

'Health and safety, Rosh,' Jean warns, getting up. 'I'll check with the bar staff. I'm not getting chucked out before we've finished this disgusting wine. Hold on a minute.'

She goes, and we look at each other.

When you've missed someone like this, you want to be wearing black. Whippet-waisted couture. You want to have long, shiny hair, not a mass of black pincurls topped with little-girl butterflies. You want to be rich, loved, or at the very least, indifferent.

'This is amazing,' he says, and I feel something loosen inside me. It doesn't matter what I look like. It never did. 'How have you been?'

'Good,' I lie. 'Really good, yeah. Still gigging, you know, busy as hell. Still doing the publishing PR thing. How about you?'

Yeah, yeah ...' He points the camera at me. 'Just keep talking, tell me what's been going on ...' I steady my hands on the table and pray I won't start crying. 'Interesting look you've got there. Very ... feminine. Nice. God, you're ageing well, Evie. I don't want to think what that picture in your attic must look like.'

'I know what it looks like. I keep waking up with it stuck to my face.'

He laughs, puts down the camera and looks at me. 'Turn a bit to the right.' As I do, he says quietly, 'I've thought about this so many times.'

I know he asked me to move so I can't meet his eyes.

'Me too,' I say to the wall.

'I thought it might, but ... how did you think it was going to happen?'

'Not like this.'

'No,' he says quietly. Then, urgently, looking over my shoulder as Jean comes back to the table, 'I never knew so many girls in London looked like you. Not … not in a bad way. Even when it was just one thing … the hair, the dress, I'd remember …' he shakes his head, as though waking from a dream, and focuses on Jean. 'What did he say? Are we good?'

'Yeah, so long as we don't sue him if she falls off.'

'Works for me.' Relieved, I get up, almost knocking over my chair.

By the window, he and I stand facing each other awkwardly.

'Give her a lift,' Jean says, grinning. 'Put your big old self to some use.'

He moves clumsily towards me. I reach up, stretching all the muscles in my shoulders to get my arms round his neck. He puts both hands on my waist and gently lifts me. He is a shock against me; solid, breathing, alive. I feel a sudden, wildly inappropriate urge to wrap my legs around his long body. He smells the same. The force of it hits me like a knee to the groin. I'd forgotten how he smells. How could I?

I don't want him to put me down, but he does, gently depositing me on the broad windowsill, my feet in their ridiculous shoes dangling.

'Oh wow,' says Jean. 'That'll work.'

'Course it will.' He raises the camera. 'Don't smile,' he says softly. I didn't know I was.

I stay a little longer after they leave. I need a cigarette before I think about heading home.

I take out my phone and check the number he left me. I deleted it so many times, but even when he'd text me out of the blue I knew it was him; somehow, against my will, I learned to recognise those last two digits, and even in text-message form, I knew his voice.

A text from Kate blips up. 'Are you coming home tonight?' Feeling leaden, I text back, 'Yes. Be there in an hour.' You're not the boss of me.

Roshan. Today, of all days. He was a couple of years above me at school, and hung out with me – a younger girl, and not one of the prettier ones – because we were both freaks. I was just growing out of my dumpling phase and into my Gothic years, but he was always gorgeous, towering above the teachers with his vulnerable wrists protruding past his frayed cuffs and a serious five o'clock shadow. He'd do, I thought, or at least he'd distract anyone from wondering why I didn't have a boyfriend. The girls around me went crazy. 'Oh my God! Evie fancies Roshan! Evie! Evie! How many phone books do you stand on to get off with him?'

It seemed easier than the alternative; that I just wanted to be mates with this tall, gangling, messy-haired boy. We spent our lunchtimes hanging out in the music block doing foul-mouthed routines from the 18-rated comedy videos that Roshan's cousin Dil sneaked out of his dad's shop and declaring our allegiance to Kurt Cobain on our bags with black markers. We shared our first bong together, followed by a family-sized pack of crisps, one bag after another as we stared at a grainy video of *Sid and Nancy* in his grey and red striped boy's bedroom. Afterwards, he doused the place with air freshener and I slipped past his mother in the hallway, mouth swollen, eyes down, stinking of burning cities.

We had the odd wet snog tasting of salt and smoke, a little fumbling; sometimes it worked, sometimes not. It seemed unnecessary, besides the point, as though we'd gone straight from being children to an old married couple who no longer saw the point in sex. For all our intimacy, our lives stayed separate. We saw each other's need for space, even celebrated it. I liked that he shared my only child's surprise that there were other human beings in the world.

I went out with him when he took photographs. He seemed particularly interested in images of loneliness and abandonment; I never asked why, you just wouldn't. We didn't always fit – the girl who loved strutting on stage, and the boy who liked life through a lens. I'd hum melodies to work into songs while he captured old road signs and sticky-faced children, a tramp drinking Special Brew in an I Heart London baseball cap, a lasershow of headlamps at night from a motorway bridge he shouldn't have been standing on. I knew my place in Roshan's world, but I'd never stopped wondering if I could change it.

Another text from Kate. 'Looking forward to seeing you.' In spite of the dread, I know what she means. I miss her. I'm used to having her in my space – the way she moves, the songs she hums, the scent of her skin. I can't imagine putting anyone else there.

'You can sit down if you like,' says someone next to me. I turn and see a middle-aged, heavy silver-blonde woman, her hands in leather driver's gloves, having a glass of wine and shielding her cigarette from the rain. Her voice is pukka, imperious, like my mother's.

'Have a fag,' she says expansively, as I hover. I sit down and relax, and we talk for a while about smoking's guilty pleasures and our pariah status. 'Oh, I don't give a damn. Life's too short to deny yourself,' she says. 'How was your day?'

'Interesting. I'm not sure I should have got out of bed.'

'Me neither.' Her face suddenly crumples, and she looks like I feel.

'I'm sorry,' I say. 'You can tell me about it if you want.'

She tells me about the fight she's just had with her husband, who's in a wheelchair inside. I'd seen him earlier in the pub, watching silently as Roshan hoisted me up onto the windowsill, briefly airborne. 'I have to take him home,' she says. 'It's been like that for years. I have to take him everywhere, so I can't just say, right, fuck it, I'll see you at home and storm off.'

She's a bit pissed, but it's more than that. Clearly she's just in a world of hurt that she can't see a way out of. 'You can go anywhere,' she says, not bitterly, just acknowledging a fact. 'You can go home, walk out of here, do whatever you want.'

I imagine her husband sitting inside, perhaps wondering if she'll come back, perhaps starting to panic. Not showing it. Waiting.

As I start on another long journey back, I feel like I just ran into some kind of oracle, telling me, 'Hang on in there a while longer. You're free now. Even this isn't all bad. You can go anywhere.'

Bright Young Things

Right now, the best thing about singing in the back rooms of London pubs is that it gives me something to do with my evenings. If it wasn't for the promoters that Kate and I used to make fun of, I would have no purpose. The show must go on. Still, it's not like I'm Judy at Carnegie Hall. I'm Evie Day, in a Kilburn pub, wearing another gaudy Camden Lock dress, having a drink with Roshan and pretending that my audience is going to show up.

Another good thing about these low-key gigs is that, because I'm meant to be working, it feels safe to bring him along. I've always loved the company of men, but not being the uncomplicated girl-next-door type, my relationships with them tend to be fraught. Some men have chased me for months, dumped their girlfriends, brought me petrol-station flowers night after night; some have taken one look, muttered 'Jesus,' and run away. Still, I honestly can't say I've spent much time worrying about men. Tonight, the whole set-up feels pleasingly innocuous. Introducing him to my small-time world feels like having someone over to play; not like a date. Definitely not like a date.

I'm still embarrassed that more people aren't here. The event organisers and the MC, who looks like the kind of girl who'll forget my name, are whispering by the door, occasionally looking forlornly down the stairs. There are a handful of punters getting restless, but the room is too empty to start playing. They're always the same, these gigs. 'No money, I'm afraid, but we can give you a couple of beers, and it's a lovely crowd. Bring your friends!' No one ever knows how to work the lights, mics, till, or crowd, and I usually have an existential crisis or two whether I'm playing to five people or five hundred.

Still, at these indie-kid nights, at least there are always plenty of lollies, crayons and Lego to keep us all amused. It helps me feel like I'm still young, and the fact that I'm sitting next to an extremely large thirty-one-year-old man biting his lip like a child as he builds a Lego truck feels somehow comforting.

'When are you going to get famous so you don't have to put up with this?' he asks mildly.

'How about you? You're a great photographer.'

'Everyone with the technology thinks they're Ansel Adams these days.' I've managed to get past his usual self-deprecation to learn that he's teaching a little, on a Master's course – 'Bunch of spoilt brats with no direction. I feel right at home. Still, keeps me out of trouble.'

As we watch the organisers struggle with the PA system, Roshan tells me he's taken up DJ-ing. I stare at him incredulously.

'What kind of thing?'

'Oh, a mix, really… ambient, electronica, bit of dancehall … sometimes I even steal my mum's old sitar records and mix them in.'

'But Rosh … you were always such a geek at school.'

He smiles. 'Live technology expert, if you don't mind. The geeks will inherit the earth.'

It's not that he doesn't have an ego – he's an artist, of course he does – but something, whether it's an Asian thing, a male thing, or a more instinctive fear of the evil eye, has made Roshan pathologically modest. We have talked, easily, for hours, but still I've noticed that, while I've told him all about me, Kate, and Cathy Holmes, I have very little idea of his life.

'Do you think this gig's going to start any time soon?' he asks.

'Probably not.'

'Wine?'

'Yeah, go on then.'

'Small? Large?'

I look around at the almost-empty room. 'Pint?'

He smiles and goes to the bar.

I try not to drink before gigs, but the waiting is stressing me out. I try to relax by driving his Lego truck through a slick of beer, making a five-year-old's brrm-brrm noises. I have truck envy. Like a typical girl, I've built a Lego house. All I can think about is finding another home.

'You can always stay with me for a bit.' Roshan's finally back with the wine, sloshing a generous helping into my glass. 'I know it's been a while, but you're always welcome. And you can't be enjoying still living with Kate.'

'I'm not. But I think I can stick it out until I find somewhere else. It'll be fine.'

Evie, Queen of Denial. I remember Pina was like this when things went wrong with Dad; I know it was awkward for her to swallow her pride, but it was still strange that, months after he'd gone, he was still, 'my husband.' It set my alarm bells ringing, my usually straight-talking mother pretending he'd just popped out for some tobacco.

I want to stop talking about this. 'I like your truck.'

'I like your house. What's that on the roof?'

'State-of-the-art security system.'

'You do think of everything. Is it … you know, OK? The two of you?'

'For the time being.' It's hell. Def Com Three, red-alert, underground-bunker hell.

'Right, yeah, well …' the MC, lumpy in a hot-pink dress, is fumbling with the mic. 'Looks like we're going to start.' Oh joy.

Roshan takes a gulp of wine. 'Hello Glastonbury.' He smiles, full lips parting to reveal the chipped front tooth that always melts me. My lovely, imperfect boy, another misfit among the Great Unsigned. He's had a couple of photography shows, been chased by some art dealers and made a couple of big sales to members' clubs and restaurants, but business has been slow since he fell out with his agent. When he refused to put his work in for a prize because he didn't think it was good enough, the guy dropped him. One of these days he'll make it, and maybe I will too, but on bad days we know we're not much better than anyone who's ever created a website to show off wedding snaps of their mates or christened themselves a 'singer-songwriter' after two open-mics in their local pubs. Bright Young Things, we ain't.

'Shut up and keep drinking,' I mutter as the MC stumbles over my name.

Once I get up there, something great happens. I find myself truly inhabiting the songs for the first time in ages, feeling the hot stew of emotions that's been plaguing me all week but not letting them take over, not letting them take any more from me. Even my anger becomes beautiful, straining in my voice like dark, bottled blood, the *fado* music of old, black-dressed women in hushed clubs. I had been scared that this, the thing I love best in the world, would be lost to me too, but it's not. Thank God, it's not.

The thing is, Kate wrote all my songs. I was the voice, the window-dressing, but the words were all hers. It used to make me feel closer to her,. Even if we were fighting or I was miles across town, those words were a thin chain between us, pulling tight. If she was there, our eyes would meet. I would raise my head and catch her eye, watching her try not to smile.

I have all the lyrics she wrote before the writer's block that descended on her like a paralysing fever, along with the depression. I sense that she won't be asking for them back, but I'll have to write my own songs in future. This would scare me more if I didn't have more pressing things on my mind, like getting a roof over my head.

I know I can't keep singing her words for ever; they feel wrong in my mouth now. Sometimes, I almost forget that. I greedily claim them, relish them between my tongue and my palate. They're my inheritance, but I know she isn't going to be writing my next album. Her name won't be in the liner notes. She won't be in the shadows, leaning against a wall, waiting for me to send her words out into the listening world.

When Roshan hugs me and whispers in my ear, 'You made tonight, Evie. Thank you,' I almost cry with relief, but instead, I kiss him on the still-stubbly cheek and get the Tube home, trying to absorb the fact that the woman who put those beautiful words in my mouth doesn't have anything more to say to me.

A Lesbian Sandwich

'Everything ends,' says Jamie, offering me a forkful of carrot cake. 'Whether you want it to or not, it's the natural order of things.'

It's Friday, and we're in our favourite deli, making the most of our lunch hours for once. I know what she's saying makes sense, but I'm finding it hard to take comfort from it. I find myself constantly clicking on to websites about being dumped where twilight hordes of the damaged offer me little consolations: a whole bed to spread out in! No one telling me what to do! And, of course, time with my friends – the friends I lost by retreating into a couple-shaped cocoon, or who used to hang out with us both and are finding things somewhat awkward.

My ex, the soon-to-be-married Jamie Silverman, falls into this category. She's looking great today in a black suit and olive-green shirt, her dark hair slicked back and her skin glowing from a pre-work gym session. If we didn't go back such a long way, I'd have to hate her, but I love her too much and anyway, Jamie and her fiancé are a welcome island of rationality in a sea of lesbian dysfunction.

We've been talking about her wedding, which is just over a month away. Almost as soon as we'd sat down, she'd asked, 'You and Kate are OK to be in the same room, aren't you?' I'd nodded sulkily, thinking that even if we were throwing crudités at each other, they'd either be too euphoric to notice, or they could just glance pityingly at us and think, 'There but for the grace of God …'

'Even if you spent most of your lives together, this was always going to end one way or another.' Somehow, when it comes to Jamie and Susie, I can't even imagine death getting in the way. Given Jamie's organisational skills, I can see them calmly checking out together rather than letting sickness, accidents or recently dumped dykes get in the way.

'I know, but did it have to end like this?' I ask pathetically.

Jamie shrugs. 'You don't have to forgive her. I've told you I'm not choosing between you; I'm still Kate's friend, but that doesn't mean I agree with what she did.'

'I'm just so angry, Jamie, it's exhausting.' The rage is like a fever in my blood, whispering under my skin from morning to night. 'I want to hurt them.'

'Yeah, I can get that, Evie, honestly. But what good would it do?'

'Why do you always have to be so bloody rational?'

'You need someone to be rational now. You look knackered. I mean, that's not surprising, but . . . you're not sleeping, not eating. You look all scrawny...' she smiles cheekily. 'And you know you looked a lot better when you had boobs.'

I gesture to my lunch; I'm trying to look dignified while eating a large foccaccia sandwich, which is difficult. Kate and I are currently alternating between not eating and trying to soothe ourselves with junk food. It's one of the things we're still managing to laugh about. Last night, I even cooked for her; one of her old favourites, pasta with white beans. Moments like this feel surreal, like we're sharing a fever dream.

'Why don't you stay with me and Suse? The spare room's all made up ... I'll cook for you. We'll even watch those god-awful old movies you like.'

'No,' I say too quickly. 'Thanks. I've got things to sort out. House-hunting, that sort of thing ...' I want to push the pain down as far as it'll go. Once it starts affecting me, that'll be it – they'll have won. Besides, Jamie and Susie are just too in love for me to handle right now.

'How's the house stuff going?'

'Yeah, all right.' Everyone's right. Estate agents *are* bastards. I'm spending my evenings being chauffeured around town in branded bubble cars with blondes called Sophie and men with too much aftershave who tell me how terrible the market is and ask, 'So, why are you moving then?' I can tell they're not sure what to make of my manic cheer, limited budget and shellshocked eyes. They drag me to look at flats I can't afford, or ex-council flats in currently-council buildings wreathed in iron grids, hip-hop and the barking of Japanese fighting dogs. The bedsits reek of age and sadness and I'm sure someone recently died in at least three of them.

'I saw Cathy the other night.' A gut-deep shiver shoots through me. 'She said she texted you,' Jamie says evenly. 'You didn't text back, I take it?'

'No, I didn't. Why should I? Anyway, she said she didn't expect me to, so she's still at least half in touch with reality. Unlike Kate. Half the time she's pretending that none of this ever happened. It's enough to drive you mad. I think she *is* trying to drive me mad.'

Jamie says quietly, 'I didn't know, of course. I mean, I don't know what I'd have done if I did. Did you, you know, suspect anything?'

'Kind of. It's hard to tell. It seems so obvious, but then again, it would now ... I used to take the piss out of Cathy a bit. It was when Kate started defending her that I knew.'

I hate to think how it must have happened. The glances they held for too long, an accidental touch, the tension building between them. It must have made them feel important for a while. Somebody wanted them, these two bruised humans, while I was running around town singing love songs about other women and forgetting to buy milk on the way home.

Jamie sips her decaf and stares out of the window. 'Cathy's a total mess.' It must be nice, luxurious, to let go and wallow. 'I know it's not your problem, but that business with Zoe really screwed her up. She doesn't trust anyone now. And she feels so guilty about you. Even a month ago, I'd tease her about Kate, and she'd start crying. I did wonder, but ...' Jamie looks out of the window, avoiding my eyes. My heart pounds. 'She told me she was sick of being the nice one, never getting what she wants.'

'Well, I hope she feels better now.'

'I don't think so.' Jamie signals for the bill. 'Let me get this. Any ideas about where you're going to live? Zoe's looking for somewhere ...'

'No,' I say quickly. 'I mean, thanks, but no.'

She nods. 'Fair enough. Last thing we need is a lesbian love quadrangle.'

I want to ask how she can stand the drama, why these women crave it. I don't; I just want what I had. I know it wouldn't be impossible to get it. We could salvage this, but I don't want to. I want her to have loved me enough in the first place.

'Evie, I want to ask you something. Listen, Susie and I have been talking, and well … we want you to write us a song. For the wedding.'

Jamie's smiling as my heart sinks. Is she really expecting me to write a love song?

'Everyone's doing something. We're going to have a big pot-luck and people are bringing instruments, so we can all jam together… and I thought at the ceremony, you could sing something for us?'

Her all-encompassing happiness trumps my darkness like rock blunts scissors. 'Sure, Jamie. I'll give it a go.' I can tell she'd like more enthusiasm. 'It'd be an honour, really.'

As we kiss goodbye, I watch Jamie taking me in, assessing my big sunglasses, lip-gloss, freshly washed hair, new black ballet flats, and reassuring herself that I must be all right. As she walks back down the street, I fight the urge to run after her and admit I'm not.

I feel like I'm being punished for trying to be strong. Cathy, with all her shyness, has stolen my life. I haven't shed a tear in front of my friends. When I tell them it hurts, it feels like I'm lying. It's like they think I'm cheating, or they're wondering if I'm secretly relieved. They think I'm hard. Cold.

I'm not – just proud. And it hurts every time I think of the two of us on our first holiday above a gay sauna in Amsterdam, naked on the bed in our tiny room, eating bread, cheese and apples, sharp and yeasty in our mouths, our limbs warm with sweat, Dutch boys talking all night outside. It hurts when I think of us in a bare room, so excited about our new life, our new, as yet unlived-in flat. It hurt last night when she came in, a little drunk from an evening out – probably with Cathy – and hugged me. It hurt when we lay in each other's arms this morning and she said, 'I've missed this,' as though we'd only had a fight. She blows me a kiss in the morning and it feels as though we can be normal again, and those moments are far and away the worst.

Cooking with the Mafia

When I get back from lunch, my boss Amanda beckons me into her office. Amanda Garvey is a size-six blonde who rules the Frederick French PR department with a rod of iron. I used to want to be her, not only because she spends her entire life having lunch and never puts on a pound. Eighteen months into my job as publicity manager for our non-fiction trade division, I no longer want to be Amanda Garvey, because she's elevated obsessive-compulsive disorder to an art form and the editors have christened her Rain Woman. Amanda doesn't shout – she doesn't need to. One stare from her and my hair spills out of its chopstick-fastened bun, my coffee cascades into my lap, the top of my pen shoots across the room and lands in a plant. She's not really the person I want to see right now.

'Evie, have you got a moment?' she asks sweetly.

'Sure.' I get up and walk into her office, where a silver-framed picture of Amanda and her fiancé sits next to the computer. Everyone around me seems to be married, or about to be.

'How's *Cooking with the Mafia* coming along?'

'Fine. I think we'll be getting some coverage in *Vision*.'

The books I handle are all faintly ridiculous, but they sell – provided we're the first to get into the bookshops. We work fast, pile high and sell cheap.

The lack of public interest in *Cooking with the Mafia* is incredible. Not because it's a bad book, but there's only so much you can do with a recipe featuring a horse's head.

'Is that it?' Amanda says – quietly, as always – and I feel myself growing cold. 'Didn't you say something about getting it in *Scarlett*?'

I did; I was just hoping she'd forgotten. Good news was hard to come by, and so I'd blurted out my one potential coup of the month before I'd really sealed the deal. Their head of department had agreed to it, but almost before I'd turned around I'd been bumped down the food-chain to a junior who hummed and hawed and vacillated for weeks of cheery phone calls and delicately worded emails, before telling me it wasn't happening.

Any sane Sloane would know that this is not a rarity in the world of PR, but it isn't meant to happen on Amanda's watch. Things don't go wrong in her world. A couple of years older than me, she's far more settled, with a large, sparkly rock on her finger and a rich, if rather odd-looking man who takes her to wedding fairs at weekends.

'They pulled out of it,' I say, trying to meet her eyes. It would be easier to stare at a dead rat, a car crash, Amanda's fiancé's wide, flat arse sticking out of a rugger scrum …

'I've told the directors now,' she says, in the tones of a low-rent Bond villain. 'Now I have to tell them it's not happening.'

I wait for this to be over so I can go back to my desk and look at more floor-plans of places I can't afford to live in. Amanda knows about my situation, but only vaguely. I'm not comfortable with telling her the full, gory details. It would feel like going to the dentist. Naked.

'It's not just that, Evie,' she says, her voice softer than usual. 'This isn't easy, because I know you're working hard, but I have had some comments about your performance.'

My skin goes from cold to Arctic. This isn't happening. I never even got a bad report at school. Despite the bad-girl look, I am not on good terms with trouble.

'Some of it's just the usual nitpicking, of course, but I've already had to pass on some of the projects I was hoping you'd do to the juniors. I can't give them to you when you're obviously so snowed under, can I?'

I swallow hard. 'Is there anything else?' I realise I'm covering my mouth, like I don't trust my voice. I bring my hands away, covered in jammy smears of lipstick.

I realise she's painfully uncomfortable. I know things have slipped recently. 'Well, you've been late a lot over the past couple of weeks, and you've seemed distracted …'

I know things haven't been going well. I'd been having paranoid fantasies about getting fired, the odd work nightmare here and there – but generally I told myself that it was OK. And it is, in a way, especially given that getting out of bed feels like an achievement. The mornings are the worst. I wake up, jangling with energy and fury, and by the time I reach the office I'm a sweaty, irrational nightmare.

'I want to take a closer look at your workload,' Amanda finishes. She's a braver woman than I am; I don't want to look at it. I smile weakly and look around at the framed book covers on her walls. 'Evie,' she says, her voice lower than usual, 'you can ask for help, you know.'

I can't. If I asked for help, I would dissolve. I would melt into a Wicked Witch pool on her oatmeal carpet. I would start crying and never stop. I nod, give her a big Mafia smile and strut back to my desk, praying for a coronary on the way.

I look around the office at the other girls. The women around me seem to be getting younger; some of my juniors look like they're barely in high school. It's not just the uniform of ballet pumps and puffy skirts, but their skin, their hair. Feeling like Joan Crawford in my pencil skirts and arched shoes, I eye them covetously. *You don't need that youth. You're not even using it.* I'm going to be hard-faced and brassy and people will feel sorry for me – 'Yes, bit of a shame really, never got over it. Apparently she used to be quite pretty. Anyway, what colour are you having for the bridesmaids?'

I don't want to know how many of these girls have boyfriends, or significant others; I can't stand to hear women my age referring to their lovers as 'my other half'. I was never, for better or worse, Kate's other half. Or, worse, 'my partner'. Why would a straight person ever want to call their lover a name for queers, businesses and cowboys? Bloody straight people. Coming over here, stealing our euphemisms.

God, I need to work, need to think. 'You are not all right,' Roshan had told me the other night with his usual Zen simplicity – and even though it was manifestly true, I wanted to punch him. Thankfully I'm too short to reach his face.

I check my phone and, speak of the devil, there's a text from him. 'Evie, are you free tonight? I need a favour.' Thank God. For once in my life, there's nothing I want more than the company of men.

The Pin-Up Parade

When I arrive at Roshan's class, he greets me shamefacedly. Clearly, my services are no longer required. He told me on the phone that one of the models for this evening's class had dropped out, but then Jack, the other tutor, also called someone. She even got here first. I'm not sure why I'm surprised.

It only takes one glance at her to see that I've been outclassed. She's lying on a threadbare couch, in a black corset and frothy white skirt, her throat and ears dripping with jet. She glows out of the darkness as if her skin has some kind of luminosity, like a vintage fabric they just don't make any more. Her dyed red hair glows against the couch's worn velvet like a pool of fire. She's stunning. Even with my recent heartbreak diet, she makes me feel like a heifer.

The photographers are milling around, crouching worshipfully on the floor in front of her, offering her props which she looks at like a bored starlet. In the background, the eighties rap they're playing shifts into a raunchy, visceral jazz so perfect for her that she could have changed the track with the tap of an exquisite finger.

'All right,' she says, in a surprisingly strong Northern accent. 'What do you think of this lot then, eh? They don't just want one gorgeous lass, oh no. Got to have two.'

Roshan grimaces self-consciously. He's looking delicious today, sleeves rolled up to his elbows, all embarrassment and tousled bed-hair. 'Sorry, Vi. Misunderstanding.'

'Who's this then?'

'This is my friend Evie. She's going to be modelling with you tonight.'

'Well, I don't share the spotlight with just anyone, y'know.' She gets up and looks me up and down. Then she pauses, takes off her black satin elbow-length gloves, and hands them to me. I've never really known what 'throwing down the gauntlet' means until now.

She turns round to the room of photographers, an exotic butterfly among grubs. 'Right, let's do this! I've got an hour before I get hungry again.'

'Incredible appetite,' Roshan murmurs as they scurry into place. He perches me on the arm of the couch. 'She's already had a cheeseburger and fries and two bags of sweets. Like, the massive ones you get at the movies. I think she's bulimic. Or mad.'

'I heard that,' the goddess murmurs, eyes half-closed. 'And he hasn't even introduced me. Bloody rude, these artists. I'm Vi.'

'Violet?'

'Vinyl. I saw it in one of the markets back home. Out shopping with mam on a Saturday morning, I see it on one of them big fabric bolts, 'Vinyl Lace.' She smiles, and I realise she's younger than I thought she was, maybe even younger than me.

One of the girls offers Vinyl a red feather boa, which she takes greedily. She wraps it around her shoulders and poses, squeezing her small breasts together to create a cleavage. Then, bored with it, she motions for me to sit down beside her and wraps it around me.

Roshan crouches to take a photo of me and I feel it again, that sense of being truly seen. I've spent the last week packing, cutting the ties of my relationship with slow, delicate snips. I am removing myself from my life. Sometimes, I feel surprised that I'm actually here; but on the couch, with him in front of me and this crazy girl next to me, I know I'm not only alive but in colour.

As I sit opposite Vinyl Lace in the pub, all I can think is, *she's so beautiful.* She even looks amazing in girl-next-door drag – faded jeans, flat boots, a white vest that clings to her cupcake-sized breasts and some kind of camel-coloured top, what the hell would you call it – a gilet? – It's the kind of outfit Cathy Holmes would wear, but what would look sensible on Cathy looks audacious on Vinyl, a plain frame for her apocalyptic beauty.

I'd dragged Vinyl, Roshan and his teaching buddy Jack to a gay bar on Old Compton Street where the other men were wearing heels and the toilets were swimming in disinfectant and piss. Vi was in her element and even Roshan didn't seem to mind being touched up by a drag queen, but Jack was less than comfortable so we let him choose the next pub. At least it looks like you could go to the toilet without contracting anything, but it's short on personality – red carpets, cheap pints, food in deep-fried lumps and a pool table.

Jack has one eye on the table, waiting for it to be free. I take a moment to look at him. He doesn't look much like an artist, or a banker – his day job. 'I love doing the class,' he explained to me earlier, 'Only way I get an excuse to leave the office before ten.' With the speed he's knocking back the pints, he's clearly grimly determined to enjoy himself tonight. He's a big bloke, with something of the wide-boy about him. I guess his clients and co-workers like that sort of thing, but his mixture of confidence and watchfulness leaves me cold. I feel like he's sizing me up, wondering what I want and how he can prevent me from getting it. His hair's over-gelled and his teeth oddly small, giving him the look of a hammerhead shark. While Roshan's body is broad but toned, Jack's is pale and paunchy. This is what we do to our brainy young men these days – sit them at desks and fatten them up as they gamble for twelve-hour stretches. Good for us.

Roshan comes back from the bar and puts a pint down in front of me, squeezing my arm lightly as he sits down – a sweet, unconscious little gesture. He leans forward, ready to ask Jack something, but Vinyl gets there first. Looking at the two of us, she says, 'So, how long have you two been together, then?'

Roshan and I look at each other, nonplussed.

'We're not,' he says, at the exact same time as I say, 'I'm gay.'

Jack blinks in that irritating too-much-information way that guys like him go in for, unaware that we're not a sympathetic audience. He gives up and looks longingly at the pool table, which is still being monopolised by two middle-aged men.

'Oh,' says Vinyl. 'Oh, I'm sorry. I just assumed … you totally look like a couple.'

Roshan laughs. 'No, no, absolutely not.'

'We've known each other for years,' I offer. 'Maybe that's it.'

'Could be.' But she doesn't sound convinced. 'I should've checked before I opened my mouth. You've been friends for ages, then?'

'Sure.' Roshan moves away from me – imperceptibly, but I can feel it. 'I even remember the day we met.'

'Can you?' I ask, surprised.

He nods, a sweet, lazy smile on his face. 'Do you remember those weird remedial reading classes?'

'God, yeah. Jesus, our school was crap, wasn't it?' I explain to Vi and Jack, 'Basically, the classes were huge and only about half of us could read properly. I dread to think what it's like now, but even at the time, it was what you'd call a …'

'Cultural melting pot,' Roshan supplies ironically. 'Even the dealers thought twice about hanging round our gates.'

'So the idea was that the kids who could read well enough would spend a lunchtime a week helping the ones who couldn't. It was grim. And possibly illegal. It also didn't matter what age you were, so I'd often end up helping out kids who were older than me. It was fine at the time, even nice, you know, we'd get these shiny new books and go through them together. Then they'd feel crap about themselves and call me a Goth wanker in the corridors.'

Roshan laughs. 'They drafted me into it, as well. They figured the immigrant kid with the funny name needed help with his English.' His chin lifts slightly and I smile to myself at this hint of princely, only-child imperiousness. 'Never mind that I went to some of the best schools in Bangalore and my people were building universities while yours were pissing out of trees …'

Vi laughs. 'OK, spare us the lecture, you.'

After My Own Heart

'I can't believe you still remember that,' I tell him.

'Course I do. I remember everything about it. I even remember that it was raining ...' he looks at me and then shakes his head, as though to clear it. 'Anyway,' he says, clearly eager to change the subject, 'how about you two?'

Strangely, I hadn't thought they were a couple, but now I can see they are. Jack puts his hand on her shoulder, where it lies self-consciously.

'Oh, our first meeting was even sexier than that,' Vi says.

'What, sexier than a stinky prefab hut in a dodgy school?' I ask.

'Try a financial services conference,' says Jack.

Roshan and I look at each other. 'You win,' he says.

'Our school was really quite smelly, though,' I mutter.

'What were you doing at a financial services conference?' Roshan asks Vi.

She takes a deep gulp of her pint. 'I was a booth bunny.'

He nods and then whispers in my ear, 'What the hell's one of those?'

Vinyl hears and smiles. 'I was, what would you call it, resting between jobs? Having a bit of a mental health break, as it were. Couldn't work regular hours at the time, especially cause I was doing a lot of burlesque in the evenings. Corporate gigs, you know. Middle-aged men in suits. Always some stand-up they'd take the piss out of or ignore, and then I'd get my tits out. I usually ended up going home with the comedians, mainly out of pity. I don't do those gigs any more. It was totally soulless, but the money was coming in faster than I could spend it. I needed a routine. The low point came when I got asked to do a porn film and I was actually considering it.' Jack puts his hand on her arm gently, but with an unmistakable enough-now hint. 'Anyway.' She pulls it back. 'I answered an ad for this job and my God, it was the worst thing ever. These big, huge conferences in Docklands and the Olympia. Wearing high heels that killed me by the end of the day and a leotard that climbed up my arse, smiling till my face hurt. I'd already decided I was going to call it a day – I was starving and bored and the lights were giving me a migraine. But something good came out of it.' She smiles at Jack.

'Some guys in finance lose their ability to interact normally,' says Jack. I want to tell him he's getting there. 'They're used to having everything they want. Putting something beautiful in front of them that they can't have … it confuses them.'

'I had enough business cards to paper my bathroom,' Vi adds. 'I'd bin 'em on my way out.'

'Some guy was talking to her about the company that hired her,' Jack says. 'Really patronising stuff. Where are they on the stock exchange, that sort of thing. Only way he could talk to her, but it just came across as insulting. When he eventually left, I stood at her stall thinking how incredibly gorgeous she was. Then she said something like … what was it again?'

'I think it was something like, 'Not over-burdened with social skills, are they?'

'That was it. And I didn't expect her to have a northern accent. It made her seem …'

'Like a real person,' Vi says dryly. 'Who would've thought?'

'I was head over heels,' Jack says. 'It was an amazing night.'

'I knew where they kept the champagne,' Vi adds. 'So I nicked a bottle and we walked along the river for hours.' They smile and squeeze each other's hands. I remember, fleetingly, what that felt like – when you had a story, something to be proud of.

'Oh, mate, the pool table's free,' says Jack, looking around excitedly.

'Men,' says Vinyl lightly. 'Go on, sod off. We want to talk about you anyway.'

They slope off to the pool table and amble around it pointlessly. Even from a distance I can tell that they have no idea what they're doing and, even stoned, my mother could slaughter them both.

Vinyl goes to get another round in and when she comes back, she smiles shyly at me. There's a strange current between me and this girl. Without her feathers and jet, she's a little more subdued, but as she relaxes and downs her pint – economically, swiftly – she gets that dangerous edge which just makes her more attractive. It's strange, this business of suddenly being allowed to fancy people, but when she leans forward and says softly, 'Can I tell you something?' I'm not remotely surprised.

Straight girls. God, I've had this conversation so many times. If you're a lesbian, it's an occupational hazard. I'm tired of their obsession with the details, their clumsy questions, the way they nod with that sweet, tolerant lip-biting gravity that makes me want to saw my head off. I still draw the line at being dragged into one of those sweaty, glittery nightclub lip-locks to titillate some watching man, but seeing Vinyl Lace squirming with that familiar urgency makes me feel strangely affectionate. It helps that she's stunning. Superficial, I know.

'I've never told anyone this before,' she says, her voice lowered. 'But it's always been a part of me. For as long as I can remember.' Vi takes a gulp of her pint. 'I'm straight, don't get me wrong, but …' she looks briefly over her shoulder at the two boys feinting with their pool cues, 'I've always fancied girls too. My sister's friends, my teachers …' she shakes her head. 'It feels so weird, saying this. Is it OK? Am I OK to tell you? I just … thought you'd understand.'

'Course it's OK. It's fine.'

'God.' She shakes her head. I love how they always make such a big deal out of this. Sometimes I wonder, who on earth *couldn't* fancy girls? Their soft arms, expensive scents, the tickling fronds of their hair?

'Have you always known?' she asks.

I know what she's driving at – whether it's possible to change. Whether it could happen to her too – like she'll go to bed and wake up tomorrow with an iPod full of Riot Grrrl anthems and a hard-to-maintain haircut. I want to tell her that doesn't happen, even though I keep looking over her shoulder at the man behind her as he leans over the pool table, biting his lip like he does when building Lego trucks or taking a picture or sitting at a desk far too small for him on a rainy afternoon, a book in front of him and a shaven-headed rudeboy beside him, one long brown finger patiently underlining the words.

'Yeah,' I say, bracing myself to trot out the same stale revelations. 'Hard to say what it was, exactly. It wasn't all about sex, it was just part of me. I had crushes on girls, sure, but the fact that I was gay was just, I don't know, like the colour of my eyes or something. A lot of the girls I knew came out when they were eighteen and sometimes they'd run back into the closet when they left college – you know, Gay Until Graduation? I know some women who've only ever fallen in love with one woman, even though they don't always call themselves gay. There's all kinds of stuff going on out there. We live in interesting times.'

She smiles a neat, closed-mouth smile. I can tell, even though she instigated this, that she's somehow angry with me for talking about it, making it real. Making it possible.

I keep talking, 'Things are different, more fluid, even now. When I was first coming out, a lot of people gave me shit for not looking gay. Whatever that means. I did get tired, disillusioned a bit I think, being told off for not fitting in. I wanted them to just welcome me with open arms and, in fairness, a lot of them did, but there was still that sense of doubt that I wasn't really what I said I was. That I had to prove myself. But I always looked really crap in flannel.'

'I never thought about that. I mean, I don't know why they wouldn't have just wanted you to look like yourself. You're so ... I don't know. You're lovely, Evie.'

'Yeah.' I throw my arms wide, taking it all in – the down-market pub, the stranger in front of me, the empty chair at my side. 'It's really working out for me.'

She raises one eyebrow. 'Yeah, so you're pissed off with your life. Join the queue, love. You think you're the only person who's ever been chucked?'

'At the moment? Yeah. That's exactly how I feel.'

'Well, you're not. That's all I'll say.' She pushes her hair back from her face and sneaks a glance at the boys, winding up their game now. 'I meant it,' she says, lower and more urgently. 'You're so…' she shakes her head, gives up. 'You're something else.'

The boys sit down, jostling and gently ribbing each other about the game, making more commotion than they need to. Jack puts his arm around Vinyl, while his gaze wanders around the room, not making eye contact with her even while she chatters and tugs at his shirt. His eyes eventually land on me for a beat too long. I stare back at him. Eventually, he turns back to her, whispering something into her ear. So, Mister, you don't like me. I think I'll live.

'I can't believe you thought they were a couple,' he says to Vinyl, too loudly.

She looks back at him, then at us, and smiles. 'I don't know. I've seen stranger things.'

Hungover Chickens

I'd thought our bed was the worst bed to wake up in. The bed where Kate and I laughed and wrestled, made love and fell asleep in each other's hot, damp arms. The bed which we now share in a tense endgame. Clearly, I was wrong.

I wake to the sound of what I think is rain, but it turns out to be the whirr of a large electric fan at the end of the bed. A poisonous fist of a hangover pounding behind my right eye, I don't know where I am, or who I'm with. In my current state, it could be anyone.

From the corner of my half-opened, mascara-and-tear-sticky eye I can see a pile of orange-spined Penguin Classics, a computer the size of a small cinema screen hooked up to some decks and other unidentifiable boys' paraphernalia. Black and white photographs are tacked to the wall: a tulip, its tired petals swirling like a ball gown; several brides, some beautiful, some not; a rusty bike-frame tied to a lamppost, both wheels missing; a terrier chasing pigeons in Trafalgar Square. I'd been there when he took that shot, sitting patiently on the warm stone, waiting for him to be done. Well, at least now I know who the man next to me is.

The bed's a king-size, with acres of limp, wash-softened sheets, but he's curled into my back, his breath slow and even on my neck, deepening into a gentle snore.

Slowly, I take stock of things. I move my hands down my thighs, realising I'm still fully clothed in that uncomfortable half-in half-out way you get after a long night's drinking and a tear-stained tumble in between the sheets. Jesus, I hope he's got some clothes on.

A brief survey of my passed-out friend shows that, thank God, he's wearing track pants and a T-shirt that would be baggy on most other people. His thick black hair falls over his face and I see threads of silver like fine jeweller's chains.

I bet stuff like this never happens to Amanda Garvey. Or Cathy Holmes. It wouldn't even happen to my train-wreck of an ex, but apparently it's happening to me.

How did last night start? The pub; me, him, Vinyl and Jack. Pints. More pints. Everyone buying rounds, glasses nudging each other, rings of chill beading the tables. 'You must, go on, I'll be insulted.' Roshan, never that big a drinker, stoically matching me pint for pint. Talking to Vinyl Lace, telling her about Kate, still not able to shake my Pollyanna act, 'But you know, it's best that it happens now rather than later. Anyway, she'd never let me out this late . . .'

Ah, freedom, as the Internet keeps telling me. I can do whatever I want! Apparently, what I want is carnage. I get a couple of texts from Kate. I send abusive replies. Roshan asks if I'm sending abusive replies. I tell him of course not. His sleeves are still rolled up and I notice he has very beautiful forearms. Jack orders some shots and then ... then there's not much.

Another moment of clarity, monochrome this time, the streets groggy with silver light. Roshan and I are staggering down the street. I'm jumping over bollards and he is trying to convince me that this is not a good idea. I grab onto him before I fall over and nearly send us both reeling, all six-foot-something of him dragged down by my five-foot-nothing of booze-and-grief-sodden weight.

I remember thinking, if anything can get me over this, it's going to have to be seismic. A bomb scare, a tumour, a blow to the head. Life, and all its half-hearted distractions, isn't going to be enough. I'm going to have to walk through fire before I feel half-way normal again.

We stand at a crossing. I have some vague idea about a taxi but as we wait for the light to turn green, he says something unfortunate. 'I think I've got some whisky back at the flat.' Game over.

Roshan stirs, murmurs, and draws me close to him. I haven't woken up in a strange bed since college. My life now reminds me of that random, structureless existence; keeping odd hours, fending off advances, long afternoons smoking tightly rolled joints on my narrow bed, blowing away the anxiety that dogged my days. I feel so far away from him; here are our warm bodies touching, our sweet, rank breath mingling, but also the panic boiling up in me, a volcano stirring beneath the bedrock.

'Hey,' he whispers, his voice even deeper than usual. 'Are you awake?'

Daylight pours through the curtains offensively. 'Rosh … what happened? I mean … what did we do?'

'Nothing. You're all right. I think I said a few things you weren't crazy about.' He yawns. 'We were pretty drunk.'

'What did you say?'

Pause. 'I can't remember.'

'I know when you're lying. Always have.' I try to dig him in the ribs but he's holding me too tight. 'What did you say?'

'I just said that you didn't have to pretend it was all right, that you could be, you know, sad if you wanted. And then you got mad at me and asked, like, if you were, what was I going to do to help? And I was like, I dunno, I hadn't really got that far … and then you started crying and called me a dick.'

My phone's on the floor by the bed. Four messages, all from Kate.

'Then you wanted to call her and I told you not to and you said you were going to so I put your phone on top of the wardrobe and then you started crying again but then we had some coffee and whisky and you calmed down. Then we had a spliff and watched half a soft-porn movie on Channel Five and I think you might have been sick before bed but you were quite quiet about it.' I feel disgusting, broken, lost. His familiar cinnamon-and-vanilla smell is stronger, muskier, as he pulls me into a hug. 'It's all right, Evie, happens to the best of us.'

It feels weird, the way we're touching each other. Roshan's always been physically affectionate, with a penchant for hugs and kisses that stems from years of being cuddled, coddled and chastised by his mother and a crowd of equally scary auntie-jis who pinched his cheeks even after he was a foot taller than them. The awful thing is, I've been craving physical contact; I'm not used to living without it, and it scares me that I have to. Living on rations, what Kate and I can manage in one of our rare good moments, has left me hungry for touch. I can't believe this is my life now, these rags of comfort.

Hot, helpless tears blur my view of his photos; I can't look at him. He hears the way I'm breathing and puts his hand on my arm. 'Hey,' he says softly. 'Don't.'

'I'm sorry…'

'I don't mind. So long as it's not my fault.'

'It's not. I just … give me a minute.'

I get up and stagger to the bathroom – a disturbing experience in itself. It looks like it needs a few months' steam-cleaning and the closest thing to decoration is a stack of dusty photography magazines next to the toilet. I pee as quietly as I can, splash cold water on my face and wrists, blow my nose on some of his cheap bog-roll, wipe away the smudges of black and green under my eyes and try to make my hair look marginally less insane.

When I crawl back into bed with him, he slings a heavy, solid arm across me and holds me close. 'Do you want to hear a funny story?' he asks.

I sniff and nod, feeling his sleep-soaked body warming mine. I can feel our hair mingling, my tired locks and his swathes of black satin.

'Right. Well, back when I was a little kid in India, my grandma had a whole bunch of chickens, and she also had these bushes covered in big red berries. One day, the chickens got out, and they ate a whole bunch of these berries. My grandmother comes into the yard – ay! – and finds these chickens all laid out, dead on the ground. Well, she was upset, of course, she loved those chickens, but my grandmother wasn't the kind of lady to waste time, so she had them all plucked ready to take them to market. Thing is, those red berries were alcoholic. Those chickens weren't dead, they were just drunk.'

A renegade giggle escapes me. 'Like us?'

'Just like us. Except totally bald. My grandma comes into the yard and finds all these bald, pissed-off, hungover chickens wandering around …'

I laugh. It's a weak laugh, but it's something. Satisfied, he tightens his arms around me. 'Right, I'm going back to sleep now. You're …' he yawns, 'very welcome to join me …'

I wriggle out of his arms and start looking for my shoes. Suddenly, I feel so soiled that I want to sandblast my skin.

He regards me with half-lidded eyes. 'Where are you going?' he murmurs. 'Come back. Cuddle up.' He knows it's not like I have anywhere to go.

'Home. Well … ' I shrug. 'For the time being.'

'Don't. It'll just upset you.' He yawns again. 'I can make you breakfast … I don't have anything in, but we can go to the shop …'

'No, I'll leave you in peace, babe. But thanks. Really.'

I wrestle myself back into my tights, find one shoe and pick another up from under his desk. Roshan gets up and follows me around, dishevelled and yawning uncontrollably, trying valiantly to keep his eyes open, and insists on hugging me before I go. I stand, stiff, surrounded by last night's detritus – sticky whisky glasses, cups half-full of pitch-black sediment, fragments of green Rizla packet and fronds of tobacco.

He strokes my wild hair and holds me close as we stand by the radiator which is currently drying his underwear. 'Right, Evie, you've seen my pants now,' is his parting shot. 'You might as well come back.'

On the way home, Vinyl Lace texts me, 'Hi, Roshan gave me your number, hope you don't mind! I'm doing a gig next week and we could use a singer. Are you up for it?' I smile as I tell her yes, but my smile fades quickly.

The groceries I get on the way home are those of a woman on the edge. White bread is the only thing that could be considered normal and even that's the processed stuff; the rest is unashamedly vile, bought for the trailer-trash in me. Spaghetti hoops in orange sauce, processed cheese slices, slabs of cheap chocolate. I thank God for my huge diva sunglasses. They're great at hiding tears as well as shielding me from the sun, which is poking hot fingers into my hungover eyes. On the bus, carrying my psychotic purchases, I find myself crying. Everything I pass reminds me of what's no longer mine. Organic food markets full of blissful couples; a local nursery, its walls decked with cartoon characters; the bookshops that Kate and I will not be browsing today. I can't get over how much I hate everyone at the moment. I wonder if I always had it in me, this terrible black bitterness. I miss what I had over the past five years, and what I had, without knowing it, was the absence of envy.

When I get home, Kate's sitting at the kitchen table, checking her emails and looking so fresh and clean I want to kill her. Breathing on her would probably do it.

'Where were you last night?' she asks, her face tight.

'Why?' I duck into the bedroom, get into bed fully clothed, pull the covers over my head and pray that she disappears. I can't even be bothered to chisel off the last of my makeup. She knocks on the door. 'What?' I shout as she prises the door open a crack.

'It's just … Jamie and Susie are around later and they invited us for dinner tonight, I thought if you were up for it, maybe we'd go for a curry down the road …'

I push back the covers. This fake normality has to end. We're getting too comfortable in it. 'Kate, I want you to go. Soon. Sort something out.' I don't want to throw her into Cathy's arms, but hell, she did all right without my encouragement. 'I need a couple of weeks to find a flat. I don't care where you are, just … give me some space.'

Strangely, she nods like she's expecting it. 'OK. Whatever you want.'

'Of course it's not what I want, but it has to be this way.'

A longer pause, and then she asks, her voice shaking, 'When you've found somewhere, can I visit you? Not often, just …'

Exhausted, I say, 'Yes. All right. Just leave me alone.'

Day Strippers

Something strange happens in the West End after six p.m. It's one thing to see girls clicking off to work in the mornings, clutching their lunches and thick chick-lit books the shade of sugared almonds, but it's another entirely to watch the burlesque girls going to work at night. If you look closely, there's a naughty spring in their step as they lug their innocent-looking overnight cases down Berwick Street, a little extra care taken with their glossed and rolled hair, their lipstick fifties fire-truck bright.

Backstage at the Odalisque Club, I watch the girls dress and undress, eyes fixed on the mirror ahead of me, their half-naked bodies nudging towards the mirror like pale fish nosing up to the glass of their tank. I love singing at burlesque shows; there's something backstage that makes me feel like I've come home. For someone who spent their nostalgia-sodden teenage years staring longingly at endless repeats of *The Red Shoes* and *A Chorus Line*, this hot, crowded corridor, thick with hairspray and nervous sweat, is a kind of heaven.

'They told me not to grab any crotches,' says the tiny, gum-chewing creature next to me in her croaky northern accent, as she tries to make her red bouffant hair even bigger. 'If this was real stripping, I could make some serious money grabbing balls, but here? Forget about it. Why burlesque doesn't have a decent business model I'll never know.'

A blonde ingénue with pin-curled hair stares at her with mingled admiration and horror; we're meant to be nice girls, taking our clothes off for kicks. But this is Vinyl Lace, and Vinyl's a lot of things, but she doesn't do *nice*. The other girls in this place dress like me – typing-pool dollies in pearls, Navy poster pin-ups. Vinyl dresses … well, like a stripper. Big red hair, G-string, a tattoo of a black-winged bird on her back that looks ready to take flight.

Vinyl turns to me. 'And how about you, Evie? You giving us a treat tonight? I've got some great pasties you can borrow. Only slightly used.'

I smile and shake my head. 'You know I don't take my clothes off. Sometimes I wish I could, but I don't think I can handle more rejection right now. And I can't dance.'

'Neither can most of them.' Vinyl leans over me for her bag of chocolates; Roshan was right, she devours sweets by the pound, burning off the calories by constant, frenetic motion. We've only been here for half an hour and already she's tried on five outfits, knocked over a drag queen and caused a fight between one of the singers and her boyfriend with a couple of well-timed glances. 'It's not just about being able to dance, it's about star quality. I don't know if it's just that drag queen lippy, or those hips, but you've got it in spades. Go on. I'll give you a tenner if you get your tits out. It's more than they're paying us.'

'V, isn't this for charity?' murmurs the blonde.

'Yeah, that's what they tell us.' She stands up and spritzes her flat belly with body glitter, its fruity, schoolgirl smell momentarily masking the reek of old wigs, mildewed carpet and sneaky fags. 'Saves them having to hand over any money.'

'I guess it stops us fighting over who gets to headline.'

'We had headliners. They dropped out when they heard we weren't getting paid.'

Vinyl Lace – real name, Kelly-Anne Cooper. I've seen her strip once already; last week, Roshan and I saw her at a club called Tassels. She did her 'pussycat,' routine, writhing around on the top of the bar, at eye-level with the crowd – too close for most burlesque girls – with only a few scraps of spangled nylon between her and the audience, her slim body pale and firm as plaster, her crotch a smooth fist dappled with rhinestones. Roshan did his best impression of a statue and I didn't meet his eyes until the routine was over, but Vinyl Lace turned that well-behaved middle-class crowd into drooling, baying johns. Despite her defiant humps and thrusts, her perfect, ripple-free flesh, she looked so small up there that all I wanted to do was sling her under my arm and protect her. Vinyl brings this out in people. We'd go to war for her, but we're not surprised when she turns around and bites us somewhere tender.

'Evie,' she says, drawing out my name in exasperation. 'You'd make a great stripper, love. I'm sure of it. You've just got that dirty look in your eye. And class, that's important.' She shoves another handful of confectionery into her mouth and speaks through the shrapnel. 'Shitloads of class.'

The girls here come in all shapes and sizes, but they tend towards extremes – the chiselled ballerina types with small, perfect conical breasts, and the Amazons. I'm nothing special, a squashed hourglass on strong, sturdy legs that need masochistic stilt-shoes to make them look elegant. I remember the joy of discovering stilettos in my teens; my ankles, cinched to breaking point in suede straps, the cantilevered arch of my foot and the curve of my butt, the way they made me walk, all samba and sway; metal-edged tips, tapered like the weapons they were named for, announcing my arrival wherever I went. Even Pina grabbing my scarred, swollen feet and wailing, 'Jesus, Evie, foot-binding went out of style centuries ago!' didn't get to me; my shoes weren't about subservience.

I'm wearing a delicious pair tonight; shimmery leopard-print with gumdrop hearts on the toes and scarlet lining. I can't walk very far in them, but I don't have to. Even though I'm not stripping, I'm dressed appropriately, in a corset, cartoonishly short net skirt and stockings with red garters; I love their old-school, bridal, faintly sexual pull as I cross my legs.

The MC, a corseted cross between a biker chick and Bette Midler, puts her head round the door. 'Five minute, ladies.'

'Who's she calling ladies?' Vinyl mutters. 'This isn't the pissing Savoy.'

Going on after Vinyl probably isn't the best idea, especially after a night of chaos – one of the drag queens, who looks like Bernard Manning in a platinum wig, decides to double the length of her set despite – or perhaps because of – the audience's studied apathy. Vi gets into a foul mood, muttering homicidally about bloody end-of-the-pier divas and how she's seen better drag in Bradford. The main band – a trio of gangly sharp-suited lads who collectively look about fourteen – take liberties with their own allotted time, and one of the other girl singers refuses to come out of her dressing room because all her entourage can't get in for free. All this makes MC Bette Midler look increasingly menopausal.

Once Vinyl gets on stage, clattering into the spotlight with her teeth bared and her hair a Rocky Horror fright, she's taking no prisoners. By the time she finishes, humping the stage to a hard-rock, hair-flailing number that owes less to burlesque and more to eighties strip-joints, the crowd – previously a crew of polite, middle-class kids in retro suits, are whipped into a rich, soused lather, baying for more as she pulls out red heart-shaped lollipops from her bra and tosses them into the crowd, finishing with an acrobatic tassel-shake as she twirls her bra over her head.

Watching her, I'm consumed with envy, knowing I'm hardly ever so blatant under the lights; there's often a wall between me and the audience, which only ever gets broken down on good nights, and on nights like this, I want that wall to stay there. I'm happy not to be touched by the world tonight. The conscious part of me knows that this is a shame, that on the nights when I allow the crowd to see, inspire and bruise me I'm far better than when I don't. Apart from that night in Kilburn, I haven't had many good gigs recently; it's all on autopilot. It's not easy to fool the crowd, and impossible to fool myself. 'If you're going to do this,' I mouth at myself in the mirror, 'do it properly.' But I don't feel it.

With Vinyl's applause, the first heartfelt, primal roar of the night, still in the air as she scampers into the crowd, I step out onto the stage, crack a few half-hearted dirty jokes – which the warmed-up crowd laugh at generously – and start to sing. Half-way through my first number, 'Alone in This City', which I chose because of its tinny, bluesy raunchiness, I realise something's wrong; after Vinyl's floor-humping, someone forgot about the sound, and the audience can barely hear me. Sweat breaks out between my shoulder blades. I like being up here, removed; I need to stay up here, but as my eyes adjust to the migraine-strong wall of lights beyond the crowd and faces mouthing, 'We can't hear you,' emerge from the darkness, I finally, reluctantly, forget about distance. Trying to sing while keeping my balance square on these ridiculous shoes, I head down into the audience. I only get ten minutes with these people, and I want to get it right.

Of course, I don't always do this dressed like a hooker. As I sway clumsily through the crowd, hamming it up a little, reaching to ruffle one of the band-boys' hair and aiming suggestive glances at anyone who'll look at me, I realise that after Vinyl's sexed-up triumph, it's open season out here. A hand snakes out and touches my hip, one guy tugs on the frothy hem of my skirt like a child seeking attention, and then, as I turn around and try to walk further into the crowd, another hand reaches out behind me and, accompanied by a chorus of football-ground noises from pissed, overgrown boys, reaches between my thighs.

Blackness floods my head. I stand, frozen, for a moment, the line dying on my lips, my hand falling still on the strings. I never forget my words but now my voice has left me, my throat squeezed as though fingers were closing round it. The moment seems to last forever, and then, as though the sheer voltage of my rage was enough to do it, my microphone finally comes on just in time to catch a well-timed expletive. I turn around, aim a furious dominatrix stare at my assailant – a short-arse with unfortunate shoe-polish-black hair that looks like a toupee, though he can't be more than twenty. I pick up a half-drunk pint and, without missing another note, pour it over his head.

Carnage breaks out. I stop singing; in the past, I've competed with everything from festival PA systems blasting full-volume grunge to chattering cokeheads to the roar of a dodgy generator, but even I have limits.

Shaky, confused applause breaks over me. The guys from the band are doubled over, whinnying with laughter. Then, in the heart of the chaos,

I see my new friend and modelling partner in front of me, hands on her negligible hips, wearing only her pasties, panties and a dangerous grin. To a rampant chorus of whistles and screams, she steps up to me and plants her mouth on mine.

She tastes like she smells; incendiary. Her mouth, smoky and alcoholic, has the smouldering tang of geranium petals. Vinyl plants a strong little hand on the back of my head, grinding her pelvis into mine. When she comes up for air, she hisses into my ear, 'Lowest common denominator, innit? Give the wankers what they want.' She turns on her heel, shaking her hair over her shoulders.

'Right!' Her low, smoggy voice somehow carries better than mine. 'Shut your noise and let the girl sing! One more time, now, for Evie Day!'

Relieved at being told what to do, they clap raggedly. I stand in the middle of the floor, their faces, eyes, breath too close for comfort. I'm near enough to see some of the girls looking down their powdered noses at me, a few of the guys unashamedly staring at my tits and a good helping of genuine boredom.

Why do I do this? I think, as I try to remember the next song on my fag-packet-and-eyeliner set list, and then, launching into the intro, I answer myself – why the hell not?

Enlightenment

It's so late, it's almost early. When we finally leave the club, I know the sky will be like weak tea, that pale, light-polluted flood of Camden before dawn. Vinyl and I are having one for the road, surrounded by drag queens. 'This is your proper drag,' she tells me knowledgeably. 'Ladyboys and that. Not those panto acts.' They don't seem that different to me, particularly the Liza Minnelli wannabe humping a chair onstage, but there are some real beauties too, one with her face shrouded in black lace, half mantilla, half blindfold, and one with a fall of acrylic caramel hair, eyes framed with stick-on crystals, taller and thinner-thighed than we could dream of being.

After the show, Vinyl managed to charm two tweedy, soft-faced boys who took us to a members' club and treated us to aged whiskies in heavy crystal glasses, the smooth waiters not batting an eyelid at the sight of two girls trussed up like hookers on their big leather banquettes. I listened to the house band as Vinyl charmed our Conservative Club dates, letting the wide dark night sink into me with the whisky, mentally feeling my way through my Kate-free life and wondering who I would populate it with, what shape it would be, and if anything – work, friends, singing – would really be enough to fill the space she left. I cried a couple of times in the toilets, as efficiently as I could, stumbling past the models and actresses in the tiled, oval-mirrored rooms. At some point, we lost the boys and hopped in a cab to Camden, Vinyl bouncing on the back seat, singing along to the radio's offensive hip-hop in her tiny, croaky voice.

In the line for the loos, which stretches back into the bar, Vinyl clings to my hand as she hangs out of the fire escape, having a cigarette. Behind her, I gulp the cold, nicotine-scented air, wondering if it counts as smoking outdoors when most of her is still inside.

'That was all right, that shoot the other day,' she says, stubbing her fag out and collapsing back against me, a little stoop-shouldered goddess in a garter belt. 'I don't know Roshan that well. He seems pretty sound. Flaky, but sound.'

'Yeah.' Finally we're in the loos, which are copiously tagged with local legends. *Stop Blaming the Victim. Sforza Italia. Calvin Is Gay.* 'Not a bad bone in his body. He's one of my favourite people.'

'He properly fancies you, you know.'

I can't think of anything to say. Thankfully, someone leaves a cubicle and I usher her past me, but that's not enough to stop her – I can hear her peeing copiously as she chatters, 'I thought you'd probably know, the way he looks at you.' She's out, holding the door for me. 'Honestly, how long do these women take? What are they doing in there?' She raps on the door of the next cubicle. 'Oi, love! You inserting a catheter?' No answer.

'Well, she's not coming out now,' I hiss, walking past her into the cubicle.

'Maybe she's dead.' Shaking her skinny hips to the unholy-sounding pop, she reapplies her lipstick. 'You did know that, didn't you?'

'Know what?'

'That he fancies you.'

'What are we, thirteen?' I put my fingers in my ears to drown her out for long enough to pee. Blood pounds in my ears along with the disco. My skin is so hot it'll take more than the air outside to cool it, no matter how deep into the night and into winter we are.

'Yes,' I say to the Biro-scarred toilet door. 'I know.'

Once we're outside and queuing up for cabs, she kisses me. I recognise this as what it probably is; four a.m. economics. One cab, not two. In the first flush of our sugar-and-shots-fuelled fling, friendship, whatever it is, we're not quite ready to say goodbye yet. I don't know where she went to school, or who first broke her heart, or when her birthday is. Her unfamiliarity excites me.

I'd thought I was too old, too settled for this, but apparently not. I remember the routines, the paraphernalia – the knickers inside-out on the floor, the smell of a stranger on your fingers the day after, the static that comes with missed connections.

As we cruise back to her flat, the driver's eyes wandering back to us in the mirror, riding a gig-drinks-and-dancing adrenaline high, I kiss her.

'Evie,' she says indistinctly, turning her face away. 'You do know I'm still with Jack?'

My smile stays fixed on my face. Weird, how she says that – like that's the dirty secret, not this. I had told myself I wasn't like Kate or Cathy. I'd never cheated. It was one of the things I liked about myself. I was with Kate for so long, and then before that, Jamie ... the others mostly just faded out of my life before the idea of cheating ever became an issue. I feel my moral high ground slipping away. People think men are the only ones who can't resist sex. People are wrong.

'So, what does that mean?' I ask her. I feel that ridiculous primary-school-teacher's tone coming back into my voice, the one I used when we talked about her fancying girls. As if I'm worried she'll bolt – when, at this point, that might be a relief.

'I just ... before we did anything more, I wanted you to know.'

I look out at the dark streets. 'Vi, this isn't any less real because I'm a girl.'

'I know. That's why I told you.'

No it's not. She told me because she wanted to take me down with her.

'I'm moving in with him,' she says, as if telling herself for the first time.

'Yeah, thanks, Vi. Enough now.'

'I didn't ask for this,' she says softly. I can see the taxi driver straining to listen as he turns the volume down on the football scores. 'The other girls I've felt this way about, they've usually been unattainable for some reason, you know, like they already had girlfriends, or they were straight ... but you, I've been thinking about you all week.'

I take her by the shoulders and work my knee between her thighs, kissing her hungrily as though trying to absorb her youth, strength, power, and any of the other things I've lost along the way.

'When's your birthday?' I ask, coming up for air.

She laughs. 'What's that got to do with the price of happy pills, Evie my darling?'

'Just humour me.'

'November thirteenth.' She smiles in the dim light. 'Friday, to be exact. Four-thirty a.m. Scorpio. Happy now?'

'Yes. Thank you.' I lean in for another kiss. I almost am.

Part Two: Heartsore

The Name you were Born with

I try to get out of bed unobtrusively, prepared for my second walk of shame in as many weeks, and crash into a pile of boxes by the door.

Miss Lace stirs and smiles up at me. Against the vivid red bedclothes, she looks pale and insubstantial. I know, without wanting to know, that her skin is hangover-hot, her breath has a metallic booze-and-smoke tang, and her hair, sprayed and backcombed to within an inch of its life, is sticky as fairground floss.

'All right?' she murmurs. 'Try not to injure yourself, will you? I'm not insured.'

My voice sounds harsh, ringing, like my mother's. 'Where's your bathroom?'

'Just down the hall to your right. Careful, though, it doesn't lock properly and I think Gray's up and about.'

'Gray?'

'My flatmate. Grace. Gracie May. Like the singer but backwards. I don't call her that, though. She'd have my guts for garters. Get us some water, will you, princess?'

I grab a sticky pint glass from the bedside table, rinse it out in the bathroom sink and fill it with water. I'm wearing a towel which I picked up from her floor, hot-pink with garnet hair-dye stains and the legend *Bitch Goddess* in drooping cursive. In the cold light of day, I stare at my cellulite, bruises, stretch-marks. Why would this girl, with her flat belly and wishbone thighs, want to shag me anyway?

I get back into bed with her and she wraps herself hungrily around me. It's not entirely unpleasant, but for such a small person her limbs feel strong and heavy, like a delicate vice. She leans over me, reaches for the water and downs it in a series of greedy gulps. 'How are you doing?' she asks, when she's done. 'You look sad.'

'I'm not.'

'You do remember my name, don't you?'

'Yes, Kelly-Anne.'

She laughs, trailing off into a rattling old man's cough. 'Hey, you. Only my nan calls me the name I was born with. And she's a lot harder than you.'

We lie together for a while, staring at the ceiling. She turns over, showing me her black bird tattoo, forbidding in the unforgiving light, and her small, flat, almost boyish butt.

'Is this the first time you've done it with someone else?' She turns back from the pillow and looks at me over one sculpted, inked shoulder. 'Since your ex?'

'Yep. But I did have an … an incident with one other person.'

'What kind of incident? Sounds … medical.'

'Just a bit of cuddling. Nothing like this.'

'Oh yeah?' she stretches. 'Making up for lost time? Fair enough. What was she like?'

'It was a he.'

'I didn't know you were bi.'

'I'm not. It was an accident.'

She laughs. 'Watch yourself. You'll be giving lesbians a bad name. Like those vegetarians who eat fish. And chicken. And the odd bacon sandwich. Course, they can do what they like, but making them dinner is still a right pain in the arse.'

'Yeah, well, what about you? Been with many girls, or were you just groping them to give the guys a thrill?'

'No, Miss Patronising. Chemically, blokes just work better for me. They're better at keeping me sane. And I like that … otherness you get with them. With girls, I can spend hours admiring how beautiful they are. But there's something missing. They just feel too much like me.'

I think uneasily about Kate, how we became too similar over time

– best friends, sisters. I know about Lesbian Bed Death, but still, I can't imagine the situation would have been that different if she'd been a guy; don't straight people ever have too much closeness?

'Earth to Evie,' Vinyl says. 'You never got bored of girls?'

'No. Never. They've always been more than enough.'

'Well, you say that, love, but you did have that bacon sandwich moment. Just a cuddle? You sure he didn't try to slip you the tongue? It's not exactly *Penthouse* material, love, aren't you worrying about nothing?'

'A lapse. I mean, it's not like anyone notices what I'm up to these days. It's all …'

'One big lost weekend. I know. I'm flattered.'

'I don't … I mean, I think you're beautiful, it's just … things are taking a while to settle down, I don't really know what I want …'

'Forget it.' She smiles, genuinely. 'It's all hilarious, Evie. You'll see that some day. I know you don't see it now because you're in shock. I knew as soon as you walked into that studio. I've been there, God, you name it, I've done it and most of the time I can remember it too.' She stretches on the pillows. 'Don't you think it's weird how no one talks about stuff like this? Like it's distasteful?' She reaches for the water and takes a greedy gulp. 'All we see is people's outsides but we judge ourselves by our insides. I mean, you look seriously uncomfortable now, and I don't blame you because you're probably feeling like shit and wondering what the hell you're doing in bed with me and where this mystery bacon sandwich guy, or your girlfriend, or whoever's going to save you is … but isn't it weird, how sadness is like, forbidden somehow? Like we just have to get through it?'

'Well, what else do we do?'

'Nothing, I suppose. Just accept that it takes time.'

I feel it again – the old, stale panic. I don't have time. Who does? I don't want to spend my life getting over something I never asked for. I want my life to carry on as it was – yes, there was boredom, there were compromises, but they were mine.

'So,' I say, jokingly knocking my foot against hers, 'no second date then?'

She smiles. 'You probably don't need me to tell you that, Evie.'

'And so what am I for you?' Yes, I want to make her feel awkward. She's done it to me. 'Your hen night?'

She sighs. 'Jack knows I've had these feelings before. I could tell him, if you want. Makes no odds to me.'

'Yeah. And he'd probably get off on it.'

'What, you think your man's any different, whoever he is? …Who is he, anyway?'

The silence settles between us, thick as fog.

'Oh,' she says, and then, 'Oh!'

'Look, it's not what you …'

'Oh my God! I wonder if Jack knows? Did you know he asked me if I thought Roshan was gay?' She cackles. 'You've got to watch the quiet ones, love.'

'Nothing's going on. Look, we've been mates forever, it was just one of those things … I hadn't seen him in almost a year, and … I don't know …'

She squeaks with delight and rolls back on the pillows. 'See? You've got your own little love story now. You don't need me.'

No, I think, but it doesn't mean I don't want you.

'Is it serious?' she asks, studiously avoiding my eyes.

'I don't think so. Is it serious with Jack? I mean, moving in and everything. It's a big step …'

'Well.' She hunches one skinny shoulder. 'He puts up with me. It doesn't … sometimes, I think I'd chuck it all in for something like this. I'm not lying. But he knows me. He takes care of me. It feels like home.'

I know what she means. I look around the room. It's chaos – fairy lights, puddles of satin and lace, a giant framed poster clearly stolen from a local coffee-house declaring optimistically, 'IT'S CAKE TIME.' This is the life I left behind before Kate and our starter flat. Our starter relationship.

Someone knocks on the door. We lie there for a moment, equally pale and awkward. I like to see this girl falter; it makes her seem more human.

'You there, Gray?' Vinyl asks.

'Yeah, I'm making coffee. You want some?'

'Oh, yes please.' Vinyl sounds like a little girl. For the first time since laying eyes on this woman, I'm not remotely attracted to her. It's kind of a relief.

Vinyl gets up from the bed and puts on incongruously non-sexy clothes – a grainy grey T-shirt and a pair of green pants that look suspiciously like they may be her boyfriend's. She tosses me a dingy turquoise towelling robe. 'Come on,' she says quietly. 'Breakfast.'

Even in the harsh light, she's striking, with that indefinable quality I've spent years trying to emulate with paint and pantomime. I take one last minute to look at this girl, because I might not see her again. Not like this. In a basement bar with brimming cocktails, maybe, or in the violet light of a club, other lovers holding our hands, but this will be the last time I see her like this, as the girl who laid herself open in front of me, her naked body arching like a swimmer thrashing her way to the surface.

'Coffee,' I say, my mouth dry. 'Sounds good.'

A Desirable Area

We sit down for breakfast in the living room, a wide, pine-boarded sprawl, flooded with light. Gray comes in with the coffee. Beside the evidence of our last-night shame, she looks painfully clean and well-defined, in Levis and a white vest that flattens her chest into a boyish V. Her skin is pale, lightly sprayed with freckles, her hair dark, damp and gleaming with gel, hardening into a duck's-ass do. There's something friendly in her freshly-scrubbed face, a kind of monkeyish prettiness. 'All right?' she says. Her voice has a warm northern edge that flattens out the vowels. 'Bit of a heavy one last night then, girls?'

'Oh, you know me …' Vinyl starts talking about last night's drag queens, her waving hands threatening to knock over the cups, while Gray sits and watches like an affectionate older sister. Wondering how to find my way to the nearest Tube, I look around the room, which has one dominant theme. Movies. Black and white stills from the films Dad and I used to adore cover the walls – Joan Crawford with gleaming hair and shoulder pads; square-headed Frankenstein's monster; Liz Taylor kneeling by the surf in a white bikini.

'You like the movies?' I ask Vinyl.

'Yeah, but only for the outfits. Gray's the real fan. You should see her collection.'

Gray arches an eyebrow and points at the far end of the room. Dozens of narrow plywood bookshelves, all full of DVDs, with box files of movie magazines along the top. The room is dusty, untidy, the result of more than one person living here, but while I'd been dreading returning to a flatshare, it still has more personality than the rooms I'm trying to leave.

'I've been collecting them since I was a kid,' Gray says. 'The Internet's made it easier, but in a way it's taken all the fun out of hunting. Still, it's something to do.' I can see the love, the passion, gleaming behind her calm expression. Something about Gray's clearly much-loved collection unlocks the teenage geek in me, and today the geek wants to get out and play.

'So how do you two know each other?' says Gray, a mischievous glint in her eyes.

'Photo-shoot. Evie's boyfriend got us to pose with each other.'

I dig her in the ribs. 'He's not my boyfriend.'

Gray smiles cheekily. 'Well, you'd hope not. You two can do whatever you want, of course, but I still don't want to know what Jack would say.'

Vinyl looks pissed off. 'Yeah, well. This move is happening. I've put my name on his lease and everything. Just got to wait for the survey to come through.' It's strange to hear her talking about such adult things. This little dragonfly has a more solid life than mine.

'I'll miss you,' says Gray. It's a throwaway line, not quite meeting her flatmate's eyes.

'Ah, you'll live. But I'll miss you too, love.' For a minute, it's as if I'm not there as Vinyl's eyes narrow. She reaches across the table and runs a fingertip over Gray's clenched knuckles. I know, right then, that they've slept with each other too; more than once.

Gray could be a tomboyish straight girl, but I doubt it. Unlike Vinyl – and me, I suppose – she looks unambiguously gay. I've always been envious of girls like that, who aren't drawn to any of the girlie nonsense I love.

'I'll have to get that ad up this week,' she mutters. 'Spend next week coming home early and auditioning randoms. I told you what it was like last time, before you came along. The Jesus freak, the agoraphobic …'

'The Lebanese gym obsessive … I know.'

'And no men. No more crusty plates. Not after that time with the blokes in that band. Do you think they'll mind, having 'no men', on the ad? Do you reckon they'll think I'm a man-hating lesbian?'

'Aren't you?'

'God, no. Far rather have some sweaty, farting bloke than your stripper friends twittering about the place. And my male friends are sweethearts.'

'They're perverts.'

'Vi, what do you expect when you lounge around the house in your knickers?'

'It was hot! And it's my house.'

'Yeah well, not for long. He'll have a ring on your finger before you know it.'

'Stop it.' Vinyl shudders. 'Let me finish totally freaking out about the whole moving-in thing first.'

'Don't expect any sympathy from me, love. You're the one who's shipping out to Happy Hetero-Land and leaving me here with God knows what.'

'Evie's looking for a place.' Vinyl giggles like a small, evil child and bites the tip of her finger, dirty red hair swinging over her face.

Gray looks at me. I feel ill-equipped for an audition. I want to tell her that I usually have access to a toothbrush and don't wear my mascara halfway down my face.

'Oh yeah?' she mutters, not looking too enthused. Well, screw you, Gracie May.

'It's a nice room.' Vinyl sips her coffee. 'Just saying.'

I sit back, not expecting an answer from Gray.

'She's a great cook. Makes proper fierce curries. I'll miss them.'

'Shut up, would you, Vinyl, for a minute,' says Gray slowly. I feel her stare tracing my face, finding me beneath the paint and paraphernalia.

'Why are you looking for a place?' she asks brusquely.

'I split up with my girlfriend.' I'm used to saying this now, after a few weeks of stumbling and avoidance. This might be progress.

'I'm sorry.' Her voice is still steady, but a sudden blink betrays her discomfort. 'Were you together long?'

'I think we got together when we were twenty-three, so … yeah, over five years now. Nearly six.'

'Still, that's something, isn't it? Not everyone our age has had that.'

'But I could have been with someone else. Someone I might have stayed with.' I try not to let my voice crack. 'It's a waste. I should have, I don't know, done things differently somehow.' I reach for my coffee and take a burning, bitter gulp.

'Don't think that,' Gray says softly. 'You'll drive yourself mad.'

'Yeah,' says Vinyl. 'One way or another, no point regretting any of it.'

Gray indicates Vinyl. 'She doesn't regret anything.'

'Yeah,' says Vinyl. 'But, in fairness, that's because I'm nuts.'

We sit for a while, listening to the radio, the movie stars on the walls watching us with their silver eyes.

'I've got a really busy week,' Gray says, and then we're quiet again, like no one's sure how to follow that up. Vinyl nods, slowly, as though meditating.

I clear my throat. 'What part of town … I mean, where are we?'

Gray smiles. 'You really don't know?'

'Highgate,' Vinyl says. 'Leafy Highgate. A desirable area. Easy access to a Tube. Posh people with strangely named children. Anyone mind if I smoke?'

'In the garden.'

'Gray …'

'In the bloody garden. And don't do those eyes at me, I'm not your boyfriend.'

'I forget sometimes.' Vinyl gets up. 'Well, something to think about,' she murmurs as she heads into the garden, still in her T-shirt and boy's pants.

Gray and I look at each other across the table.

'Lots to think about,' I say.

She nods. 'Definitely.'

I can't resist. 'This is forward, but …' I gesture to the racks of DVDs, 'were you planning on watching any of those today?'

She gives me a half-smile. 'Not till now. But I'm always open to suggestions.'

Eating Out

Vinyl stamps her foot about the idea of sitting in all day watching movies, so after we shower, she kits me out in a dress that must be loose on her but clings to my curves, and we head out for a walk around Muswell Hill.

Vinyl points to various pubs and tells me long stories of lost nights and Gray walks on the outside of us, her fine-boned face armoured in shades and tilted towards the sun. We eat lunch in a café full of broadsheet-reading young couples in chinos and Breton shirts. If they give me pangs for my old, borderline-acceptable life, I try not to show it, and even feel grateful for my single status when their children take one look at their carrot smoothies and scream blue bloody murder.

Being out with Vinyl Lace is like being part of a celebrity's entourage; even the overworked waiters rush over to serve us when she's only raising a hand to tidy her hair. By the end of lunch, we've racked up three free cappuccinos, the email address of an American who works for Goldman's, a sheaf of flyers, a wilting gerbera and two phone numbers. Vinyl pockets her tributes, and sticks a cheeky spoon into Gray's chocolate cake before her hand gets slapped away. I like them, these strange, salty, raucous girls, flirting and enjoying how uncomfortable they make the straights around them. Kate and I weren't like that; we never noticed the reactions. We never noticed anything but each other.

'This … this kind of feels like a holiday,' I say, and almost blush. My hands tingle. I don't know when I last said something like that to strangers. Londoners tend not to.

Gray grins at me. 'Good God, love, you need to get out more.'

I laugh, run my hands over my face and through my hair. 'Yeah, I did just embarrass myself a bit, didn't I? Oh well. Just going to the loo.' I get up, squeeze past Vi and head to the Ladies.

As I move through the café, I see them both, but I don't even fully register what I'm seeing until my mind starts screaming at me. I move in what feels like slow-motion to the toilet door. I know they've clocked me.

Cathy Holmes, girlfriend-stealer extraordinaire, and her ex Zoe. They look as miserable as they should. Zoe's holding Cathy's hand, her head bowed. Zoe's number one haircut is growing out in patchy tufts, her skin so translucent it's like some chilly underwater substance, not flesh at all. Her back's hunched like she's waiting for a kick.

Cathy doesn't look much better – colourless, hair falling in dirty blonde clumps over her face. There are deep shadows under her eyes. She looks weary, bored, and not much like a femme fatale. When she sees me, she looks horrified.

I keep my face blank as I turn away from her and into the toilet, which is mercifully – and miraculously – empty. I feel like someone is stamping my heart into pulp. I can't breathe. Well, I always did wonder if I'd die on a toilet. Rock and roll.

In the blue, gold-mirrored little room, I thrust my hands between my knees, try the old Buddhist chant I use before going on stage. *Breathing in I calm my body. Breathing out I smile.* A rictus grin, but it's something. Act as if, I tell myself. Act as if you're OK and your life will catch up with you. Yeah, right. My life's not that stupid. I wish it was, that I could convince myself I was moving forward, moving on – and suddenly things would start to make sense again, my future limping up to me like an eager old dog, simply because I'd whistled.

Shaking my head to clear it, I finally get up and leave the cubicle. Cathy and Zoe are still sitting there, completely silent now as I walk past.

'You look bloody awful,' says Vinyl. 'Is it your hangover? Have some sugar, that'll sort you out.'

I shake my head. 'No, I'm all right.'

Gray pushes her cake towards me. 'Go on. Have a bite.' Her eyes widen. 'Sorry, you're not going to puke, are you? I didn't think you were that bad.'

To my horror, I feel tears in my eyes. 'I'm sorry,' I say, trying to make light of it. 'It's that cake. It's so … beautiful.'

Gray hurriedly pushes it towards me. 'Have it. Please. I'm full. I don't know why I'm still eating it, to be honest.'

'Yeah, Christ, have it, so long as you stop showing emotion for the love of God …' Vinyl gives her a look. 'Calm down, Gray. She's only human. Evie, you go for it, babe.'

'No, I'm fine. Thanks.'

Still, my heart doesn't stop pounding for a good half hour. When Zoe and Cathy walk past me, instead of feeling better, I feel worse. Every sight of this girl ruins me a little more. I turn and watch her flat, narrow arse swing out of the door. Cathy is, of course, wearing jeans – a sagging, nondescript blue. I wonder what made her pick them off the rack, whether she thought – Oh, yes, these unremarkable jeans will do me nicely, I don't have to think about that for another couple of years now. They're the most annoying item of clothing I've ever seen in my life, and my mother wears Afghan car rugs.

Something about those jeans flicks a switch in me. Enough. My life cannot be ruined by a woman who dresses like a Communist foot-soldier.

I look at Vinyl Lace, ploughing through the remains of Gray's cake. I'd thought I was all-right-looking – pretty, sometimes – but I've never been a woman like this. If I had her expensive skin and eyes, I could charm and kill as the mood took me.

I should do what Cathy did to me. No one would blame me; it doesn't even feel like anyone's blamed her. I can turn this from a death throe into a blip. A couple of years down the line, Kate and I won't even mention this. Unless, maybe, I want something.

It won't be easy. It'll be messy. But it's possible. I feel an excitement surging through my blood that not even my biggest gigs have given me. I think of those glossy-faced women I watched Sunday after Sunday on the couch with Dad. It's not enough to wonder what they would have done in a situation like mine. To get her back, I have to become one of them, with velvety eyebrows and fan-dance lashes, a mouth like a sucked cherry.

Not forever. Just for long enough for Kate to notice me again.

With my fingers, I steal the last mouthful of cake. I grin as Gray laughs and Vi squeaks in outrage. She flounces up to pay at the counter, and while she's up there, Gray says, not looking at me, 'It's a nice room. Gets a lot of light. I'd swap, but I can't be arsed.' She names a figure, which is slightly more than I paid Kate, but what the hell. 'Near the Tube. I work odd hours, but I'd try to stay out of your hair. And she's right, I do make a great curry.'

I stare up at the ceiling. I don't know why, but I can't look at her. 'Thank you. You have no idea how grateful I am.'

I feel all right again. Not totally better, not healed, but as if it might be possible.

'It gets better,' Gray says, her voice soft and steady. 'It really does.'

A Handbag

'I'm so glad you asked me to dress you up!' Vinyl claps her hands. 'I've wanted to do that for weeks!'

I hadn't planned to ask her yet, but then Kate asked to see me and it had thrown me into a frenzy. I'd gone into the ladies' loo at work and looked at myself in the mirror – just one look was enough to convince me that I was going to need an expert. Even though I'd moved into the new place and it had been a month since I had even spoken to Kate, I still looked like I'd been in a car crash; pale, drawn, dead-eyed. I'd gone back to my desk and sent Vi an email, begging her to make me over. I knew I needed more than paint, but it was a start.

Kate's text hadn't been particularly romantic, 'Drink? You left some stuff at the flat, when can I give it back to you?'

I had thought it would feel final, that as soon as I stepped through the door of the Highgate flat I'd realise it was truly over, and be able to breathe again. None of this had happened. Instead, I started rationalising that we'd only broken up because we were around each other all the time. Now I'd gone, she'd realise how much she missed me.

We're sitting in Vinyl's old room, surrounded by her old things and my new ones. She's been evasive about when exactly she's going to move the last of her stuff to Jack's gleaming Canary Wharf gaff, and I'm starting to sense that she wants to leave them here. That's fine with me. This is the kind of décor Kate would never have stood for. Fake Tiffany lamps, jacquard cushions and a swathe of dusky pink satin that only Vinyl Lace and her showgirl forebears could ever dream of using as a throw, pooling luxuriously at the end of the bed. When I come home from work, I slip gratefully into her world, enjoying the feel of satin against my skin, the soft rose-shaded lights. On Saturday mornings, I lie here under her home-made canopy of net curtains – pure Bradford Market, a mock four-poster for a pound-shop princess. I lie in the wintry sun and tell myself I'm all right. Sometimes I even believe it.

She takes my face in her hands, turns it left and right. 'I'm thinking Ava Gardner,' she says. 'Pissed off her face in the Mocambo, driving Sinatra mad. Have to pad your knockers a bit, but we can get away with it.'

While I take off my makeup – 'Blank canvas, love, please,' – she moves round the room with a dancer's easy grace, putting away childish things – or, rather, passing them on to me, heaping my arms with her vintage prints, the Camden girl's skulls, stars and tattoo brocades. 'Try these on for size. They're a bit big on me anyway. I don't want them back, it'll just make me feel like I can eat.'

Once we've chosen an outfit – a simple sea-green dress with a nipped-in pencil skirt, I don't want to look like I'm overdoing it – she gets serious. She rinses my tired hair in something that gives it the soft coal shine of the pin-up girls' hair on vintage cigarette cases, anoints the new, shorter do with gloss and shows me how to roll it back like a Shoreditch showgirl, pinning a cigar-thick roll behind one ear with a fake orchid. I look like I'm from another era, like I could have had another life. She works on me from my head to my neglected toenails, turning them into ten perfect petals. She plucks my eyebrows into fuck-you arches, gives me cheekbones with a few sweeps of a brush. When she's done, I barely know myself. I look expensive, classy, with a subtle all-over bloom.

When I come downstairs and twirl in the living room doorway, Gray mutters, 'She's always threatened to do that to me,' but she looks at me for longer than she should. Vinyl grins and nudges me. Our mission, whatever it is, feels accomplished.

In her slinky dress and my own high heels – Vi's feet are size three and mine are definitely not – I shrug on my jacket over my finery and head out of the door. Walking to the Tube, I take a moment to breathe in the fresh air. The sun's shining and it feels like spring. I wonder how long it's been like this.

Not the most hopeful setting, meeting your ex in a pub for the old hey-you-forgot-this ritual, but you've got to start somewhere. I'd tried to be careful about not leaving anything behind, but I did, and some of Kate's things intertwined with mine. Even if I hadn't been three-quarters of the way down a bottle of cheap white wine at the time, it probably still would have happened. Surely something this big needs a post-mortem at the very least, but I didn't come to this pub for a post-mortem. I came because I wanted my life back, and I came armed.

Kate's sitting by the window, at the table we always used to try to get. She's reading, and I take a moment to look at her. She looks well, but close up, after our first excruciatingly awkward hug, I can see she's got the exact same car-crash look that I'm trying to disguise. She wants this too, I tell myself. It might be easier than I think to talk her round. This is all a mistake – people get through things like this, people whose relationships aren't as strong as ours.

As well as the supermarket bag of my belongings, she has another bag with her; a white, crackling, designer-labelled paper bag. I don't remark on it.

After the first awkward hug, Kate and I are surprised to find ourselves actually smiling – some rogue part of me is pleased to see her and I feel it spread out, relax and breathe. After all, she understands me better than anyone else – of course she feels like home. I don't have to ask her if she feels the same way. I can tell she does. Slowly, our faces soften and our guards drop; I forget that I can't just say anything to her any more.

We make small talk for a while about our friends – Jamie and Susie's wedding, mainly, and Jamie's upcoming pre-wedding party in Paris. Only a few of her closest friends, not including Kate or Cathy, thank God. The last time I was in Paris, I was with Kate, and I know she'll be on my mind as I walk around with the girls; in the flea markets, the Sacré Cœur, the portrait artists and fake flowers. Still, I can't spend my life avoiding Paris. There are only so many cities to go round.

Kate touches my hand. 'You're all right, aren't you? You don't want to go yet? It's just that … this is all a bonus.' She smiles at me. 'I didn't think you'd stay this long.'

I don't want to tell her that, for once, I don't have anything else to do. 'No, I'm fine.' I can afford to try and be graceful. It helps, when her last memories of me must be of a screaming, open-mouthed harpy, smelling of pubs. It's like being on a really good second date – that formality, that shyness, but with someone you already know and think you might like.

I hear her phone beep, and she says, 'Excuse me,' before she checks it. I feel myself freeze up inside, thinking – Cathy. The one thing we're not talking about. As she plays with her phone, I check my own and see one new message. Roshan. 'Hey Evie. I know it's a bit short notice but I'm doing a DJ thing tonight in Hoxton and this bar is totally deserted. Feel ridiculous. Fancy coming if you're free? Buy you a beer.'

I've got more important things on my mind right now. I text him a short, 'Sorry, got something on, see you later this week?' and get back to the business of trying to look pretty and non-mad for the woman I – still, damn it – love.

The wine softens the room's edges and we sit in the faint, pinkish glow from the fairy lights around the bar, Kate looking at me like she used to. Out of nowhere, she shakes her head and says quietly, 'You're so beautiful.'

It's what I've been waiting to hear, but it sounds more like an accusation than a compliment. I see how pale and worn-looking she is, and hear the subtext loud and clear – she wants to know why I'm still all right. I want to tell her I'm just doing the only thing I know how to – put on a good show. We say none of this, though; we just drink and smile at each other, speechless as the first night we met. I remember how we stood outside the Boudoir Café in the dark street, how we were fizzing and brimming over with promise. How she'd held the door for me and stood waiting outside, and then when we were finally alone, we had looked at each other, and laughed. Even for two people who loved words, no words would do.

I haven't managed to let go of all my hope, and she's not making it easy. It's not just that I miss what we had – the Sunday mornings, the movie nights, the day I'd had the flu and she read me the whole of *Winnie-the-Pooh* in one afternoon – but I miss what we were going to have. We'd talked about children, and sitting there with her, somehow it matters less that we could never agree on their names.

She asks me, 'Are you seeing anyone?'

'Not really. One or two, you know.' I'm not sure that a one-night stand with a stripper or a Platonic fumble with a hungover photographer really counts, but I don't want her to think I'm just staring at the walls night after night.

'One or two?' She raises an eyebrow. 'Fast worker.'

'You should talk.'

She sighs. 'I know, but … I'm not a bastard, Evie. And it wasn't fast.'

'I don't want to know.'

'I'd like it, one of these days, if you could forgive me. I'm not expecting it to happen right now, but … one day.'

I stay silent. I can, now. What's she going to do about it?

Kate pauses. 'Who are they? These two?' Then she checks herself quickly, 'I know, it's none of my business. You don't have to answer that.'

This all sounds very final. I fight an irrational urge to cling to her while I still have her, the usual poison singing through my brain – 'See, you're being punished. You wanted some time to yourself, well, you've got it now…'

'Are you?' I ask suddenly, pathetically. 'Seeing anyone?'

She pauses for too long, looking ashamed, biting her already chewed-looking lower lip. Why did I do that? No matter that we've been ignoring it all night, Cathy still exists. And Kate's going home to her tonight. All the paint and perfume and sultry Ava Gardner dresses in the world won't change that. I feel like the plain, angry girl I used to be, armpits drenched in sweat, bowels loose and hot. How can this woman have this effect on me, when I haven't even liked her for months? How come I still care?

'We're giving it a go,' she says evenly. 'Just seeing what happens.'

'Right.' I nod. 'That must be nice for you.'

'It's not. Not really. ' We stare at each other across the table, Mexican stand-off style. I wish you could still smoke in pubs. She always hated it. 'I'm not always … I'm not very good to her. I can't be. I miss you too much.'

She'll probably stick around anyway. That's the thing with girls like Cathy; they're like creeping bindweed, a pale, throttling flower.

'I miss our life,' Kate says.

'Me too.' I might as well be honest about it. 'I just can't believe how fast this happened.'

'I know. I feel … shellshocked. But still, it was happening for a while.'

'To you.'

'Yes. To me.' She looks up at me with some of that old fire, which I haven't seen in months. Strange that she's finally getting her spark back. Maybe it's the thrill of having someone new to push around. Maybe she really is better off without me. I'm glad that she's not being good to Cathy, but it's a pretty hollow consolation. I could cope with our not-so-great love, so long as I had the security. Most shameful of all, I'd already decided to. I'd chosen to screw myself over, and in the end they hadn't even let me do that.

'I got you something,' Kate says suddenly. She's smiling. How can she be smiling? I watch as she reaches under the table for the big, rustling white bag and hands it to me.

'You said I had a package,' I say foolishly. I know this bag is for me; I've known since we sat down. 'This isn't a package.'

She's really grinning now. 'Well, it kind of is.' I haven't seen her look like this in months.

It's a bag. A Phil Sidley handbag, big, black, smelling of expensive leather like the inside of a city boy's car, clasped with an old-gold replica of his signature loose bow. I don't want to think about how much it cost. This is more than Christmas, more than a birthday. Still lost for words, I open it and trace its spotless, sea-grey lining which rasps against the pad of my finger. She's never spent this much money on me.

'Kate, it's beautiful, but no.' I try to stuff it back in the paper bag but it's out now, preening, more luxurious than the whole pub. The paper crumples in my lap. I feel a sudden urge to whirl the bag around my head like an expensive shot-putt and let it fly out of the nearest window. I want my life back. I want warm, lazy mornings with buttered bagels and light gathering in the windows, someone to do the crossword with in coffee shops, someone to make soup for, someone to give me back my peace. I don't want a fucking handbag.

'Just take it,' she says. 'I know it doesn't make up for what I've done. I just can't get my head around the idea that I can't give you anything any more.'

I shake my head and hand it back to her. Once, she'd have known better than to try something like this.

She shakes her head, looking hard-done-by as she puts the bag, half-in and half-out of its wrapping, under the table. 'You didn't have to keep it. You could have, I don't know, sold it or whatever. I wouldn't have minded.'

'Even so. No. Thank you.'

We're quiet for a while. I look at my phone again. Roshan's texted me: 'OK you. Filling up a bit in here now. Still nervous though. Have a good night. X.'

'So,' she says, 'you're not going to tell me about these other ones, then? The ones you're seeing?'

'None of your business.' She was always the transparent one, her needs and urges closer to the surface than mine. She was the poet, I was the performer, the tough one. A lifetime ago we used to joke about it.

'Feel free to tell me to fuck off, but I'm jealous,' she admits. Kate's face is still bright, but there's something subdued in her voice. 'This is all right, isn't it? Coming out with me? Do you think you might want to do it again? I mean, I never thought …'

She pauses for a couple of seconds. 'I never really thought you'd come,'

Sophia Blackwell

she says. I feel like an idiot for coming in the first place, but still relieved that she's said it. It feels like the most normal, human thing she's done all night.

'I wasn't sure I would. But it feels OK, I mean, weird, but still OK.'

'Better than your other two women,' she muses teasingly. 'Well, well. Anyone I know? ... OK, so you're not going to tell me.' She pauses. 'It's not Zoe, is it?'

'No, Kate, strangely I am not shagging your girlfriend's ex.'

'She's not my girlfriend. I didn't leave you for her.'

'It kind of looks like that from here.' I take another gulp of wine. 'All right, it's not her. It's not even two women, and it's not a big deal. I mean, one of them's Roshan.'

'Really?' She looks horrified. 'Are you ... what, you're actually seeing him?'

Why am I trying to spare her feelings, for God's sake?

'No, it's just ... you know, he's been paying me a lot of attention since we split up. Gets a bit much sometimes.'

'He's not giving you too much grief, is he?'

I shrug, wanting to stop talking about this, making it seem dirtier than it is by handing it to her as if it didn't matter, when it's one of the few things that still does. 'I'm not really in a position to tell him to sod off, am I? I don't have any other friends.'

'You know everyone! You're a musician, you work in PR, you never came home before midnight, for fuck's sake!'

'They're not friends, they're work. Not like ... not real friends, anyway. I gave up a lot for you, you know. I moved here, left my job ...'

'Don't give me that,' she says, but without malice. 'You wanted London. The flat, the security. As soon as you'd got it, you disappeared every night. When you weren't working you were out playing in bars, meeting up with people ...'

'Any thoughts on what else I should have been doing with my life?'

'You could have been with me. You could have been living like a grown-up.'

'And look how happy you are. I'm going for a fag.'

I take my bag out with me, and for a moment, I think about running away – but as if she knows somehow, she comes to the door and asks if I'm OK. My answer is uncalled for and perhaps even physically impossible, but it's the best I can do.

She seems perversely relieved that it's got uncivilised again; we both find it easier than our polite divorcees' dance, so we have a brief slanging match where we say everything we've already said, only louder and with more choruses.

'You took everything,' I hear myself say, 'everything, even the songs, you even took my songs … you wrote them for me and I can hardly sing them now.'

She looks puzzled. 'What are you talking about? We wrote them together, didn't we? I don't even really think of them as mine. You underestimate yourself, you always have, but you'll be fine.'

I start to cry again. I don't want to be fine if it means being without her.

'You'll find another crappy wannabe poet somewhere, but I think you'll do just fine on your own. You'll forget me.' She reaches out and brushes a tear off my cheek. 'You can. I don't want you to, but you can.'

The Misfits

Once she's gone, I sit at one of the tables outside the pub and try to pull myself together. There's something disturbing about women weeping in public. Tears, hot and sticky, sting their way through Vi's carefully applied pancake makeup, leaving black-edged runnels on my cheeks. I dab at them with a wettened finger, stroking my mask back into place. I'm not ready to go home yet. I need to scream, sing, do something … dance. I could dance. Getting up from the bench, I grab my phone and send Roshan a text. 'Where in Hoxton?'

It's a beautiful night. I head past the fried chicken shops and Cash Converters, up past the fire station towards the pubs. Even before I see him outside the bar, I know something is going to happen tonight; that maybe the miracle I dressed for wasn't with Kate, but him.

He looks good enough to eat, in black jeans and a hot-pink shirt that sings against the dark plush of his skin. We duck our heads, trying to avoid an awkward stare across the road while we wait endlessly for the light to turn green, but we can't pretend we haven't seen each other. He's the first to give up pretending he hasn't seen me.

'Wow,' he mouths, his hands caressing the outline of a pin-up girl in the air. A gauche schoolboy's gesture that takes me back fifteen years.

He smiles and I smile back – not bashful any more, but a straightforward grin. I feel myself bounce slightly on the balls of my feet and while the rational part of me asks, 'What the hell am I doing … ?' it's all I can do not to break into a run as the lights finally change.

'Good timing,' he says. 'If a little late, as usual.'

'Sorry, babe, I was just … finishing something up.'

'Are you OK? Your eyes look a bit red.'

'Just tired. But still up for a dance. Want me to get you a drink? Calm your nerves?'

He shakes his head. 'Nah, I'm like you that way, I try to stay sober before I go on. I need to know what my hands are doing. But if you could line one up for afterwards, that would be amazing. Have you eaten?'

I shake my head. Suddenly, I realise I'm starving.

'There won't be much open by the time we're done,' he says. 'Otherwise I'd take you to this Vietnamese place … but I think we might have to make do with chips.'

'That's fine. Seriously.' I give him a long-overdue hug. 'It's all good.'

While he's on the decks, I watch him. Hanging around in the corners, for once enjoying not being in the spotlight, I love every minute of seeing Roshan in his natural environment. Comfortable with the crowd, he finally looks like he's grown into his considerable self. There's something in the way he moves, something comically close to arrogance, and, remembering that gawky, awkward boy at school, I feel so proud as the girls admire him and the boys nod grudgingly when they look his way. Another victory for the misfits. We didn't turn out so badly, him and me. I want to go behind the DJ booth and whisper into his ear – What were we so worried about, back then? Look. We did all right.

His tracks, their skewed fusions singing under his fingers, are as quirky as his photographs. It's amazing what they do, those huge hands with their long fingers and cracked palms. Above the throbbing bassline, a sitar whines like a fly on a glass door. I remember his mother's old Bollywood movies, their sound effects oozing upstairs on those long afternoons. The screaming, the dancing, and upstairs, two kids getting high and dreaming together.

The chorus kicks in, an exploding punch of bass. The sitar stops, the glass of the high notes cracking and showering the crowd. Silver crystals spread through my veins. Someone yells, 'Tune!' I bounce in my tired shoes, wait for him to look up and see me, and when he does, everything funnels in on itself like a dying star. Blinking at the intensity of it, he looks away, but not nearly fast enough.

We sit at the counter of a fluorescent-lit kebab shop on Old Street. Two gypsy kids out on the town – him in his girlie pink shirt, me in my sea-green fifties finery. We don't say much – too busy eating. I'd forgotten my hunger until now, but it's all I can do to eat slowly; if I was alone, I'd be cramming these chips down in handfuls, they're so salty and crisp-skinned. Nothing's tasted like this in weeks.

'Good gig,' I say. It's an understatement.

'You think so?' He turns to face me. His eyes are so dark they stain the skin around them. 'Yeah, it was OK, wasn't it?'

'More than that. Is there anything you can't do?'

'Let me think. Maths. Contact sports. Holding onto a girlfriend.'

'Mmm. Same as me, really.'

'You've got special talents, though. Like bollard-jumping.'

I remember that drunken night with Vinyl and Jack. 'Don't remind me.'

He shrugs. 'I like it. You make me feel alive.'

A couple of hours ago, I was feeling battered, but now I feel high. Invulnerable, like nothing can hurt me again. It's how I felt when I was running down the street with him, jumping over bollards in the dark. I remember enough of that night to know that it's dangerous.

'So, that track you sampled,' I start to ask him, 'the one with the kind of Cuban feel to it, where'd you …'

He leans closer to hear me, looking over my shoulder at the women at the counter, who are making a commotion. Real cockney queens with dangling earrings and big hair, laughing like drunken squaddies as they flirt with the tired, black-eyed men behind the counter. 'Here, you should give her extra,' one of them shouts, gesturing to her friend. 'It's her birthday!'

'Shut up!' yells the birthday girl, who's forty-something and built like a pyramid.

'Happy birthday,' says the young man behind the counter soberly.

The guy frying the chips mimes applause with his free hand, waving the iron basket from side to side. The one who does the salads starts singing in a nasal drone that reminds me again of Roshan's mum's favourite movies, 'Happy birthday to you …'

The kebab shop crowd – students, cab-drivers, two girls with Harajuku hair – join in, in that typically abashed, British mutter.

Then, swinging around from the counter, Roshan starts to sing too. My shy boy – where did he get this shamelessness? Unlike everyone else, he sings loudly, naturally, straight from the heart. The birthday girl's eyes widen. She'd expected extra chillies, maybe – not this. Suddenly, it feels like we aren't just a crew of random wankers in a kebab shop. We're sharing a state of grace.

For once in my life, I don't sing. I can't take my eyes off him. It hits me, with the force of an angry child throwing a rag doll against a wall.

I'd thought of him, on and off, over the past couple of weeks. I'd thought idly, at work, at late-night launch parties, on the Tube, about how it would be if I really loved him. In the pub, reading pulpy free music papers and laughing at the band names, watching Roshan chat politely with every deadbeat who wandered into our orbit, I had wondered. Lying on the couch with him on Sunday afternoon, the TV soothing us into a post-lunch coma and his head sweetly heavy against my shoulder, I had wondered. Watching him on the decks, head and shoulders moving up and down to the music, almost-but-not-quite-dancing, I had wondered.

But now, watching him sing, 'Happy Birthday,' to a middle-aged woman in a voice like Jeff Buckley, I stop wondering and start to know.

Saying Yes

It's starting to feel like summer. I'm shooting a music video with a new director, Lucy Swift, a chatty, pretty lesbian who's looking to boost her show-reel with some films of emerging artists. I don't want to think about quite how long I've been emerging, but when she asked if she could include me, I said yes right away. While we were splitting up, Kate had tried to make me see the bright side, telling me I had the freedom I wanted now, that I could say yes to everything, though I did point out that this hadn't served me well in the past. Then I threw a plate at her.

She's been getting in touch every couple of days, checking up on me. Making it clear she still cares. 'It's confusing,' I'd told Roshan, while we were lying on his couch watching old footage of Bill Hicks, both of us elated by his righteous, loving anger. When we spoke about the big stuff, we usually did it while the TV was on, looking at the screen rather than each other.

'Way simpler if it's a guy,' he said. 'Most of the time, we don't show our feelings. Maybe one night we get pissed and stand on your lawn. We usually go after you call the police.'

Lucy picks me up from the flat and we head for the basement club she's booked for the early evening. Because of the traffic and her dodgy SatNav, we end up taking a scenic tour of market stalls and God-themed hairdressers.

While I'm failing to improve things by telling her about my disastrous love life, my phone starts to vibrate with texts, first from Kate, 'Thinking about you – wondering how you are,' and then, just as I'm puzzling over how to reply to that, Roshan texts me about our plans for later. I'm going over to his place; he's cooking us dinner. He's an excellent cook, even if he does use every utensil in the kitchen to make one meal. I'm bringing the beers and we've got a box-set marathon planned. It's almost like my old life, except with a large hairy man where my girlfriend used to be.

Since our night out in Hoxton, he'd been texting me two or three times a day, usually the kind of texts that needed proper answers. I'd find myself picking my phone up, wondering how to respond, putting it down again, my mind still half on him. Today, he'd been asking me what I wanted to drink, to eat, what time I'd be over, what I felt like watching – and my mind was elsewhere. I'd tried to refrain from looking at my phone, knowing he'd have found something else to say – 'Evie I'm getting the chillies out now. I'm going to make at least one not too spicy thing cos I know my cooking makes you sweat like a horse. Any requests?'

This latest text, though, is something else. I'd told him I'd crash on the couch as it would be late by the time I got there. He wouldn't hear of it, he told me; I could have his bed. I refused – there was no way someone his size could fit on the couch, but he insisted I could take the bed. Sitting in traffic between rafts of plantains and phone-unlocking stores, I look down at my latest text: 'Hey my back is playing up today and I need my bed. You can always join me x'

I don't think so, and send him an abrupt message to that effect.

Immediately, he gets defensive. 'Okay you can have the couch. You don't have to be like that about it. Just let me know when you're done if that's not too much of a problem.'

'I am not sharing your sweaty bed, you dick,' I say out loud. 'Not again, anyway.'

Lucy, swinging the car through lazily blaring traffic, turns to me. 'Everything OK?'

'Yes. No. Just a friend of mine being a bit weird. Or maybe I'm over-reacting. If someone wants to share a bed with you, does that always mean …'

She bites her lip, staring out at the traffic. 'Pretty much. Unless you've, like, known them for years.'

I have, of course. But somehow that doesn't help.

Lucy sets up her lights in the basement of The Blue Door, Dalston's finest lesbian pit. I change into a little black dress that I wish made me look like Audrey Hepburn but really makes me look like a gangster's wife on the razz in Marbella.

My focus is hazy. I hate conflict. Even this minor fight with Roshan reminds me of recent bigger battles, and my hands are shaking as I try to keep them still on the edge of the pool table, making a mess of the nails I'm trying to paint. Lucy thinks the red will look dynamite on camera. Anything to detract from my sleep-deprived face. I hope he's not angry with me. I can't take it if he is.

I perch on a stool. We tool up, me with my guitar, her with her lights balanced precariously on beer crates, and get to work. 'Three takes, max,' she says apologetically. 'I need to be in town at eight.'

That late already? I fight the temptation to look at my phone and begin to sing, enjoying each stolen-feeling moment as everything else fades. Oh Lord, that old bargain-basement magic. How can I give this up? How could I have thought of staying at home, when I could have been doing more of this?

I was right, I tell myself, staring into the blank keyhole of her camera. I can write my own songs, find my own way home. Out of the corner of my eye, my phone flares with light, but I keep playing. They can wait, all of them. Time will prove me right.

Rock and Doris

Still in my Marbella-moll drag, I knock on the downstairs door of Roshan's flat and Dan the Weird Landlord lets me in. Dan is some kind of software genius. He keeps odd hours, smokes a lot of weed and has trouble making eye contact with women, especially women in hooker shoes clutching blue corner-shop bags of clinking six-packs and a bunch of tired irises. Don't ask me why I'm buying flowers for this boy as if he's my disgruntled girlfriend. They were sitting outside a Turkish shop, wilting bravely, their perfume almost gone, their luscious, lolling petals shot with gold. I felt a twinge of desire, something almost sexual, binding me from throat to crotch. I had to have them.

I smile at Dan, take off my shoes and climb the stairs. I knock tentatively on the door, but he doesn't answer.

I knock again, and realise the door's open. He's probably got his headphones on. Roshan likes mixing tracks in his free time but when Dan's being particularly odd, he spares him the worst of his pounding, liver-quivering basslines.

'Hello? Babe, you in there? I'm sorry I'm late, I was nowhere near a Tube…'

I slip off my shoes and pad into the immaculate room, which smells delicious from simmering chillies, fresh with citrus and coriander. He's sitting at the table, looking intently at his laptop, a pair of huge black headphones cuffing his ears. He doesn't see me. He's already bought flowers, arranged in a plain glass vase on the table; exactly the same irises as mine. He must have felt sorry for them too. Sometimes I think he's gayer than I am.

Roshan's eyes are glued to YouTube. As I get closer the pixellated cluster comes into focus. There's something familiar about the girl he's looking at. Not her face exactly, not her hair, but the way she raises her hand to brush it out of her eyes, how she dips her head to smile as the song ends. Another night. Another grainy video shot by a stranger as a favour to someone else, some organiser. Someone with a wobbly camera whose thoughts about the singer they were filming may never be known, though I'd put my money on indifference. I clear my throat and he turns around, so slowly I know he's already realised I'm there.

'What's that?' I ask as he hurriedly takes off the headphones.

'Just killing time. Good song. Have you ever thought about, uh, slowing it down a little?'

I haven't had a proper conversation with anyone in weeks. I do enough pretending with Kate, or at work, and I'm not going to start doing it with him. 'I don't know, I never watch videos of myself. Cringey. Which one is that, anyway?'

'I forget what you called it. The one about family secrets.' He stands up and stretches, towering over me. 'You want a beer?'

'Yeah, that would be … that would be great.'

I let him stride past me into the tiny, plate-filled kitchen and watch him as he pours us a couple of beers, his cheeks faintly mottled with red. I feel an urge to stand behind him and lace my arms around his waist, press my face into his broad back. I want to tell him it's all right, but I'm not sure it is. 'I brought more beer,' I say. 'And flowers.'

He smiles, not looking at me. 'Well, you are spoiling me.' He hands me my drink. I clink my glass against his and hand him the irises. He looks down at his own vase of flowers and pushes it gently towards me. When he looks back up he's biting his lip. I wonder if his gift somehow cancels mine out. 'Coals to Newcastle,' I say.

His forehead furrows. With his grammar-school-and-MTV English, he doesn't really do idiom.

'Nothing. We shouldn't have,' I say.

'Oh, I don't know.' He smiles, and finally I can see him relax. 'I think it's perfect.'

After he's given the bubbling pots a quick stir, he seems calmer, as though the flush on his cheeks might just be from steam and alcohol. We settle into some sort of normality as we root through his DVDs.

'How's your back?' I ask, and he looks at me, slightly mutinous, like I'm trying to catch him out in a lie. I suppose I am.

'Ah, still not great. I think I slept in a weird position or something.'

I imagine him sleeping. I know what that looks like now, his mouth slightly open, the bold, swooping lines of his features softened. I know how sweet his sleeping flesh smells. I think of him in his big, crumpled bed, holding me like I was about to break in two.

'I can always go home. Or take the couch. Either.'

'Let's talk about it later.' He holds up a fan of DVDs. 'OK, I'm down to five. You choose.'

'*8 Women* … *Mildred Pierce* … *Harold and Maude, High Society* and *The Hours*?'

'What do you reckon?'

'That you're really, really gay.'

'I bet the sisterhood would be pleased to hear you say, "gay" like a twelve-year-old boy. Anyway, you're meant to like this stuff. You're a girl.'

'Closet case.'

'Muff-diver.'

'Not *The Hours*, I saw it last week.'

'All right. I think the food's nearly ready.'

'Ah, fuck it,' I say, 'Let's just watch some of the old Rock and Doris.'

'Right.' He raises an eyebrow. 'Because that's really heterosexual.'

'Shut up, Rosh.'

We shuffle around his kitchen, happily playing house before settling down to eat. Having lived in India for ten years and England for more than twenty, Roshan is the undisputed king of fusion food, with a genius for curry-themed leftovers. His special skill is creating the best hangover cures known to humanity, including Indian-style omelettes with cumin and coriander and my personal all-time favourite, baked beans with garam masala, chilli and brown sugar. I love watching him eat, his lower lip glossed with sauce. There's something boyish about his delight in food that always softens me.

'You should have more,' he says. 'You've been working hard.'

'No I haven't. And I'm fine. It's lovely. Stop channelling your mum.' I don't know what my problem is. I never used to have trouble eating in front of him.

The couch seems smaller than ever and as we sprawl out and relax, he takes up more of it. Once we've pushed our plates away, mouths stinging and bellies full, he puts his arm around my shoulder. It's not like he's never done this, but this time it makes us as awkward as the ungainly teenagers we were. I catch him watching me, mirroring my gestures, resting his head on his hand like I do. I rub my nose and, a minute later, watch him do the same.

As usual, we talk throughout the film in a low, rustling murmur; when it's the two of us, it just feels like the characters are only there to provide us with material. We used to switch off the sound and provide our own disturbing dialogue:

'Excuse me, can you direct me to the nearest cruising spot?'

'Over there by the church. That's an interesting hairpiece.'

'Thank you, it was my mother's.'

Tonight, we're quieter, watching Rock Hudson and Doris Day endlessly misunderstand each other. Everything's hilarious, the way it probably always is when you're experiencing chronic sexual tension and everything in front of you is unfurling in full cheesy Breathtaking Cinemascope and you've had at least three cans of strong European lager.

He stretches. I hear something in his back click ominously. 'You OK?' I ask hurriedly, touching his arm. My hand stays where it is and I'm strangely all right with that.

He laughs, through a wince. 'Fine.' As I pat his arm, relieved, he pulls me towards him. We're silent again. I'm very aware of myself – the tight, straining black dress, the gobs of makeup, the musk of sweat the day's laid over my skin. My breath smells of cumin-tinged embers doused with GBH-strength beer. Roshan smells of clean laundry and shampoo. I thought boys were meant to be the disgusting ones.

He pulls a bobby pin from my hair. 'Can I … ?'

I nod, not knowing what I'm agreeing to.

His hands roam over the back of my neck, a roughened fingertip buzzing against my ear in a sketchy caress, as he undoes my hair from its rickrack of pins.

'Pretty.' He combs my hair with his fingers and I feel myself shrinking, doll-small beside him. I smile sideways at him, sip my beer, wish I was somewhere else.

His hands are on my shoulders now. 'You're not watching,' he says quietly.

'No. Well, I have seen it a few hundred times.'

'Could you … Evie, could you please look at me?'

I do. Whatever he sees in my eyes makes him step back a little, but he doesn't move his hands. His touch hovers on my skin, warming it. Even my skin betrays me. His jeaned thigh brushes mine and I feel suddenly, ridiculously turned on. He bends his head and all I can see for a moment is the dark blur of his eyes, the soft sprawl of his mouth dangerously close to mine.

'Don't.' All the conviction is gone from my voice. It's been a long day.

'It's OK. Just …' his hand rises, tracing my cheek. 'Just let me …'

'Not again.'

I feel his hand falter and he moves back. We don't talk about that.

'That was a mistake,' he says eventually. 'I felt … well, I needed a couple of cold showers, but no harm done, we didn't …'

'Go through with it? No.' I think of Kate and Cathy. It's not the sex I mind so much, it's the intimacy. How their eyes must have lingered on each other. How they must have laughed at each other's jokes, even when they weren't funny. Especially then. 'There's more than one way to cheat.'

'Yeah, but you've got to draw the line somewhere. And we didn't …'

'So what are you saying, I owe you one now?' I ask angrily.

'No! You know that's not it, you just said, back then … if things were different …'

'Yeah. Like if I was straight. You know we don't talk about that time anyway. You never mention it. You don't even like saying, "Wardour Street." We sure as hell don't drink there any more.'

I scramble away from him and stand up. Even at my not-so-full height, I don't exactly tower over him. And he's sitting down.

'And whose fault is that, Evie?' He rubs his mouth, as though we'd kissed.

'Mine, OK? But if you want a trip down memory lane, I'm not going to stop you.'

He takes a deep breath. 'You're right. We don't talk about it.'

'About what?'

'Wardour Street.'

'Sorry?'

He glares at me. 'Wardour Street!' I have never in my life heard him shout. In my head, the waves of his voice rise, gather and blur.

When I open my eyes, he's looking at me. 'Sorry. I don't … like shouting.'

'You're pretty good at it.'

'Come back here.'

I think about it. I think about going back to my strange new house. I think about the mess humans leave as we rampage through life, our trash streaking behind us. I know if I go to him, I'll do something I can't undo.

'Wardour Street,' he says. 'Wardour Street, Wardour Street, Wardour Street.'

'I love it when you talk dirty.'

'Come back here, Evie,' he says again. 'I'm not messing around this time.'

His phone starts to ring. He stays where he is, staring as though he can see beneath my skin into my loops of neuron, my soft, red cavities, my innermost scars.

The vibrating bleat seems to rise, the phone trembling on the arm of the sofa. I stand for as long as I can – he's waited a year. He can wait a few seconds longer. The phone rings. And rings. And rings.

Just a Kiss

When it happened, I blamed myself. It was easy. I blamed him for being a man. That was easy too. I'm not sure which of us was the victim when we were writhing and tussling in the doorway of a Soho pub. Maybe neither of us.

It was a year ago. He'd looked at me that way men sometimes do and I knew it wasn't me he was looking at, Evie Day with the hippy mum and the battered guitar, no longer the girl who debated the theology of *South Park* with him or made fun of Picasso's ruder etchings in the Tate Modern; a girl he wanted to fuck. I wanted him that way too – not to be had by him, but to devour him, to brand his smooth skin.

I remember the soft bath of his lips on mine, and how I felt nothing at first, and thought – it's OK, I can salvage this, it's a mistake – but it wasn't, even as my conscience screamed at me. It wasn't a mistake.

We broke apart before any real damage was done. I went home to my long-term girlfriend and told her nothing and he went home to one of his less long-term girlfriends and did the same. It felt like the end; once we'd had a safe place, but we realised it too late.

I miss that place. I want to go back there now.

'What would you do? If I came over there?' I realise I'm flirting with him. It's my default setting. I learned it from Pina, watching her night after night from the top of the stairs – the toss of the hair, the hand raised to the throat.

'I don't know,' he says, looking like he's surprised by his own honesty. 'I'd like to kiss you. I can't really think of anything else right now.'

'And the whole gay thing … what, you haven't really noticed? It's not a problem for you? What do you think, we're all secretly straight anyway?'

'Don't give me that. If you feel that way, why are you flirting with me?'

'I'm not. No more than I do with everyone, anyway.' This, at least, is true.

'You had no reason to keep seeing me,' he says.

'You're the one who kept asking. You're always on at me. Like I haven't got enough on my mind.'

'Sorry, Evie.' He bristles. 'I didn't realise I was such an inconvenience.'

'You're not. That came out wrong. I like having you in my life again. I don't want to lose that. I really don't. But, come on … we hang out a bit, go to some gigs, watch some movies and then you turn around like all the other blokes I've ever met and go, 'Yeah, I know you're a lesbian and everything but do you want to see my knob … ?'

'It's not like that. Anyway, I had no idea this would be a surprise. I thought I'd made it clear enough.'

'How? How did you make it clear?'

'Texting you all the time. Wanting to see you every week. The way…' frustrated, he rubs his hands over his face so his words are muffled as he says, 'For God's sake, Day, haven't you seen how I look at you?'

'No,' I say softly. Though it's not true.

'Really?' He takes his hands away from his face. He looks tired, suddenly. With his bright, plushy skin and little-boy smile, he's always seemed young. This is the first time I've seen him look older than he is.

'OK, I had some idea, but do you have any idea how insulting that is? And how many times it's happened in my relatively short life?' I stare down at my bare feet. 'I know girls who are friends with boys. I know it happens, whatever the movies and chick-lit say, men can be friends with women. So how come it never happens to me? I'd do so much for you. I want to show you how happy I am that you're back in my life. I'd … I'd like to cook for you, you know that?' I swallow some salty, lager-tasting tears. 'If you even felt a bit down I'd run across town to hug you. We could have so much more than this. But this is all you want. Can't you see how that kind of hurts?'

He shrugs. 'All I know, Evie, is that yes, I'm sorry, but I do want this. There's something between us. I don't know whether it's that I want to take care of you too ... can you stop looking at me like that? Little avenging angel. I won't lay a finger on you. Sit down.'

I sit beside him, staring ahead of me at the screen, arms crossed protectively over my breasts. As he talks, I bring my knees up and wrap my arms around them. I want to seem invincible, but I know I don't. Everything about my posture screams, 'scared little girl.'

'I broke up with someone a couple of months ago,' he says slowly. One hand reaches out and holds my foot, tenderly as you'd hold a new egg. His whole hand can wrap round it. 'It's still a bit raw. I think about her a lot. I just wanted something to get me out of the house. When we met in the pub for that photo thing and heard you talk about your life, I remembered how you throw yourself around town ... how you never sit still. I recognised that in myself. I knew you just didn't want to think.'

'She was cheating on me. Of course I didn't want to think.'

'I know. And with mine ... there wasn't any of that, but it still hurt like hell. That night after I'd seen you, I just went home and thought, I don't want to be like this any more. I want to breathe. I want you to breathe too. You're so ...' he reaches out and brushes my cheek.

'No,' I say. I'm hollow. I can't move.

'You're so lovely.' He strokes my foot, his long fingers navigating the arch, making sparks on my skin.

'You said no touching.' I turn to face him as he obediently takes his hand away. 'I don't need this. I need you to be my friend.'

'I'm still your friend. I can't stop being your friend. But I can't turn this off.'

'Yes you can. You think I don't mind doing without love? Knowing my girlfriend – my ex, whatever, prefers someone else? Sometimes you don't have a choice. Move on.'

'I don't want to.' He stares at me, his voice low and even, his gaze steady.

'Too bad.' I get up clumsily. 'I'm out of here.'

'Evie, don't. Come on.'

'I think I should go.'

'Can I get you a cab? Or walk you to the bus stop? Please. It's not safe out there.'

'It never is.' I sling my guitar over my shoulder. 'If I thought like that just because I'm a woman, I'd never do anything. Bad things happen all the time, Rosh. No matter how safe you think you are.'

'Text me when you get in,' he says quietly. 'You can do that at least.'

'You're a dick,' I say, eloquently, from the door.

'Yeah.' He presses his lips together, not meeting my eyes. 'I was starting to notice.'

Getting over Hope

For all his warnings, the neighbourhood's silent and the air in the street is clear and cool. I gulp it like champagne.

I don't want to think about losing another friend. I don't want to think about how easy it would have been to stay, how I'd wanted to be close to him at all costs. I remind myself not to think about Wardour Street. I try to forget about my body, how loose-limbed and warm it feels, the sparks of hunger and excitement in my belly, constellations forming between my thighs.

I'm so busy trying not to think that it takes me a while to realise I'm lost.

Nothing looks familiar. Run-down buildings, darkened playgrounds, off-licences lit like hospitals. No people, no cabs. All I can hear is my own breath. Unbidden lyrics spring into my head, but I'm not sure whether they're for Roshan or Kate. *What you said happened accidentally / leaves me mentally scarred / getting over you will happen eventually / getting over hope is hard.*

I take a moment, standing on a corner, vainly scanning for anything that looks like a taxi rank. I take stock of myself. High heels, warpaint, guitar – all the usual props, but I feel very delicate, very small. I think of Cathy and Kate in our old bedroom across town, dreaming together. Bastards.

I've walked up a lot of streets like this. I used to, when I was a teenager, fearless. When the nights were a drug. These days, I play it safe – or I try to. My breath speeds up and I feel tears welling hotly behind my eyes. I want to scream at the sky. *Don't I deserve a fucking break? My lover, my flat, my friend … what else do you want? A couple of limbs?*

I have no idea where I am. I just know that I want to be exactly where I was, back in the warm room with him beside me. It feels like everyone else in the world is with someone tonight. I'm tired of fighting. I'm tired of trying to be good.

I turn back and start walking towards his flat, but either I take a wrong turn or I'm just too confused to think. I can't find the way. I fumble in my bag for my phone and keep walking, like suddenly the streets will start to make sense if I just keep on.

I wonder what he's doing. I think of him running the dishes under the tap, walking alone into his bedroom. Sadness and longing hits me like a velvet punch in the gut. I want to comfort him, breathe him in, feel his skin against mine.

I take out my phone, bring up his number and call. He picks up right away, as though his phone was already in his hands.

'Evie.' His voice is guarded. 'Are you all right?'

'I'm lost,' I say, hearing the scrape of panic in my voice.

'OK. You can't have gone too far. Just …' I hear some fumbling in the background. 'Right. What can you see?'

'Er… some kind of corner shop, green sign, just says Groceries and Off Licence, sorry, that's not helpful … I can see a nail bar, seems to be called Polish You Off… er, some clothes stores … and some kind of sign, I think it's in Urdu or something.'

'Right. What's it say?'

It takes me a moment. I laugh. 'Fuck you, Rosh.'

'OK, well, specific as all that was, I'm going to need a street name. Can you do that? And don't worry. You're all right.'

I look up, and somewhere among the breezeblock and shuttered shop fronts, I see it. 'Linen Street. Must be, I don't know, in some old textile area or something.'

'Linen Street. Fine. Stay where you are, don't move. I'm already trying to do this without a sense of direction.'

Before too long, he's coming round the corner. The sight of him floods me with relief and I get a rush of some of that happiness I didn't manage to feel when I first saw him tonight, hunched over his laptop, watching me sing. It's like we're starting again.

'Hey,' he says, once he's close enough. 'Are you all right?'

'Yeah. Yeah. Thank you, I … I'm fine. I don't know what …'

'It's OK. I made a bit of a mess of that, I know.'

'You didn't.'

We stand there for a while. I listen to his deep, hectic breathing. I look down.

'You're not wearing any shoes,' I say quietly.

'No. And I think I may have trod on a lit cigarette. But that's kind of irrelevant.'

'I'm sorry.'

'Don't be.' A slow smile lights his face. 'Are you coming back?'

I nod.

'Because you want to? Or just because you're lost? I mean, it doesn't matter, of course you can crash, it's just … I should have called you a cab. But you just went. I …'

'Ssh,' I say. 'It's all right.'

He puts his arms around me. 'Is this … I mean, Evie, can I … ?'

'Yes,' I say. 'You know you can.' And finally, he kisses me.

It's awkward. Of course it is. In the half-light of his bedroom, we're awkward high-school kids again, all fumbling and questions. We are children clinging, beyond gender, beyond everything. I feel like my skin's blossoming into colour, like those cheap books I had as a kid where you trailed a wet brush against the paper and pictures bloomed to the surface. That's how it feels, coming to life. You can't choose the pictures or the colours, but it still doesn't seem right to complain.

It still seems natural, especially when we fall slowly asleep at the same time, dreaming in each other's arms. I know we're not having the same dreams, but I tell myself that we might be. We start drowsing when we're still on top of the covers and eventually slip under them together, still speaking but half-asleep, his body folding around me, big and protective. His hand on my back is the size of God.

I don't know what this is. If you asked me, I couldn't tell you. But I know I haven't felt so safe in a very long time.

Sleeping Together

I can't believe it's Monday morning already. I look over at the man sleeping next to me and want to laugh – at the silliness of it all, but also the joy. Now I know why they call it a crush. I'm flattened, incapable, bruised, a Victorian heroine in need of a lie-down and some smelling salts. I can't believe how beautiful he's become right in front of my eyes.

We'd had one of those Sundays – the kind you only have in the first flush of lust, a slow, underwater day, lying together, whispering, kissing and touching, telling each other our life stories until after dark. We ate last night's leftovers in the middle of the afternoon. In the evening, hungry again, we went out and looked for food in the corner shops with their garish tins and packages and their lights so achingly bright that we blinked at each other like recently released prisoners, trying not to laugh.

Sleeping with Roshan – in the most literal sense – is the best thing on earth. The ease with which we fold into each other and drift off surprises us. No sweat, no dead limbs, the odd gentle snore quickly quietened by a shift in position. We could be the poster-children for sleep. I sometimes wonder if that's when we communicate, if the part of him I don't get to see talks to the parts of me I hide, but as soon as we wake up, we start returning to our separate selves. Even as he snuggles into my back and murmurs, 'Can we just stay here all day?' I know he doesn't really mean it. I wonder what he'd do if I said yes.

'I'll make some coffee in a minute,' I murmur untruthfully.

'Don't.' His sleep-deep voice thickens. 'Not yet.' He pulls me closer. We look into each other's eyes and smile. In the half-light of early morning, he holds my face and traces the outline of my lips with his thumb. I feel them pout and plump like apricots under his touch.

'You want some water?' I reach for the glass on the bedside table and pass it to him. Propping himself up on one elbow, he drinks and politely passes it to me to finish.

'Evie,' he says, 'I don't want to be personal, but was that your ...'

'If you say, 'first time,' I will have to emasculate you.'

'Yeah, but ...'

'Was it? Like that, yes.'

'Jesus. I don't think I've ever been the first.'

'You weren't, love. That was Sandra Atkinson. I was seventeen. She was, I don't know, twenty-something. Red hair. Nineties tattoos. You know, those Celtic bands everyone had?'

He rolls onto his back, looking mildly shell-shocked.

'Stop looking like that. You did not just de-virginise me.'

'I wish I'd known, that's all.'

'Why? Would you have done something different?' Then, telling myself to shut up, I put my arms around him and burrow in. 'It was ... I don't know. If I was going to do that with anyone, I'm glad it was you.'

'My fifteen-year-old self is very glad it was me too.'

'And how about the thirtysomething version?'

'Blissed out.' He hauls me up onto his chest. I luxuriate in his warm, silky skin, the current of his breath.

'Did you want it to happen back then?' I think of the two of us scrabbling under teach other's clothes, fifteen, weak with dope and desire.

'I was a teenage boy, Day. I would have screwed anything that stood still. But I'm kind of glad this is now.'

'Have you had a lot of girlfriends?'

'Not a lot. But they stayed for a while. Bit of a serial monogamist. How about you?'

'Only two serious girlfriends. Jamie and Kate. Jamie for two years, Kate five, a lot of whoring around in between.'

'I should have done more of that. How about boyfriends?'

'Not really. One or two … one when I was sixteen, after you went to Uni … a couple of fumbles in college. I love the company of men, always have, but you can count the ones I've actually fancied on one hand.'

I smile at him, sprawled unselfconsciously on his rumpled linen. It tickles me a little, how comfortable he looks. How it's the boys he wants to know about, when they're barely a chapter in my life, usually forgotten. I'd bragged for years that I'd never once slept with a man. Now I had, I didn't feel it as a loss – or a gain. Still, something about it nags at me; that I've done something momentous, but he doesn't see it that way. I'm sure he thinks my sexuality is an illusion, something I'm growing out of. I know I'm not exactly helping the cause by having just lost my heterosexual cherry to him, but I want him to know that he's my exception – not the other way round.

'I'd better not tell my mum about this,' I say. 'She always said you were gorgeous.'

'God. I'm your mother's idea of an exotic shag. I'm really going to need counselling now.'

'You can't blame her.'

'I bet if we had a baby she'd want to adopt it.'

'If we had a baby, it would be far too beautiful to give anyone.'

We're silent for a while.

'You'd be an amazing mum,' he says softly.

'Maybe. Maybe even in this lifetime.'

Kate and I once talked about babies this easily. We'd go round to our married friends' places and beg for a hold; I remember how natural she looked with them, how one sleep-deprived couple after another would look at us holding their babies and nod smugly like we'd just caught their wedding bouquet. I can't think about that now.

I turn away from Roshan and gulp the rest of the water, giving myself a minute. I feel his hand on my spine, stroking as I swallow, like I'm a baby myself.

I breathe again. I don't know how he does that.

'You're really young,' he says evenly. 'Why would you be so worried about that?'

'Not that young. But you're right, I don't need to worry about babies at the moment. So don't start thinking you don't have to put something on it.'

'Right now,' he says, 'I'd be very happy to.' He rolls me into his arms again and we move back into each other's rhythm. If he tastes salt on my mouth, it's quickly tempered by his own burnt-sugar sweetness.

I wonder what people will think, of course. I want to take him out, play him songs, but I can't imagine his mates or his mother would approve of me even without the back-story.

As for my world, it's just as bad, if not worse. Jamie and Gray will be deeply unimpressed and Kate will probably assume that I was straight all along and that's why things never worked. But right now, I don't feel any of that. I just feel happy and impatient to breathe his skin, bury my nose in his charcoal-soft hair, feel his laugh rumble through me as he asks if we can stay in bed all day. I wish we could stay here for the rest of our lives.

We lie together, exhausted. 'I don't even want to look at the clock.'

'Don't. What's your excuse?'

'Breakfast meeting,' I say. 'Yours?'

'Eye appointment,' he says. 'I do actually need one.'

'You'd look cute in glasses.'

'I'd look like a brown John Lennon.'

'My mother would definitely fancy you then.'

'Yeah. Let's stop talking about your mother now. God, you're hot.' He kisses his way down my belly. 'Literally. I could cook breakfast on you.'

In summer, Kate used to huff and throw the covers off us because my skin gave off too much heat; Roshan treats my heat production with a kind of amused wonder, like my body's doing something clever by keeping us warm all night. 'I can't wait for winter,' he murmurs. 'You could be my central heating.'

'We're late,' I say groggily. Light's rolling across the ceiling in great unforgiving slabs.

'I know,' he says. He's looking at me intently. 'You look … Evie, just give me five minutes, OK?' He gets up, slides back into his shirt and jeans and grabs his camera bag from on top of my bookshelf. 'Stay where you are.'

'Naked pictures?'

'Doesn't have to be. Pull the sheets up.'

'I look awful.'

'You really don't. I don't take pictures of awful-looking people. Stop – no.' He swats at my hand. 'Don't do anything to your hair. You're perfect.'

I'm very aware of myself – smeared mascara, lips raw and stubble-swollen, eyes damp. He takes picture after picture, moving around the bed while I stay where I am.

'Come back,' I say. 'Be with me for a moment.'

He's already gone. 'Just a minute. Please. I'm nearly…' he clicks for another couple of minutes. 'Raise your head.' I do. 'Not so angry. What are you looking at me like that for?'

'I'm not angry. I just want you to stop.'

'I'm nearly there.' There is something sexual in this. Something in the way that he sees me. Not as a person, but an image. It reminds me of Kate. How she stopped seeing me. My idiosyncrasies. My flaws. She saw me as a catch that it was a dumb idea to let go of, but she still let me go, and I'm still gone.

'That's it,' he murmurs. 'That is totally it.'

Strangeness over, he perches on the bed and hugs me to him. 'You OK now? I'm sorry. I wanted you to know how you looked then. You'll understand when you see.'

'I wish I could take pictures. I'd like to dress you up and immortalise you.'

He laughs. 'Don't tell me. Eyeliner and lipstick. Maybe a skirt?'

I look at him, weighing him up. I'd like to coat his eyelids in soft kohl, heap cheap gemstones on his skin. 'Eyeliner maybe. It'd look pretty striking.'

'Funny you should say that. I think I've got an old eyeliner pencil in my bag.'

'A man after my own heart,' I say. Kidding, but there's a grain of truth there.

He stops and smiles, and for a second, it's like he's really seeing me.

The Three R's

I love the smell of Soho in the morning. Even when it's stinking like a pub carpet, it's rich with life – sleaze, heat, hunger, a great hot-mouthed tart. In twilight it can feel tragic, but in the morning, it's always new and feels like it could, just possibly, be conquered.

Every morning I walk up the stairs to the Frederick French offices, I know how lucky I am to work here. At the door of the office, I pause and tell myself, as I have every day for the past month or so, that this will be the day I get it together.

Somehow, though, I doubt it. Within an hour, once I've got over my usual morning horrors about Cathy and Kate, I'll be bogged down in demanding writers, writing endless urgent press releases, wishing I was lying on a hillside somewhere hot with Roshan at my side, all the time in the world our own. By the end of the day I'll be as annoyed with myself as I am with everyone else, trailing back to the strange-feeling Highgate flat, telling myself that tomorrow, it'll all be different.

It hasn't rained in days and the heat is making everyone crabby. Two of the younger executives have cried this week, and the accounts seem to be drying up – everyone's afraid of spending money, and PR, like so much else, is a luxury. It feels like my new rawness is what everyone's been waiting for. They can smell it. Journalists never return my calls, I've been missing meetings and deadlines, and Amanda's talking to me as though I just finished primary school.

Still, Angelo Giannini, with his triceps, photoshoots and terrifying dinners, is finally out of my life, and I've been doing all right with my latest job – the ghosted biography of Plato J. Reilly, also known as Rebel, a hot young American hip-hop star. Rebel's story is the usual one – Ghettos-to-Gold. In his white puffa jacket and jewellery he looks like a cross between a snowman and a Christmas tree. He's been tearing up the summer charts with his second single *Urban Girl*, notable for the lines, 'Bitch, don't think you gonna snare this Rebel / you got a big fat ass and a heart like a pebble.' The Last Poets' pioneering work was clearly not in vain.

Our shareholders are all rubbing their hands and, even though he's not coming over here – he wouldn't, for a company as small as Frederick French – we're the first on the market and, as Amanda optimistically thinks, about to make a killing, though I can just see the book marked down to three pounds in the impulse-buy section of music stores. Given my recent performance, I wouldn't even have got the account except Amanda thrust the manuscript onto my desk after the first few pages, throwing up her manicured hands, 'You know me, Evie – my idea of an edgy act is Take That!' Sadly, this is true.

I got all the coverage we could have, and more. I've been patting myself quietly on the back over the impressive list of magazines I've forwarded round to Amanda and the big bosses, not that they'll know who I'm talking about. All I have to do is wait.

Unfortunately, Rebel – like many celebrities before him – does something dumb. I come in to work on Monday to a heat-stunned silence and he's scrolling through my Google reports like descending stock figures. 'Anti-gay… Rebel puts his foot in it again … one-man PR disaster.' Except now it's not just his disaster, it's mine.

Gay magazines and bloggers are now ripping Rebel a new one for a foul-mouthed Twitter update on Friday night, in which he referred to a sports team whose performance had displeased him as 'a bunch of fucking fags.' It gets better. There are at least twenty tweets following that, trying to justify himself and putting his foot in it even more. 'Whatevs, yo, it ain't natural,' he concludes like a hip *Daily Mail* columnist before thankfully disappearing into the ether.

I know the three R's of PR disaster response – regret, responsibility, renewal – and I know that's what Amanda's expecting of me. The only R I'm interested in now is Revenge. Or Reality. I want something more real than this. I've done some pretty unscrupulous things in the name of press coverage, but the hunger of my early twenties has started to fade. I'm sick of Rebel. I'm sick of anyone who gets away with anything.

There's a press-ready statement from his agent already sitting in my inbox, apparently provided by Mr. Reilly.

'An unfortunate lapse in judgement sparked by a moment's frustration … like many men, I have struggled to understand homosexuals, but I love all my fans, gay and straight. I have learned from this unfortunate incident and am ashamed of my insensitive comments. With God's help I will continue to become a better person and put all this behind me.'

I'm expected to farm this out to everyone who calls me, and my phone's ringing off the hook, my inbox filling with questions from allies and enemies alike. 'Evie, can we have a statement? When is the book out again?' If only he'd got this kind of attention before.

Jamie texts me. 'Rough day at the office babe? Ur not going to let him get away w that are u?' I refrain from pointing out that he already has. Behind me, I can feel Amanda pacing in her kitten-heels, watching me as I text her back – on office hours. 'Just figuring out how to handle it. F-ing nightmare. Usual drill I guess.'

She fires back. 'What? Just go w the flow? Aren't u gonna do something?'

'Like what? Pulp the book?'

'No offence but it's gonna be shit anyway.'

'Course it is. I'm busy Jamie. Hook up with u later.'

'OK. Don't let bastards grind u down etc. Good luck darlin.'

During lunch, I check my own email. Apart from Jamie sending me unflattering pictures of Rebel with the subject line, 'Douche,' the only other thing of interest is an email from a promoter called Anna that Vinyl Lace had turned me on to, who signed me up for an AIDs benefit gig at the end of August. 'Your songs do not have to be directly related to HIV/AIDS,' the email says chirpily. That would be a bit of a stretch, to be honest, but my alarm bells start ringing when the email ends:

'All of you, I ask that you please keep your songs clean, the purpose of the evening is to send out positive messages, not to stir things up. Please don't swear, talk about sex, sexual acts, or sexual rights and please don't make negative references to religion. Thanks for reading and taking part in this benefit, I hope I haven't put anyone off, but as I'm sure you know as writers and performers, words are powerful!'

Is she having a laugh? Does she know how many deaths have been caused by religious nut-jobs spreading lies about the virus? No queers, no sex, no God … AIDS without sex? AIDS with the 'undesirable elements,' removed? Not on my planet. I can feel my own voice, the fuck-you voices of my mother and father, struggling to get out as I type.

'Hi Anna, I am quite alarmed having read your guidelines for tomorrow's event. I do have some 'clean' songs that don't involve swearing, sex or religion but still I don't think anything I have to say will fit the bill. Sorry, I'm obviously not what you're looking for.'

I turn back to my inbox and the Rebel saga. I feel very old. I think of the bullied, the beaten, the dead, the disappeared. I think of my fifteen-year-old self crying in her room, telling herself that because of what she was, things would never be all right.

I wouldn't sugar-coat it, if I met my younger self. I'd disappoint her by not being a big star, not rich, not married, but I'd tell her that I was loved, that there were people who supported me, that there was a whole world out there that largely didn't give a damn what I was. I don't know what I deserve – failure, sell-out, Z-lister, bullshit artist that I am – but that girl deserved better than this.

Stop it, I tell myself, this is your job. You've done far worse things than collude with some big-mouthed kid whose words – or whose ghostwriter's words – are buying your shoes. But somehow I find myself getting up from the desk and walking into Amanda's office.

'How's it going?' she asks, commiseration in her voice and marble in her face. Her sympathy doesn't reach her eyes.

'Not great.' I sit down, uninvited. 'I'm not comfortable with this. I think perhaps we should take it a bit further. Say we disapprove. It's our reputation at stake as well.'

'Evie, people have heard of him. No one's really heard of us. When a book comes out, the first thing people think about isn't who published it. You know that. Anyway, it's not surprising he feels like this. You know what it's like. It's a, you know, it's a cultural thing.'

I don't even want to start unpacking that statement. She keeps talking. 'All that macho stuff, it's just how those rappers all are. A bunch of little boys.'

'Seriously, though, doesn't it make you mad? They're loaded, powerful, dripping in jewels, the world's listening to them and all they come out with is this shit?'

'People buy that shit, Evie. And no, that doesn't make it OK. But it is how it is.'

I'm tired of her talking to me like this. 'I know that. But gay people have Twitter feeds too. And they have blogs, and magazines, and they are going to name-check us.'

'It's not like they would have bought the book anyway.' She pushes back her hair. 'Look, Evie, I know this is personal for you.' She manages to pack a lot of distaste into the p-word. 'But it's not our job to judge. He'll be judged by people out there, anyway. They can choose whether or not to buy it. The bottom line is – no one cares.'

'No one who matters, you mean.'

She looks at me like she could keep staring for years. 'As far as this is concerned, yes. Are we done?'

'Yes,' I say, numb-tongued. 'We're done.'

I get back to my desk to an email from Anna. 'I'm sorry! I didn't mean to offend you. I must have struck a chord. It's just there will be people with kids there, Christians … it wasn't anything personal! Can you give me a call if you're free this afternoon?'

I sit at my desk, hot, hungry, doused in the rank sweat of panic, and think about the people around me. Rebel's arrogance. Amanda's chilly indifference. Jamie's outrage. Somehow, though, Anna puts the tin hat on all of it. Another well-meaning, amateurish girl, just trying not to offend anybody.

Given the choice, I'd choose Rebel – the foul-mouthed, plastic-dressed man-whore – over her. People like her scare me. They can't see what they're doing with their silence. They genuinely can't see.

My phone rings. Anna. A text comes up – Jamie. Followed by Kate – why Kate? Why can't she leave me alone? Anna emails me again. Then another message – Roshan. I breathe a sigh of relief. He's exactly what I need – but when I read it, a coldness seeps through me strong enough to overcome the office's rainforest heat.

'Evie. I hear I'm chasing you and you're not interested? You just had to say.'

Kate. Again, Kate. I feel my world tip. My ex, the asset-stripper. She left me with nothing and she apparently wants more.

I storm out into the corridor, clutching my phone. How did this happen? We don't even really have any mutual friends. I try to figure out who she told, how he heard about it. Small town, this London.

She picks up right away.

I dive straight in, no pleasantries. 'Kate, can you just stop trying to ruin my fucking life for five seconds?' Amanda chooses this moment to walk past. Brilliant. I lean against the wall and close my eyes.

'What are you talking about?'

'Roshan's pissed off with me because I'd said he was stalking me or something. I only told one person that. You. So what happened?'

A long, horrified pause, then, 'I don't know, it must have been ... I was in the bar the other day and I got talking to some girl, I'd seen her around before ... she wanted to know all about you, kept asking questions. I'd never have done that if I'd known she knew him.'

I feel overdue tears burning as I think of the camera holding my face. His big hands.

'It just came out. I'm so sorry.'

I turn around and rest my head against the wall. Even the building seems to be sweating. I liked him. I really liked him.

'I can talk to him,' she says evenly. It's the same tone we adopted when we were talking about who was going to get what in the flat, whether I still owed her for the bills. 'I mean, I don't really know him, it would be a bit weird, but I wouldn't mind, honestly. I'd tell him I got it wrong or something. I'm sorry.'

'No. Let me handle it. I handle everything else.'

Without saying goodbye, I press the button on the phone that sends her back into the stratosphere where she belongs. I walk down the corridor, sit at my desk, and write something that takes me even less effort than Rebel's Twitter outburst – 'Fuck you.'

Pithy, but I don't see how it can be improved on. I won't need my copywriting manuals for this one. Before I go ahead with it, I reach for my mirror and lipstick and make sure I look nice and unrepentant.

I send my two-word parcel of offensiveness – first to Anna. Then to

Amanda. Then to the shareholders. Finally, to Rebel's agency. Then, in the heat-dazed instant before Amanda's heels come clicking up behind me, I enjoy a hard-earned moment's silence.

Going Back In

I'm lying on my single bed in our Montmartre hotel, watching the ceiling spin, when someone knocks on my door. '*Bonsoir, mademoiselle? Je voudrais un ... pamplemousse?*'

'Who is it?'

'Me, genius.' I hear a belch, then a hiccup, then Jamie giggling outside. I let her in and she swings unsteadily towards me in a black sparkly top hat, her one concession to bridal wear, and her plain black dress. The hen night's been a mixture of straight and gay women and we've made quite an arresting picture stomping around Paris. Eight girls, some in flowered baby-doll dresses, some in jeans and tank tops, led by me in cats-eye sunglasses and one of Vinyl's vintage dresses, a full-skirted gown patterned with oranges and lemons. My French isn't great but I have heard the locals wondering if we're transvestites.

She gives me a hug and lurches past me. As she collapses on the bed I can see she's wearing blue Diesel boy-shorts under her dress. Clearly her taste in pants hasn't changed since our college days.

'This has been such an amazing day,' she says. 'I don't want to think about how much all this cost. Please let me give you some money.'

'No, your money's no good, Jamie. Do you want a drink?'

'I shouldn't.'

'Go on, it's your hen night. You need to be more pissed than the rest of us.'

'Stop calling it that. And all right, go on, just the one more.'

'Speaking of pissed people, how's Susie doing?'

'All right. I put her in the recovery position to be on the safe side.'

I crack one of the bottles of Cava we brought with us, standing next to the window. It's a beautiful room, if a little on the small side. When Kate and I came here, we stayed in a boutique gay hotel and the boys who owned the place put us in a baroque pink room decked with swirls and swags that Kate had instantly christened 'Vaginatown.' She'd surprised me with that trip, stolen my passport and presented it to me at St Pancras after work. 'You've got to be more careful with your things,' she'd grinned. I probably should have listened.

Here, everything's perfect; the wrought iron railings, the splash of scarlet flowers on the building opposite – all we need is a Gauloise-smoking baguette salesman in a striped T-shirt. Once or twice tonight, when we were downing Tabasco-spiked shots in a tiny café or driving back to the hotel in a taxi, the windows down, the warm night whispering against my skin, I thought – this is perfect. I felt like this all the time once. Maybe I can feel like this again.

Jamie stretches out on my bed and accepts a tumbler of bubbles. The French have standards – no plastic glasses. 'Just wanted to check in on you,' she says, slurring slightly. 'Are you all right, Evie? I mean ...' she pauses awkwardly, 'really?'

Let's see. I don't have a job. I don't have a girlfriend.

I live in a house I can't afford with a girl I barely know.

I had one person, apart from Pina, who was on my side. So I slept with him and then told my ex he was stalking me, which at least means I'm not sleeping with him any more. I've tried to patch things up and think I partly succeeded, but I know even the biggest barrage of apologetic texts wouldn't be enough. I've bruised him again and I don't know what to expect when I get back to London, or if he'll even want to see me.

Sometimes I cry myself to sleep, which I wasn't aware was physically possible.

On the plus side, I have friends, I have a fiercely protective mother, and Gray's all right with my situation – not wild about it, of course, but she knows I'll be all right for a while financially, even if I'm spending a chunk of money giving my friend the send-off she deserves. Unlike me, Jamie has worked hard at being a better person, opened herself to another human being. While I'm still jealous as hell, I know she deserves this.

'I'm OK,' I say hesitantly. 'It's not perfect. But then again it never was, even when I thought everything was just fine. I was in denial about it.'

'Do you miss her?'

'No. I don't even like her.' I'm lying, but I can't bring myself to be sad about it yet. Self-pitying, absolutely. Humiliated, of course. So neurotic that people are talking about what a loser I am that I'm burning holes in my stomach lining – naturally. Sadness is harder.

'And you are still OK, with, you know, the wedding …'

'Yes, Jamie. You don't need to worry about that.'

She clears her throat. 'You do know Cathy's going to be there too.'

'Yes. Zoe told me.' Why does Jamie have to be so scrupulously fair with the people in her life? Would it kill her to take sides for once?

She nods, looking relieved. 'I thought maybe you didn't know, so I wanted to check. How's the song coming along?'

'Umm. It's all right.'

'Evie! You haven't written it, have you?'

'I've been a bit busy, Jamie. Moving house, getting fired, holding bags for you to be sick in on the Eurostar, stuff like that.'

'Yes, we did overdo it a bit on Friday. Sorry. I know you've had a lot on. It's just that you're like, Superwoman. You fit so much into your life.'

'Up to a point, maybe. After a while it just sort of … implodes.'

'I love Kate,' Jamie says. 'I love you both. Doesn't mean I'm not mad at her for doing this to you. And Zoe's starting to look like she won't be our photographer, on account of the whole Cathy thing. I keep asking her to tell me for definite and she says no, no, she'll be there. She wants me to just let her off the hook. Well, I'm not going to.'

'You know nothing could keep me away, but you are asking a lot, Jamie.'

'I'm asking because I know you can do it and I'm not having my wedding ruined by a bunch of grown women behaving like schoolgirls.'

'Easy for you to be grown-up, though. Your life's perfect.'

'It wasn't always.' Jamie sits up and runs her fingers through her dark hair. 'And it may not be again. Some day, it won't be this good, and I'll be able to live with that because it was wonderful once. And for now…' she reaches over and taps me on the knee, 'I'm going to enjoy it.'

'Good for you, babe.' I take a gulp of cheap Cava, tiny fat fireworks exploding through me as we lie together, like we used to lie when we were nineteen and more afraid than this.

'Are you bringing a date?' Jamie says. 'You can, you know. that's one of the reasons we're going pot-luck with the food. I didn't want to be all anal about place settings …'

I stop her before she starts talking about aubergine dip again. That's fifteen minutes of my life I'm not getting back.

'No. It's not like I'd ever subject anyone to the whole Kate-Cathy-Zoe triangle. Not if I expected them to shag me afterwards.'

Jamie smiles. 'I don't know. I bet there are people who'd put up with worse from you.'

I pour her more Cava and we clink glasses.

'I love you,' she says, her voice squeaking a little.

'Are you going to start crying?'

'Um … possibly, yeah.'

I reach out and grab the pink helium balloon tied to the bedpost. It originally read, 'Bride-to-Be,' though one of the girls has blocked out the first B with a marker pen so now it says, 'Ride-to-Be.'

'What are you doing?' Jamie sniffs.

I punch a hole in the helium balloon with a sharpened nail and take a belt of the helium. Jamie creases up with laughter, her dress riding up her thighs.

'Nice pants, Jamie,' I squeak.

'Gimme, gimme …' she reaches out for the balloon and presses her lips to the puncture. 'I do love you,' she says, sounding like one of the Chipmunks. 'You're my best friend. I …' her voice suddenly drops back to its normal register and that makes me laugh even more as she says, surprised, 'Oh!' and takes another hit. 'I want you to have a girlfriend,' she says, her voice cartoonishly high. 'Even a rebound thing. That would be ...' her voice drops again, '... good for you.' She giggles and takes another gulp of Cava.

I take a deep breath and finish it off with some helium. 'I was seeing someone,' I squeal breathlessly. 'Sort of.'

'Tell me!' she squeaks. 'Oh my God, that's really cool, is it your new flatmate? She's hot! I'd totally fancy her, if I wasn't getting married to the love of my life and all that, but I think she'd be great for you. Have you seen her eyes? I mean, course you have, you live with her, but they're gorgeous ... nice arse too ... I might be in love but I'm not blind.'

'It's not her.'

She reaches out for the balloon, takes a helium hit and cackles demonically, 'Tell me! Tell your Auntie Jamie!'

Half-way through my sentence, the helium runs out. 'You don't ... you don't know him.' The last three words, in my normal voice, hang in the still air.

We're silent for a while.

'Wow,' she says, shaking her head. 'Just ... wow.'

'It's nothing serious. Just a couple of nights, that's all. It's not even like we're seeing each other any more.' I don't tell her that this is my fault, or that I regret it.

'Like a real him with, like, man bits and everything?'

'Yep.'

'But you're ... you're really gay, Evie. Really, really gay. You've never even slept with a man.' She looks at me. 'Well, you have now, clearly.'

I try not to think about how gentle he was, how he held himself as though scared he might break me until I reached out and pulled his head down to mine, the full weight of him coming to rest against my narrow bones. Kate and I used to say we couldn't handle how that would feel, to be submissive, crushed under someone, but I didn't feel like that with him. I felt like I ruled the world.

'Jesus.' She reaches for the bottle. 'Please, not another one. They're dropping like flies.'

'I'm just having a bit of fun. Don't straight girls have flings with women when they're having a crisis?'

'Yes! And it's really annoying! You were on my team, Evie. I liked you there.'

'I'm still on your team, Jamie. I always will be.'

She shrugs. 'I know, but ... there aren't many of us, like, proper lesbians left, it seems sometimes. Everyone's doing some kind of queer metrosexual postmodern thing. Like it's all a big game, like ... like it doesn't really mean anything. I just didn't think you'd go down that route.'

'I'm not. I just got close to someone and I wanted something a bit different. Some comfort. I wanted to feel sexy again. What bits he has are pretty immaterial when I'm never even going to walk down the street holding his hand.'

'Yeah, yeah. I'm just surprised, that's all. I never got that vibe from you. Course,' Jamie says, over-compensating now, 'I know it's not all black and white. Like, even Susie freaks me out sometimes when she looks at some bloke on TV and goes, 'He's nice,' or whatever. I've told her I wish she wouldn't do that but that's how she is, you know. I just get tired of hearing, 'ooh, everyone's a bit gay,' whether it's from her or you or daft women's magazines with articles like, 'Could you possibly be with a woman? Urgh, how could you stand it, mind you, might turn your boyfriend on, continued on page sixty-nine ...'

'Maybe there's something in that. Not the stuff about pulling girls in clubs to get your man excited, though, you know how I feel about that ...'

'I remember you were on the receiving end of it for most of Uni, yes ... still, you did take some of them home, from what I remember.'

'The stuff about everyone being a bit gay, though. I don't know if it's even true, but if it is, where's the harm in me acting a bit straight for once?'

'Just trivialises it, I reckon.' Her face is flushed in that patchy, childlike way that always means she's angry. 'I'm sorry, but … everyone might well be a bit gay, but you don't just get a bit discriminated against, do you? Bit of death threats, bit of kicking to death in public places …'

'Jamie. This is your hen. Stag. Wedding party. Let's not talk about that now.'

'It is happening. It's happening out there as we speak.'

'I know it's happening. I got bloody fired because I was tired of it happening.'

'Evie, you got fired because you're a nutter.'

I laugh. 'I know. Pina said I was just like my dad. But in a good way, which in itself was a surprise.'

'Is she OK about it?'

'She's worried. But she's a mother. That's what they do.'

Jamie's laughing now, shaking her head. 'Honestly, the thought of you telling Pina you're straight …'

'I am not, Jamie! Jesus!'

'I think she's the one parent I know who'd be devastated.'

'My daughter the deviant.' I pour the last of the Cava. Jamie clinks glasses with me.

'God, coming out was bad enough … can you imagine going back in?'

Now isn't the time to tell her I have thought about it, before last week when Roshan and I were still waking up in the same bed. I knew I was letting my imagination run wild, but it's hard not to think about some sort of future when you wake up day after day to the same face next to you, smoothed with sleep like a child's, when you bury your nose in the back of their neck and breathe the smell of their hair like a wine-taster seeking a bouquet. I miss his big body, the space he takes up in my life. I miss the way I stop hurting when I'm with him.

Next morning passes quickly and I'm glad when Jamie, worried about pickpockets, quickly drags us through the square near the Sacré Cœur that reminds me of Kate. I picture our younger selves, content and unconcerned, thinking about lunch, not knowing how it would end.

Exhausted, we stagger from the baked summer pavements into the Gare du Nord and battle with fiercely inept passport control. On the train, Jamie and Susie fall instantly asleep, Susie's head tucked in Jamie's neck, my ex's long, elegant body folded around her girlfriend's as though she was born to protect her. The afternoon light covers them in a defiant blaze before it fades. The other girls drowse, magazines abandoned on their laps, hair falling over their faces. I'm the only one awake.

I look out at the huge fields in the glow, the warehouses, the scaffolding, the cranes, all beautiful in this sudden light. I take my phone and turn it between my palms, thinking of his uneven smile, the wild-honey smell of him first thing in the morning. In my head, I hear Kate say, 'You've got to be more careful with your things.'

The phone feels like it's burning a hole in my pocket all the way to St Pancras, where I hug the girls goodbye and then stand in the street, bringing up Roshan's number on my phone and taking a deep breath as I wait for it to ring.

Before it does, though, I hurriedly end the call. I'm trouble. I'm a mess. The only way to be careful with him is to leave him alone.

Having your Cake

'Evening, ladies.' Gray walks into the kitchen and puts down her shopping bags. 'Vi, I hate to break it to you, love, but you don't actually live here any more.'

'I love you too, Gracie May.' Vinyl gives her a frosting-sheathed finger. 'I'm doing something important here, if you don't mind. I'm helping with the cupcakes. For the lesbian wedding.' Sitting on the worktop, she bounces excitedly. Everyone loves a wedding, even angelic-looking, foul-mouthed burlesque artists who aren't even going. We've grown closer in the past couple of weeks; Vinyl's freelance, or, as Gray would mutter, 'living off her boyfriend's fat wad,' and she's living like a lady of leisure, who takes her clothes off a lot.

Vi can turn anything into a treat, meeting me after I spend a morning waiting in the Job Centre, distracting me with a rummage through Vivian's of Holloway or a hazy afternoon of tea, roll-ups and old records, which she always finishes off by picking up my guitar, bashing away enthusiastically at it while I try not to flinch and then saying, 'Right, let's go to the pub.'

'Oh yeah, the wedding.' Putting away her groceries, Gray looks around doubtfully at the sugar-dusted kitchen, cupcakes on every available surface, me with my hair in a bandana and a dab of frosting on my nose. 'Job hunt going well, then?'

I can tell she's starting to get tired of my self-pitying, sugar-loading funk and I feel terrible about having saddled her with an unemployed housemate, especially when I know she likes to work at home. This month I've gained five pounds. Jamie says I look much better, that I looked 'all skinny,' before, but I'm not sure. I've joined the cheapest gym I could find and spend the hours between job applications sweating out my anger; not so much to get thin, though in my weaker moments I imagine Kate seeing me in a club and thinking how good I'm looking these days. I do it to keep myself on an even keel. I will get along on my own. I'll have to.

'She's being really good,' Vinyl says. 'Honest. How many applications today?'

'Ten. I don't want to talk about it.'

Sometimes I just lie in bed, waiting for Gray to leave the house, before I do what I did as a teenager and spend the day in a haze of TV movies and self-loathing. I'd never liked taking sick days, precisely because they felt like this. Heaviness settles in me like a low fever. Being out in the daytime is strange; it's like the world's been taken over by the elderly, the ill, the stay-at-home mums and excluded teenagers. I'm one of these people now.

At least my frantic preparations have been taking my mind off the prospect of seeing Kate and Cathy together, the endless dull ache of knowing I'm losing Roshan, and of course, being unemployed and apparently unemployable.

My life was once all book launches and business meetings. Now it's all downloading application packs in Turkish and African internet cafés, booths at the back full of anxious women. It's Job Centre rooms full of angry young men and churning out applications to PR companies that go largely unanswered. Faced with the Job Centre, or the option of weeping over another kid-with-cancer movie, no wonder I've channelled my energies into the wedding. I still have contacts; I've managed hundreds of events, and I know where to get fabric, fire-retardant spray, rose-water flavouring for the cupcakes, wholesale bunting. In this small way, I feel like a player again.

'Something'll come along,' says Gray. 'Bright girl like you, you'll be fine.'

'It will. But you know it's not easy out there at the moment.'

'You could always just take whatever comes along, then move on when you find something better,' she says, her face shielded by a cupboard door, 'Get you back on track.'

'It's got to be right,' says Vinyl. 'It might have happened for a reason.'

'Not necessarily. This happened because my brain went a bit wrong.'

She shrugs. 'Yeah, well, maybe that happened for a reason too. Can I have another cake? Just one of the crappier-looking ones.'

I thrust a cupcake towards this girl, my unlikely saviour, who laid herself down in front of me, bare and open, just that once. I won't say I never think about doing it again. 'I'll make some tea. Gray, why don't you sit down, I'll put the shopping away.'

'It's all right. I know where things go.'

'So do I. Go on.'

Gray looks at us both, confused, then sighs, pushes back her dark, messy hair and walks into the living room, where she flops down on the couch. Vinyl follows, trailing icing sugar behind her like smoke. 'I always said you needed a wife,' she says chirpily.

'God, give it a rest, would you, Vi?'

The two girls clamber onto the couch and Vinyl leans against Gray, twisting a skein of red hair in her hand. They're not doing anything intimate, but looking at them still stings a little, as though they'd shared a joke I didn't understand.

'You have to see her dress,' Vinyl says, as I bring in the tea.

'I'm sure I do,' Gray says dryly, channel-hopping. We sit on the couch together, Vi curled between us. Moments like this, it feels good being an adult, when you're allowed to put your feet up on the couch, slurp your tea and eat all the cake you want.

'Is everything else ready?' Gray asks me. 'Seems like you've been running around like a blue-arsed fly ever since you got back from Paris.'

'Nearly. Just thinking about the decorations for the service itself. Well, the celebration, ceremony, whatever they're calling it.'

'We got tea-light holders from the pound shop,' Vinyl says proudly.

'Are you working at the moment?' Gray asks her. 'Sticking sequins on thongs again? Making hats, or, what is it you call them, fascinators?'

'You're in a charming mood today, aren't you, lady?'

Gray rubs her eyes. 'Yeah, just a bit tired. Thanks for the tea, Evie, by the way.'

'When are you off to Brighton?' Vinyl asks me.

'Tomorrow. They're getting married on Saturday, but we're having dinner the night before, so … yeah, I'm just going to put all the Tupperware together and go.'

Vinyl looks around at all the cake, the garlands, the tea-light holders, the fairy lights. 'Evie, you can't get all this down on the train.'

'I'll be fine. I've got some serious suitcases. I'm used to carting equipment about anyway, you know, for gigs and …'

'Why don't you give her a lift after work?' Vinyl asks Gray.

'To Brighton?'

'For God's sake, Vi, she's got more important things to do.'

'An evening in Brighton,' Vinyl murmurs, playing with her hair again, not meeting either Gray's eyes or mine. 'Might be nice. I'd do it.'

'Well, you can't. And you might want to stay in with your boyfriend at least once.'

'He's never home. He gets up at four-thirty, checks Bloomberg and CNN, and even when he's got nothing to do at work he still stays there waving his face in front of his boss. Then when he does come home he tells me he hates his life. It's bloody boring.'

'He's keeping you in the style to which you're rapidly becoming accustomed.'

'Yeah, well, I'm twenty-seven and I'm going off cheap wine.'

'Don't call me when he has a coronary.'

'Go on. Give her a ride.' Vinyl smirks and nudges her. 'It's not going to kill you.'

'You could come to dinner,' I offer. 'It'll just be pizza, but I'll pay for yours and … I don't know, you can stay for the whole thing if you want.'

Gray shakes her head and flips channels. 'I don't know. The things I get myself into.'

Vinyl leans behind Gray's back, looks over at me and winks like a dirty old man.

'I saw that,' says Gray, deadpan.

'Did you? Well done. Right, that's sorted and it's past five o'clock. Let's go to the pub.'

It's late, and the house is quiet. Gray's upstairs in bed. I've packed up the last of the cakes, snug in their plastic boxes, and wiped the worktops clean, though the kitchen's still warm from baking and that safe, childhood smell of vanilla lingers in the air.

Mellow from a night of wine and conversation, I hum a little as I work, then start to sing – a sexy, teasing blues that bubbles up like laughter in my throat. When I turn around, I see Gray standing in the doorway, in pyjama trousers and a vest, her face softer and blanker than I've ever seen it.

'Sorry,' I say, 'I didn't wake you, did I?'

'No. No, you didn't. I just came down for a glass of water.' She moves past me in the small galley kitchen, her hip almost, but not quite, brushing mine. My heart starts to beat faster. It feels like the space between us is shrinking, as though someone's draining the air out of the room.

She turns back and looks at me. Whatever this is, she can feel it too. My heart stops for a moment, the way that birds seem to freeze in the sky when they're turning.

'You're good,' she says, once she's reached the safety of the doorway.

As she pads back upstairs, I stand there in the bright, sweet-smelling kitchen, wondering.

Taking Orders

Gray takes the afternoon off and we embark on our road trip. I feel awkward, loading up her neat little car with my wedding paraphernalia, but she seems softer somehow, almost excited in her faded weekend jeans and battered olive-green leather jacket. She's even bought a family-sized bag of sweets. 'Force of habit,' she mutters as, 'I'm used to driving Vi to burlesque gigs in the arse-end of nowhere and you know she can't function without sugar.'

As I settle into the passenger seat, she hands me a silver stack of CDs and asks me to DJ. Half-way there, a song comes on; a Motown song that Kate and I used to love, Little Jimmy Wilson singing, *This Is My Love*. Not quite Our Song, but one of them – enough for Kate to write scraps of the lyrics in my diary, leaving them for me to find. Enough for her to smile and catch my eye if we heard it at a party. I remember it coming on the radio one morning, the two of us dancing in the kitchen, all bed-hair and wash-softened robes and stale, night-smelling skin, and how it felt like there was nothing else in the world, that there would never be anything but this. I reach over and skip to the next track, then settle back into my seat like a chastened teenager, praying she won't comment.

'You're all right,' she says dryly. 'I've had plenty of women ruin songs for me too.'

As we drive into Brighton, that old bitter-sweetness fills me, as the townhouses, headshops and winding streets tug at my memory. Kate and I lived here for three years without knowing each other. We'd been here once for a weekend, but if I'd known how many places, how many jokes and sayings and even words that losing her would taint, I guess we'd never have done anything. We'd come here four years ago, staggering over cobbles, window-shopping in the Lanes, trying to look mature in sex shops – we'd been poor, young and crazy for each other.

I tell myself I'm being silly, torturing myself. This world isn't an album, a series of tracks I can choose to skip – it's all here, all around me, and in the evening light, it's too beautiful to close my eyes to.

I tell Gray the name and address of the pizza restaurant where we're meeting. 'I'd like to get your mate something,' she says. 'Shout if you see anywhere open.'

'You don't have to. She doesn't expect that. You're doing me a huge favour transporting me and all this wedding crap, that'll be enough for her.'

'Still,' she says. Even with just one word, I can tell she won't be argued with.

In the end, we do find somewhere a couple of streets away from the restaurant. A hippyish gift shop, all jangling glass and moonstone rings. Gray, looking slightly uncomfortable as she browses the cramped aisles, picks up candles and looks at them critically. Eventually, she goes for a beautiful teal-coloured bowl that seems to glow in her hands. I almost covet it, but it's too classy for me. I'd never have seen it, let alone picked it out – I guess that's one of the things that makes us different. She shows it to me, looking touchingly young for a moment, and I nod my approval.

She follows my gaze. 'What are you eyeing up there, Miss Day?'

Embarrassingly, I'm in the children's section. I point to what I'm looking at – a shelf of snow globes. They're all different, hand-made, one with a traditional Christmas tree and snowman, one with a ginger cat rolling in drifts of glittery snow, one with an elegant, Gothic Victorian lady in crinolines, a bird perched on her wrist. The one I love is the simplest – a black, skeletal tree in a drift of white, a single red apple in the fork of its branches.

'Snowstorms,' I say. 'I don't think I've seen one since I was a kid. My dad used to bring them back for me when he went travelling. I had quite a collection.' I pick up my favourite and weigh its glassy heft against my palm. 'I don't know where they are now. My mum's moved a couple of times. It's been a while since I even thought about them.'

'Can I … ?' She takes the one I'm holding from my hand, lightly tickling my palm. A jolt I wasn't expecting rushes through me.

She shakes the globe and watches the snow fall. I watch her forehead furrow.

'Pretty,' she says. 'But I've got to say, I never really saw the point in these.'

'They're so sealed, I guess. So perfect.' I think of the bubble I lived in when I was with Kate. How there were so many signs I could have seen, but I'd wanted that bubble so badly. I'd longed to thicken its walls, even if it meant I couldn't have seen outside it any more. 'You want to take it apart, but you can't. You can't get inside it without ruining it. That's what I like. How you can admire how beautiful they are at the same time as wanting to smash them.'

When we arrive at the restaurant, Jamie gives me a happy, eyebrow-raised smile as she sees me with Gray. I whisper in her ear as I hug her, 'Any spare rooms tonight?'

She nods. 'Sure. Zoe's not here yet. Your mate can have her room, and not everyone's staying tomorrow so we can all shuffle round a bit. She's not sharing with you, then?'

I give her a dirty look. 'Bit early for that.'

'Still,' she says. 'Nice to see you're back on the straight and narrow – well, not … you know…'

'Thanks, Jamie. But I don't know if I'm anything at the moment. Except hungry.'

As we move from the bar to the table, I try to stick close to Jamie and Susie but instead we end up sitting opposite two women I barely know. One, at least, I met on the hen weekend – a dirty blonde, in more ways than one, whose name I forget, so I have to go through that boring ballet of dodging potential introductions. The other woman introduces herself as Antonia, a friend of Susie's from work. Rich husband – a lawyer, apparently – big house, two kids, Harriet and Orlando. She tells us all this within five minutes, talking about her husband and kids like she's name-dropping celebrities at the members' clubs that Vinyl likes to blag her way into. It's obvious that they're the reason for her existence. I'm quite glad she's made this clear as otherwise I'd be tempted to think there wasn't one.

'Are you married? Seeing anyone?' she asks us almost immediately.

Gray, amused but detached, shakes her head at Antonia and scans the menu. 'How hungry are you, Evie?' she asks solicitously. 'Reckon you could squeeze in some garlic bread? I'm game if you are.'

'How about you?' Antonia's clearly undeterred by Gray trying to catch that bullet for me.

I shake my head. 'Terminally single.' I don't need to give this woman any more details, though the facts might shut her up – 'I've always thought I was totally gay but after a brief one-night stand with a burlesque artist I started bedding some bloke who used to be my friend and now isn't returning my calls since I accused him of stalking me. Ooh, is that chilli oil? Yummy!'

'Yeah, I'm single, too,' says the Dirty Blonde, contentedly. 'More fun that way.'

'Oh, you can't really think that!' Antonia declares, with all the tact of a flasher.

'I do.' She bites into a breadstick in a disturbing manner. 'I like having a bed all to myself. If I want some affection, I can go out and get it.'

She's good-looking, in that way guys seem to like – despite her long hair and full lips, there's something rough-hewn and mannish about her, like she used to be a crew captain or killer rugby prop, the kind that played dirty.

Antonia looks put out. I give her the old once-over. She doesn't seem to realise that, out of the four of us, she's the least attractive by a very long way. I'm in another of Vi's old dresses, a pretty, red, polka-dot number, my hair done forties-style. Gray, beside me, is fresh-faced and handsome, muscles in her bare arms like the fluted bones of a bird's wing. Along with the Dirty Blonde, we could be a trio of sexy, ass-kicking babes. Antonia, on the other hand, exudes the aggressive casualness of a woman who no longer tries. No makeup, hair like a middle-aged aunt's, dumpy frame encased in a flowery fabric that reminds me of three-piece suites.

'Isn't that a bit, you know… shallow?' she asks the blonde.

I try not to listen, holding my menu up like a shield as I point out my potential dinner options to Gray and she nods, sweetly grave, as though I'm telling her something important. I can tell she's trying to tune Antonia out too.

'Not really,' says the Dirty Blonde. 'I'll worry about that later. What are you having? I just saw someone get one of those four-cheese pizzas. They look nice.'

'I need to fit into my dress tomorrow,' I say. 'But I am starving. Might even have a pudding.'

Gray laughs softly. 'You go, girl. I tell you what, you know how to live!'

I swat her on the arm.

Antonia and her self-satisfied mouth aren't giving up so easily. 'What about kids?'

'What about them?' Gray asks, her voice cool.

'Well, don't you want them?' Antonia addresses all of us at once.

'I did just say I was single,' I say, taking a gulp of water. 'And I don't see any willing sperm donors around.'

'Would you do that?' asks the Dirty Blonde, interested – or perhaps just keen to pull Antonia's focus towards me. 'I've had such crap boyfriends, I think about it sometimes.'

'Best thing that ever happened to me,' Antonia says smugly.

'Sperm?' Gray murmurs, trying to catch the waitress's eye.

'Children!' Antonia's looking a bit desperate now. 'Of course, my two are exhausting, but they're wonderful. What are you all, twenty-seven, twenty-nine? You want to get started, you really do. I started pretty late, and I wish I hadn't. You're getting less fertile by the minute and it's actually good for your body, having children, did you know that? And for your soul. You never see the world in the same way again.'

'I'm sure.' Gray succeeds in flagging down the waitress, and with some relief, we place our orders. Antonia starts, thank the Lord, to pursue a more normal line of conversation. 'How do you know Susie?' she asks me.

'I used to shag her girlfriend.' It just slips out. It feels like it wasn't sad, redundant Evie Day who said that but the chubby, crazy kid inside me with the big boots and the voice like Ma Rainey. Gray coughs helplessly and takes a gulp of water.

'You're a lesbian too?' The Dirty Blonde looks elated. 'God, just think, I hung out with you for a whole weekend, and I never even knew!'

'Imagine that,' Gray murmurs, looking apologetically at the waitress.

The Dirty Blonde leans forward, exposing another inch or so of leather-tanned cleavage. 'There's something I've always wanted to know,' she whispers, ignoring Antonia's look of abject horror, 'How do you, you know, *do* it?'

'Madame?' Thankfully, the waitress is next to me. No 'Mademoiselle'. Evil Antonia's right, I'm not getting any younger. I look at her, wrapped in her warm, cosy self-righteous cocoon. I wonder whether I'll ever feel like boasting about anything again, if I'll ever be secure enough. Then I check myself. Whatever her reasons are for making me feel small, I'm pretty sure security has nothing to do with it.

'I'll have a Four Seasons, please, and the tomato salad. And some olives. And Gracie May?' She looks surprised to hear me call her by Vi's old nickname. 'Honey, did you order the bread?'

She blinks. The Dirty Blonde looks like she's just died and gone to heaven. 'Are you one of *them* too?' she asks Gray.

'Yes,' says my long-suffering flatmate. 'Yes, I'm gay, and yes, I did order the bread.' She looks at the lone bottle of white wine we're sharing like good girls, and then asks the waitress, 'Could you please bring me a whisky?'

'What kind, Madame?'

'Just a Scotch.' Gray shoots a dark look at me. 'Straight. Straight up.'

'Haven't you ever had a boyfriend?' The Blonde asks me. 'You look so … girlie.'

'No. Well, once. Sort of.'

Jamie leans over, giggly and wine-flushed. 'Don't listen to her. Evie loves the cock.'

'Jamie!'

Gray stares at me. 'What? I mean, do you?'

'I do not love the cock!' On the tables nearby, a couple of heads turn.

'I do,' says the Dirty Blonde, forlornly.

'Any starters?' the waitress asks me.

'No, I don't think so, thanks,' I say, blushing.

'Got to save room for that pudding, Evie,' says Gray, and she touches my arm again. Almost fondly.

'That got to you, didn't it?' Gray says frankly. We're sitting in the hotel bar, the last two standing. The Dirty Blonde and her new friend, one of the three men in the wedding party, just vanished upstairs. He looks overwhelmed by his good luck and I don't want to think about what's going to happen tomorrow when at least two more men show up.

And Kate. I don't want to think about that either.

'A bit. It was pretty insensitive, I guess. It didn't get to you?'

Gray shakes her head. 'Nah. No one judges me but me. I'm glad I'm not her. I'm even gladder I'm not one of her kids. Hatstand and Orgasm or whatever they're called. I'm sure they'll be in therapy by the time they're five.'

It's quiet in the bar and the two gay men who run the bed and breakfast blatantly want to go to bed, but we're not causing any trouble – just sitting here in the darkened front room, talking. Upstairs, my ex is sleeping with the woman she'll marry tomorrow. Beside me, my flatmate is talking to me like a friend for once. Outside – way outside – Kate is probably getting ready to make her way towards me.

'I just want to survive tomorrow,' I say.

She nods. 'Do you know what time she gets here?'

'No. It's not like we're really in touch at the moment. She was for a while, but, I don't know, it tailed off.'

'Do you still love her?' Gray asks matter-of-factly.

'I don't know. I honestly don't.' Everything's so confused – my different loves, all mixed up in my head. The wave of shame that's been threatening since dinner finally breaks over me. 'So many of them know,' I say, pathetically. 'About us. It's just so bloody embarrassing. Even the ones that don't know are as bad as that Antonia woman.'

'I don't want to pry, but … how come you're so ashamed? As far as I can see, you've got nothing to be ashamed of.'

'I should have known. I should have seen what was going on. I must be stupid.'

'I wish you'd stop saying things like that,' says Gray softly. 'Why should you have known? I bet if you'd suggested it to her, she would have acted outraged, am I right?'

I nod. I had, a couple of times, and it had always ended badly, with the two of us telling half-lies to each other, me tugging at her sleeve, apologising, desperate for things to go back to what they'd been, unwilling to accept that this was no longer an option.

'What I don't get,' I say, 'is that there's no reason on earth why this should have happened. It doesn't make sense. It doesn't accomplish anything. I've tried and tried to see the positive side, but maybe there isn't one. Maybe this is it. It's like wasps. Or sharks. Or the Tories.'

Gray smiles gently. 'There doesn't have to be one, Evie. So stop looking. It's just random, that's all. It's horrible and random, like so much else in the world. I'm sure she didn't mean to fall in love with this other girl …'

Even months after the break-up, the words jolt through me. Love? I'd never thought I was anything other than the love of her life, even with all the evidence to the contrary. This was the one piece of information I couldn't take in. I couldn't handle the idea that I was a paragraph in Kate's life, maybe just a footnote. I had to be more than that.

'It's not love,' I say, knowing how pathetic it sounds.

'It might be. You don't know.'

'It's not. She still loves me. I know she does.'

'Evie …' she sighs, and then she's quiet for a while. 'You need to accept this.' Her voice rushes out fast, words landing like karate-chops. 'I was just thinking that, at some point, you might want to be sane again. You can't keep pushing people away. I've seen you do it. You do it to me, you do it to Vi, maybe you even do it to your mum. You're angry, I get that, but you'll be fine. You will. I can guarantee you that. All you have to do is let go.'

'If it was that easy, don't you think I'd have done it by now?' I get down from the bar stool. She climbs down too and stands beside me. In the kitchen behind the bar, one of the hotel owners gratefully flicks the light off.

'There's just you, Evie,' she says. In the darkness I feel her reach for my hand. 'There's no her any more. Only this, and you, and whatever you do next.'

End of the Pier

Jamie's wedding day dawns overcast and grey, but I still wake up buzzing with excitement. My friend, who I love, is getting married today and it feels like nothing can go wrong. I didn't sleep well, even after several strong drinks after dinner, but it's not entirely the sleeplessness of anxiety – more like a child's excitement before Christmas. I pick up my phone and there's a text from Gray, 'Gone for a run on the beach. Hope you're enjoying a lie-in.' I smile to myself.

I sit up in bed and listen to the seagulls mewling outside. The registrar is prepped, the food awaiting its final touches. The only thing left to do is to write this bloody song. I've got the tune and some tired lines that I scribbled down, but I know it's the one thing that really matters to Jamie, and the one thing I'm failing at.

'It's a wedding,' Gray told me, gently exasperated. 'It's the thought that counts. They don't care if the song's any good or not.' Maybe not, but it matters to me. I reach for the remote, turn on QVC and stare in a trance for ten minutes while a wide-boy and a holiday rep convince me I need a mother-of-pearl watch – only fifty-eight left!

I try to think of lyrics but all I can think of is an early poem of my dad's – a young man terrified by how light his daughter is as he picks her up in the middle of the night. 'This is the life force,' he'd written, sounding as stunned as he must have felt, 'this fierce, hot, endlessly ticking clock.' I couldn't write like him, or Kate. 'A bloody Irish poet,' I mutter in my mother's voice, and decide to stop scribbling Hallmark horrors and go down to breakfast. I can never concentrate when I know there's semi-free food in the building. I slip my feet into flat pumps and throw a hoodie over the vest and track-pants I slept in. No makeup. I'll dress to kill later.

Downstairs in the lobby of the little gay B&B, Jamie and Susie are looking curiously regal as their guests start to arrive. Between them, just moving back from a hug with Jamie, bright-eyed and beautifully groomed, is Kate.

When she sees me, emotions fight for control of her face – happiness and shame. Her posture shifts into scared little-girl mode, her hands clasp over her crotch as she bites her lip. I feel like a vengeful, all-powerful bitch, but this is not the time to make a scene. Fuck it. I should have trashed everything while they'd still have understood.

Instead, I stick my tongue out at her – a reflex action, something we did when we were in love. Looking relieved, she sticks hers out at me, and some of the tension ebbs away. Jamie and Susie swap anxious glances, then laugh.

'Hey,' she says quietly. Jamie grins up at me and ushers me into her arms while Susie does some over-enthusiastic and probably tension-related jumping and squeaking. My appetite has suddenly left me. Another couple of guests arrive, ready to check in. In the flurry the hall gets very full and Kate climbs up to where I'm standing.

'How are you doing?'

'Fine. Fine. Good. You?'

'Yeah, good.' We smile at each other in a parody of functional adulthood. I hope Jamie's paying attention but when I look down, I can see she's too immersed in this opportunity to organise everyone. Looking down at my friend's flushed, shining face, I silently wish her all the happiness in the world.

'This is weird, isn't it?' You'd think an award-winning poet could do better than that.

'Just a bit, yeah.'

'You look good.'

'No I don't. I just got out of bed.'

'That's what I mean.' She smiles. 'I forgot that it's nice to see you when you're not quite so polished. Makes the rest of us feel better about ourselves.'

I want her to feel like a stranger, but I know that's not possible. There's too many shared years between us. I wonder when it'll stop, that sense of homecoming when I see her. Maybe never, terrifying though that is.

'Do you want to get out of here?' she asks. 'I'll buy you breakfast.'

We don't talk about anything that matters. We catch up on our families, compare horror stories from weddings we've been to. I tell her about the song and she reassures me, telling me her poem also isn't up to scratch. We were always like that. Exacting with ourselves, but forgiving with each other. Now the white heat of our breakup is over, all we're left with is a dense, somehow comforting sadness, as though we've both gone through a bereavement.

It's only after a breakfast of egg and chips in a pensioners' greasy spoon that she mentions Cathy. We're on the deserted pier, walking off our breakfasts. I'm thinking of the girls we'd been, clutching each other at the top of a creaking fairground ride at the end of the pier, near the hungry edge of the sea.

'She's coming later,' Kate says quietly. 'She had to work today. I got some time off in lieu, so ...' her voice trails off.

I could ask a lot of things – are you still together, how's it going, do you love her, what has she got that I haven't? – but I stay quiet. I know she said that to prepare me, that she knew I'd been hoping Cathy wouldn't come at all. I still have my doubts about whether Zoe's going to show up.

'I'm sorry,' she says suddenly.

I stare out at the water. 'You've never said that before.'

'I know. I felt it, though. I should have said it. It's the least you deserve.'

I could come up with a smart-arsed response, but I just say, 'Thank you.' I mean it. I even appreciate it. Something in me lightens when I hear those words.

We're silent for a while.

'It's for the best,' she says.

'Don't push it. You were doing pretty well there.'

'I was a mess, Evie.'

'I remember,' I say.

'I was holding you back. I resented you.'

'Resented what, for God's sake? My pissy little gigs? My daft PR job?'

'You cared about them. And they're not much dafter than anything else. They were what you wanted. They must have been worth something.'

'But they're not.' I stare at my battered ballet pumps. My feet are cold. 'We were worth something. Now, I … I go to the same open mic nights, nothing comes of it. If I was a real success, this would almost be worth it, but I'm not. And you know about the job.'

She pauses for a moment and then says, 'Yeah. Great way to resign, though.'

'I didn't resign. I did it because I was stressed out of my mind and I made a crap decision. Ever thought about how that might have happened?'

'I told you I didn't mean to mess things up for you and your boyfriend.'

'He's not my boyfriend. I don't think he's even speaking to me now. You had no business messing that up. It was my life.' The bitterness rises again, stirring sluggishly after a morning of companionship and comfort-eating. 'You apparently dumped me because I was too busy gigging and now I don't even like it any more. I can't write this crap song and it's not like I can ask you for help.'

'It'll come back. It would've been worse if we'd stayed together. I don't think I did ruin your music, but I was on the verge. Wanting you around all the time, making you feel guilty for going out and doing your thing … I was depressed. I know that now.'

'And what, you're better now? She's better for you?'

'She's more like me,' Kate says.

'Great. Another set of lesbian twins. You're already like some weird two-headed monster in sensible shoes.'

She smiles reluctantly. 'We're not that bad.' That, 'we,' makes me nauseous, panicky – like I've still got something to lose.

'You know what I hate? That Cathy got all the good stuff from you and then you'd come home and treat me like crap. You were different with her. You made an effort.'

'You made an effort for your audiences. I didn't notice you making one for me.'

I can't deny it. 'It wouldn't have been like that forever.'

'I didn't know that. You don't even know that.'

'No,' I admit. 'I don't.'

We stand together at the end of the pier, listening to the tinny burble of the fruit machines, the grind and chink of falling coins. The air smells of fried onions, hot sugar and rain.

'We're not together,' she says quietly. 'Not properly. Cathy and me.'

I'm not sure how to feel about this. Slightly relieved, I guess, but it still throws the sheer ugly waste of it all into relief. She has no idea what my life is now, the way the weekends stretch, how if I haven't made plans with friends by Saturday morning I'll be alone on Saturday night. How dinner parties are full of women giving me dirty looks if I talk to their partners. I have to leave at a reasonable hour. I don't get to cook. I don't get to stay in the warmth and light. She doesn't know the hot weight that lands on my chest when I open my eyes in the morning. How sometimes I dream that I'm still with her and, on waking, it takes me a moment to identify what I feel as happiness. She sees me, painted and battling, because that's what I want her to see, but for a minute I want her to see my desolation.

'I've got something for you,' she says.

'Another handbag?'

Kate grins. 'Yeah, I know I made a bit of an arse of that. It's in the car. We should go back, come on – Jamie's going to start worrying in approximately ten minutes.'

Once we're back in the warmth, she turns the music on and hands me a folded letter. 'You left this,' she says. 'I'm pretty sure you did it on purpose. But everything in it's still true. I'd like you to keep it.' Her voice thickens. 'I … just humour me, OK, Evie, I can't live with it … even if you burn it, just take it with you.'

She wrote letters in the last month that we were together. It helped her to do that when she was down. She wrote to her favourite aunt, her old teachers, and me. Mine is more of a litany, really. More like a poem. I love you because …

Words jump out at me from the page. *Because you buy terrible celebrity magazines and don't take the piss out of me for reading them. You make the best mashed potatoes. I love you because you drink pints and I drink wine and the barman always thinks the pints are for me. I love you. I love you because you believe in your horoscope. Because you talk to the plants, even that orchid that gives you so much grief, because you fill your days until they strain at their seams. I love you because you're the only person I know who can't stand bubble-wrap. Because you swear like a trooper. Because you always surprise me and I think you always will. I love you because you never stopped singing.*

'I'm not going to burn it,' I say.

The music doesn't mask Kate's sobs as she slides down in her seat, shaking her head as though to shrug it all away. I reach for her and we clutch each other, awkward and scared at once. She pulls back, and for a crazy moment, I think she's going to kiss me.

Then my phone rings. Jamie. Fuck. I motion Kate away and answer it.

Jamie, at first, is an incoherent as I am, and it takes me a while to realise she's having a meltdown. Zoe, and her camera, are not coming. We've got several well-meaning poseurs with expensive cameras in the wedding party, but we do not have a photographer.

'Bloody Zoe,' Kate mutters as she starts the car. 'I knew this would happen.'

'It's going to be fine, Jamie,' I tell her. 'We've got plenty of time.' I look out of the window at the rain. 'It'll be all right. I know someone.'

Shipping Forecasts

He's not the first person I call. Given that we've never been seen together by any of our friends, I know this won't be the gentlest introduction to my world, a room full of women I'd slept with, but it's too late to book anyone else. One of my photographer friends has the flu, one has a press pass for a gig and two just don't answer. So he's not the first, but he is the one I'm sure of. I can hear him trying to pretend that this isn't remotely strange while Kate pretends she's not listening to the telltale softening of my voice.

When we pull up at the community centre, Kate and I carry our new-old closeness safely between us. We head inside to reassure Jamie, both of us smiling. I want to turn to her and say, Look, I'm not useless after all, am I? I'm fabulous! Some people think so. You used to. Isn't this all just a big mistake?

Then I see Cathy standing with Susie. She looks as pale and awkward as when I saw her in the cafe, but her obvious discomfort doesn't melt anything in me. Susie reacts immediately, throwing herself in between me and Cathy like a rugby player, chattering excitedly about how she's so looking forward to wearing her new dress and how she hasn't managed to lose any weight this week so it's going to be tight but who cares, and other comforting girl-talk nonsense. Kate breaks away from me and walks with Cathy to the other side of the room.

'Suze?' I ask, interrupting her monologue. 'Can you just tell me something quickly? What do you love most about Jamie?'

'Most? Oh, God, I don't know… everything. There's so much.' She grins. 'She's amazing. She's kind, funny, and so smart, she's like the smartest person I know…'

'OK. Yeah, we know that. What I want is – I don't know.' I try not to look at Kate and Cathy whispering in the corner. 'Something random.'

'I love how she can't get to sleep without the radio on.'

'Really? That used to drive me nuts.'

Susie laughs. 'I know. But I'm quite into it now. There's something weirdly calming about shipping forecasts. And you do hear some amazing things at four in the morning when you get up for a wee.'

'OK. What else?'

'Well, she's really calm, really organised? But she drives like a maniac on crack.'

'True. Keep going.' I put my hand on her arm and steer her out into the foyer.

'You enjoyed seeing Kate, didn't you? You look really... really happy. Like, you're actually glowing.'

I don't want to tell her it isn't Kate, but the prospect of seeing Roshan. 'Just resolved a few things. Now come on. More Jamie stuff, please.'

'I like her contradictions. Like she's a Jewish atheist and she loves sacred music, like Christian music. Even hymns. She sings them in the shower. She always wants to eat things that bring on her migraines and sometimes she gives in, but nowhere near as many times as she'd like to. She has Marmite on toast for breakfast every single morning. Never seems to get tired of it. Would you ...' she laughs, 'I don't know, do you want to write this down?'

'I can remember it. Go on.'

I barely notice Cathy and Kate sliding past us as I listen to Susie talk about the girl I used to love. It feels OK, like one day I could feel like this about Kate. I find Jamie, sit her down in one of the tulle-swagged chairs and ask her the same thing about Susie. I watch her relax and smile as she speaks. Then I jump in a cab back to the hotel, a wad of community leaflets and a pen in my hand, writing like a maniac before we pull away.

I meet him at the station. When I see him walking towards me, his head ducked slightly, I wonder if I'll be able to speak. He smiles shyly and draws me close for a clumsy hug. It's been weeks. His hair is still messy, black and silver-threaded, kinking into fat finger-curls in the damp air. His shirt needs ironing. His eyes are still beautiful.

'Good to see you,' he says.

'You too.' I hug him tightly, hanging around his neck. 'You're so amazing to do this.'

'Hey. My first lesbian wedding. How could I resist?'

'Yeah. I have to warn you, it is going to be pretty weird.'

'I don't know. I went to a *Lord of the Rings* themed wedding once. *That* was weird.'

The awkwardness between us thaws a little.

'You look beautiful,' he says.

I did make an effort, of course. The dress was a last-minute find in a Brick Lane vintage boutique, a fifties bridesmaid gown in raspberry satin. It fit like it was made for me and I'd carried it around town like treasure, high on strong coffee and my cleverness in finding it – but looking at myself in the hotel mirror before going out, I'd had my doubts. It was just too bloody much, but I couldn't go back now. I was stuck with it.

In the taxi, I say hesitantly, 'So, Kate's going to be there. And her new girlfriend, well, I don't know if they're really with each other any more, but ...'

'None of my business,' he says too quickly. 'This is just a job.'

'OK. I just wanted you to know.' I look out of the window. The rain's calmed down. It's the hour before night, what the French call the blue hour. A dusk so beautiful I'd like to bottle it.

'I'm sorry about what happened with us.'

'It's OK.' He reaches for my hand and brushes it lightly. 'I probably didn't take it the way it was meant. I just felt like I was putting too much pressure on you.'

'I can't imagine you putting pressure on anybody.'

'No. But you needed some space. I should have known that.'

'I've had plenty of space.'

We lean back and look out of our separate windows.

'And you used to date the bride?' he says, smiling to himself.

'Yes.' I pause. 'She's the only other one who knows about you. But … she doesn't know it's you, so it'll be OK.'

'I don't know,' he says gently. 'I don't think it's that easy to hide.'

I know he's right. No one could watch me watching him, and not know straight away. No one could share a room with us. You could put me in a burka or have him in the next room like a Hassidic wedding. Everyone would still know.

We finish the cab ride in silence. I pick up my guitar and my scribbled lyrics, and in we go. In a side room, the girls are getting ready. Jamie's neat and glowing in a black suit, Susie's in her pale green scalloped dress. Behind them, at a table, Cathy and Kate are sitting, not touching, looking lost. I can tell they have nowhere else to be right now.

'I like to take photos of the bride and, uh, the bride, before the ceremony,' Roshan explains. 'So just relax. Keep doing what you're doing. Pretend I'm not here.'

'Good luck with that,' I tell myself, as I go to tune up.

Frocks and Beards

The wedding is a wonderful flurry of tears, laughter, cheering and the muffled sounds of other people's children screeching and falling over. Jamie and Susie bow their heads and light candles, faces lit from the inside. I sit uncomfortably between Kate and Antonia. Roshan crouches in the aisle, his camera trained on the happy couple, and while I wish he was next to me, my hand nestled in his, I draw comfort from the fact that he's there at all. After Kate reads her poem, it's my turn to get up and sing.

Gray was right, it doesn't matter if the song's any good. It probably isn't, but at least it was made especially for the happy couple. I sing about all their little quirks and rituals as they squirm and laugh, glowing with recognition. I look into his camera, its flashes flowering in front of my eyes, and I can't see the man behind it but I still think as I sing, *this one's for you.* I swore I wouldn't let him in again, that I don't want to be touched – but watching the brides, the middle-aged husbands and wives, the babies, I know I do. I'll be bruised and broken again, if that's what it takes. Anything but this half-life.

When the registrar pronounces them married, there's a mad scuffle of action, a rush of whoops and cheers that becomes a standing ovation. We scramble to our feet, calling out *congratulations, mazel tov, yay,* cheering that this thing we were all promised has happened to someone.

The teary-eyed girls turn to face us, hands clasped and arms raised in an unrehearsed salute. I give in and burst into hot, grateful tears. One of Antonia's kids rubs a half-chewed handful of organic rusk into my skirt.

At the end, after we've cheered Jamie and Susie for the last time, people get up and start to leave slowly. Kate and I stand patiently, not moving or acknowledging each other, until she turns to me.

'That was beautiful,' she says.

'So was your poem. I can't believe you told me it was crap.'

'I'm never sure.'

The crowd still isn't moving.

'I know,' she says softly. 'This was supposed to be us.'

We hug fiercely. Over her shoulder, I catch a glimpse of Cathy, hurriedly turning her face away like she's seen an accident. Gray is standing patiently behind me, Roshan ahead of me. I wish I could shield them from this mess.

'Kate, you know Roshan, right?'

They shake hands, looking each other up and down like prize-fighters.

'Well done for doing this,' she says, her voice light and clipped. 'I know it was short notice, but you've made our mate's day.'

'Ah, I don't think she needs me to do that.' He gives me a not-so-secret smile and I can tell he's doing it to wind Kate up, but I relish the small moment while it lasts.

'Is this the first time you've done something like this?' she asks.

'Weddings? No. I do them all the time. Shame I'm not better at blending into the background, really, but there you go...' He puts his hand on the small of my back as he steers me towards the door. 'Kind of makes you think. To see two people who've found each other like that. Like, no matter what's happened to you, it still restores your faith.'

'I need a drink,' says Kate bluntly. I can't help but agree.

It takes me almost all night to catch up with him. Between the photo opportunities – the frosting-smeared kids, the trailing ribbons, the terrible dancing – and the girls from the hen night dragging me around the dance floor, shoes discarded, handbags in a pile – I just keep losing sight of Roshan. Every time I turn around he's disappearing, a black-haired, black-jacketed blur in the corner of the room.

Gray and I talk for hours; she's always at my side, holding my elbow, refilling my glass. At some point she nods at Kate and Cathy, having an intense-looking conversation in the corner. 'That's her, right?' she whispers in my ear. I nod. 'Thought so. Do you want me to get off with you? I don't mind.'

I laugh. 'I'm all right, love. Thank you, though.'

'We can dance, though, can't we?'

'Course we can dance!' A cheesy, campy Studio 54 anthem fills the dance floor, and I grab her by the hand.

She groans. 'Not this!'

'Yes, this. Who cares? Come on, it's not like you know anyone here!'

She rolls her eyes and starts to dance with me. She's good. Tipsy and delirious, lighter somehow, I'm dancing like a six-year-old, swishing my heavy satin skirts in the jewel-like lights.

'I've never seen anyone dance quite like that before,' she says dryly.

'I know!' I pull her close and shout in her ear. 'I'm happy!'

'That's good,' she says. I wait for the put-down. 'No, really,' she says. 'It's good.'

Eventually, I leave her talking to Jamie – they're getting on like a house on fire, unsurprisingly. I get the feeling that my mother would approve of Gray too. I break free from the hot, scented fug of the room and go to find him in the garden outside. He's sitting at the table, scrolling back through the night's photos, a frown of concentration on his face. Before he sees me, I allow myself to watch him for a moment.

He's so beautiful. Ridiculous, given the amount of time I've spent thinking about him in the past few weeks, but somehow I've still managed to play this all wrong. I've dreamed of holding him, tried to identify the particular scent of his skin, wondered what he looked like as a child, but not once have I really thought of how this would ever work out. My feelings are primal, animal. I love his body like it's mine, or like something I created. I want him, I know that, but then what? Would he bore me? Would he want to settle down too fast? Would I? Would I scare him with my 'exotic,' past? What can we be to each other, really?

'Sit down,' he says, without raising his head. 'Those heels must be killing you.'

I sit opposite him. We look at each other.

'Interesting friends,' he says.

'No need to judge.'

'I'm not judging, Evie … that being said, the blonde one is filthy.'

'She is,' I agree.

'She said she thought I'd be great in bed.' He raises an eyebrow. 'Apparently, I look really *spiritual*.'

'Oh dear.' I smile. 'She should have asked me. I could have told her that you spend your life in front of the telly eating pizza and watching robots fighting. I bet she'd like to know that you are great in bed, though.'

We grin conspiratorially. I toss my hair, a flirtatious reflex action, though I probably look like a smeared nightmare by this point in the evening.

'Do you often get that line?' I ask.

'Sometimes. I'm really not spiritual. Makes me feel like a rubbish Asian.'

'Yeah, well, I'm a rubbish lesbian, so …'

We sit in silence for a while. Surprisingly, it's not awkward. It feels like the silence we'd share sitting together on his couch, or walking home from school years ago.

'Your friend's so happy,' he says. 'I liked seeing that. In fact, I'm glad you brought me to a lesbian wedding in the middle of Brighton and I have no idea how to get back and I'm not entirely sure what gender most of these people are.' He pauses slightly. 'I didn't even know how much I'd missed you till now.'

'I'm glad.'

'I'm not,' he says, 'I thought, I don't know, that this would be easier.'

'Well,' I say, lamely, 'don't worry about having to get back. I don't even think the trains are running by now. I've got a room.'

'Yeah, but that's the thing. I can't share a bed with you.'

'Why not?'

'Because you know what'll happen,' he says.

'And that's bad, why?'

'Evie. You know why.'

The minute he reaches for my hands across the table, I know we're lost again. I take hold of his hand – so different to Kate's, hot and dry with faint dark streaks at the creases like charcoal, stroking the dense silk of his wrist, unable to meet his eyes.

'This is hell,' I say softly.

'I want to kiss you so much,' he says. 'It's killing me.'

'So do it.'

'You've got your ex here, your friends. You don't need anyone judging you.'

'I don't care!'

He breathes out, exasperated. 'OK. I want you to take a look at something.' He takes the camera in his hands, scrolls back through the photos, a flick-book of blurs that doesn't hold my drunken focus. He catches me looking away. 'Jesus – give me a moment, will you? I'd forgotten you've got the attention span of a squirrel.'

In between the slide-show, he shows me photos of Kate silently, like evidence pushed across a table. First, there's a shot of me dancing with her. 'We're just being civilised.'

The next one he pauses at is Kate, looking at me, her face open and fragile.

'She could be looking at anyone.'

'No she couldn't.' He flicks through some more. Me, dancing, my arms thrown up – not the most flattering pose. Me turning to see her. Our faces changing. Click.

'She's looking at you. And this is *how* she looks at you. And this one – well, this is you, looking at her like she's the centre of your universe.' He puts the camera down. 'I'm trying here. OK? I really am. But I've wanted to be with you for so long, I can't just be … something that happened to you.'

'But you are,' I say softly. 'And it was amazing.'

He sighs, looking suddenly tired. 'I thought this would be easy,' he says. 'Either that, or impossible. I didn't know it was just going to be hard.'

We sit and look at each other, an island of silence, eighties pop blaring from the doorway. The air's getting colder, spiked with sneaked cigarettes, the remnants of perfume and sweat. I wish I knew the right thing to say.

'Thank you for bringing me here. No, really, thank you.' He looks over my shoulder at the light, the silhouettes and smoke. 'We've always lived in our own little private world, haven't we? I never really thought I'd see your life. Now I can see how much this matters to you. Your history, your girlfriends.'

'Of course they do.'

'Evie … just out of interest, what do you call yourself at the moment?'

'Gay.'

'Not bisexual, then.'

'What, you think your mum's going to prefer that?'

He gives me a sad, flat smile. I hear Susie and her Dirty Blonde friend staggering out into the garden behind us; Susie's champagne giggles and her friend asking her about sex toys. I see him stiffen. He holds out his arm to me. 'Shall we?'

I get up gratefully, take his arm, and we walk further into the garden, our gait uneven, given his height and my heels.

Away from the noise, he seems more relaxed, but I can tell he's still far from happy. 'Your friends are looking at me like I'm a sap,' he says. 'Some big stupid bastard who can't even tell that he's your beard.'

'Frock.'

'What?'

'You'd be my frock. Beards are girls.'

'Jesus.' He brushes his hair out of his eyes. I watch the moonlight picking out his strong features, like it's pleased with its work. If I was the universe, I would smile on him. There's a faint crackle of autumn in the air. I remember him saying that when winter came I could be his central heating. I know we're not going to make it that far.

'I don't think …' he says, 'I don't think it can last. I can't keep looking over my shoulder, wondering which girl you're checking out. You were right. We shouldn't have done this. We were each other's rebounds.'

I break away from him. 'I'm not exciting any more, is that it? Not forbidden fruit. Not a fantasy, just a mess like everyone else. You've gone off me.'

'I haven't.'

'So what is it, then? Let me guess, it's not much fun pulling a lesbian, is it? I'm putting myself out here too, you know. I mean, what did you think was going to happen? Are you just waiting for my hot blonde best friend to show up and start fondling me?'

He smiles reluctantly. 'Damn. And I didn't bring my pool cleaner's uniform.' He laughs, and some of the tension fades. I hit him lightly on the arm and he takes my hand, swallowing it up with his like a catcher's mitt. We keep walking.

'I've known you for so long,' he says. 'I could never go off you in a million years. I knew you as this mad, sparky girl, and then when I met you in that pub you seemed so hurt, so vulnerable … I just wanted to scoop you up and keep you safe for a little while … and then it was like you were changing, you were becoming who you would have been if you weren't trying to keep someone else happy, and you were dazzling. But now… every time I see you, you're better. And I feel like, the better you get, the closer you are to leaving me and I can't live like that, Evie. I can't.'

We're deep in the garden now, surrounded by darkness.

'Do you know where we are?' I ask.

He looks around and then shakes his head ruefully. 'Sorry.'

'Typical,' I say softly. 'No sense of direction.'

'That's another reason we shouldn't be together. We'd never find anything.'

Blocking out his words, I bury my face in his shirt. We hold onto each other. Babes in the wood.

'Listen,' he says. In the dark, we pick out the voices, the static of the music, and we start walking again towards the smoke and the noise. As the lights come into view, I finally find what I wanted to say, but I think it's too late.

'Look, I don't know how to explain how I feel about you. If I could, it would be … like that song I wrote for the wedding. If I love you, it's not because of the body you were born in. It's not that. I love how gentle you are. I love the way you can't eat anything without chilli sauce. I love our crap private jokes, especially when we can't quite remember where they came from, or why they ever made us laugh like that.'

'If? You said, if you love me?'

'That's about as good as it gets right now.'

'That's the thing.' He strokes the inside of my elbow. 'I think it always will be.'

It's getting cold as we walk up the lawn. I shiver, crossing my arms over my breasts, like I did on his couch when I knew he was about to kiss me. He takes off his jacket and drapes it over my shoulders – it comes almost down to my knees. I laugh, in spite of everything, shrugging my arms into the sleeves and twirling in the middle of the path.

He pulls me into his arms for a hug. I cling to him, every last vestige of my pride gone. I breathe him in with what feels like my last lungful of air before I plunge back underwater.

'I've never met anyone like you,' he whispers in my ear. 'Never will.'

I might be wrong, but it sounds a hell of a lot like *goodbye*.

I wake up at four in the morning, two hours after we finally go to sleep, my eyes stinging from makeup and tears. I get up, go to the bathroom and wash my face. I hear my pit-of-the-stomach gulps as I down water from the plastic hotel glass, refilling it again and again. I stand and watch him sleep in the faint glow from the bathroom light.

We're still geniuses at sleeping together. I know him best this way, dreaming his secret dreams. When I get back into bed, he shifts and folds back around me, though he's still fast asleep.

Something in him knows to wait for me, knows the rhythms of my body like blood knows the clench and push of the heart. And something in me knows him so well that, when I wake up again, the room drenched with light, I don't need to open my eyes to know that he's gone.

Part Three: Heartsong

That Way Inclined

No crying. I've done enough of that. I sit on the rumpled hotel bed, his pillow pressed to my chest, my head up and eyes dry.

I consider the positives. I survived the wedding, without making a show of myself. Gray and I had a good time – I hope she's OK, that she's not angry with me for abandoning her last night. I'm aware that people have been treating me more gently than usual, but for Gray, Jamie, and even Kate, their patience has its limits. I can't trade off my wounded woman status forever and God knows I don't want to.

I run myself a bath. Not often I get the chance to luxuriate in a real tub. Our Highgate bath is narrow as a coffin. I take my beautiful dress, slightly stained from wine and sticky-fingered kids, roll it up lightly and pack it away in my evening bag. I can't imagine wearing it again. He said I looked beautiful. I press my lips together hard.

I fill the bath to the brim, so the water slops over the sides as I slide in. As I lie in the water, my mind starts to wander somewhere it doesn't usually go.

Fifteen years ago, Pina and Dad had asked me exactly what Roshan wanted to know – just how gay was I, exactly? Of course, there were other questions hovering under that. How did I know so young, had I been abused, was it Pina's fault for buying me trains instead of dolls? – but all they really wanted to know was how much of a choice I had.

I cried the night I told them. In those days, tears came more easily; I didn't have many other outlets apart from staring at camp celluloid classics. I'd blurted it out at dinner and run upstairs in tears. Dad was sitting on my bed, waiting for me to stop crying. Pina was standing in the doorway like a censorious angel.

'I always wanted a girl,' she said, as if to herself. 'I thought they'd be easier.' It was a summer evening, too hot to endure my mother's judgement. Or her lentil curry.

'Well, I'm not like those shitty boys in school. If you had one of them, you'd know about it!' I reared up from the pillows, hair stickily smeared across my forehead. 'I wish I was like that! I never do anything I want to do!'

'Plenty of time for that, Evie.' When I stole a glance at Pina, her face was unforgiving. 'And you give me plenty of grief sometimes. Like tonight. Can't we get through a meal without you having to turn it into some big production? Can't you give it a rest for one night?'

And how many nights after that? Sometimes, that was all I wanted to know – how long this limbo would last. Maybe if I knew that, I'd manage to behave.

'You don't know what you are yet,' Dad said quietly. 'There's no point in getting yourself into a state now. Life can surprise you, you know.'

'He's right.' Pina was still standing in the doorway. Light streamed from behind her. I could tell my mother had always known what she was; she was strong like that. I was clay. 'You were never a tomboy. I couldn't even get you to kick a ball about.'

I was a sexless, genderless kid in many ways. Pina wanted me to have as much of a childhood as possible, and everything that brought me a step closer to the murky, sexual world of adulthood – shaving my legs, buying deodorant, even my first pair of nylon tights turned into a battle that had Dad retreating, newspaper in hand, to the café where the Turkish gangsters gave him considerably more respect than we did.

Pina still wasn't talking to me, but to her invisible audience, the one she sometimes muttered to when she was painting. 'I tried to be the best mother I could,' she said. 'I've always been proud of you. I always will be, so long as you're true to yourself. I'm just saying, you don't need to go broadcasting it.'

'It's a dangerous world out there.' Dad squeezed my foot. 'Sometimes, you just don't want to give people any more ammunition than they need.'

'It's quite normal,' Pina went on, 'in girls your age. I never had that myself, but I know it's common. And of course, some of my friends are that way inclined ...' Her feminist friends, with their ironic *Guardian* cartoons tacked to the fridge with rainbow magnets. I saw glimpses of myself in the rambling women's movies that Pina rented on weekends, the plaintive country songs she played on car journeys, but I knew my mother was rampantly heterosexual. She loved men – Pina was always drawn to things she didn't understand. 'I mean, are we talking about sex here? Like, you feel ... sexual? About girls?' If I hadn't already known this was a big deal, hearing my usually articulate mother sounding like a translation from the X-rated Bulgarian would have tipped me off.

'Yeah. Yeah, kind of.' My crushes were sexless, but dreams, graphic and unbidden, would startle me out of sleep. I'd find myself checking the sheets for damp patches, not quite believing that these dreams had left no mark.

'It doesn't matter. Not to us. I just want to tell you, Evie ... if you do have a choice ...'

'What your mother's saying is that she doesn't want your life to be any more difficult than it has to be. I'm not an expert, but all I want you to know is that, however strongly you feel right now, that choice is there.'

'Are you going to be all right now?' Pina asked brusquely. I looked at her. We had a strange moment of recognition; seeing each other's flawed strength, our identical pride.

I was starting to feel ridiculous, and there was only so long I could writhe around on the bed. I nodded, and she nodded back. Briefly, we were equals. Dad got up and left; she moved back to let him out of the way. She wasn't looking at me, but at the wall next to my head, when she said, 'I'm not ready to lose you yet, Evie.'

I wasn't sure what I was agreeing to, but I nodded. I didn't want to disappoint her any more than I already had.

Telling them I fancied women, though I did, wouldn't have summed it up exactly. I knew I was gay before I knew what gayness was, what sex would be. Having read a lot of dismal lesbian fiction and seen some terrible movies in my short life, I knew that kissing, cuddling and back rubs were involved, and perhaps something to do with nipples.

When I was eleven, Pina had shown me a book about lovemaking, illustrated with pictures of a woman who looked like a younger version of her and a man with inexplicably lavish facial hair, but she'd never enlightened me on the finer points of girl-on-girl action and there was no Internet in those days, though in retrospect typing, 'teenage lesbians' into Google would probably have been too educational.

What I was then is what I am now; queer. And when you grow up queer, whatever form that takes, you enter your adult life with a backbone. For that reason alone I'd never regretted the choice I'd made. Even after what happened when I was sixteen.

It was the week of my birthday. I'd behaved badly for months leading up to it; I was allergic to my mother, too forgiving of my often-absent Dad. After a fight over the corner-shop birthday cake my mother had absentmindedly got me and another argument between her and Dad, the two had summoned me downstairs from my room.

I'd clicked downstairs in the stilettos she hated, my heart like a falling rock in my chest. I sat on the sofa between them while they told me they loved me but they weren't making each other happy – the same hollow words Kate had doled out to me and, when it comes down to it, the only words there are. I had begged them to stay together. I'd told them I'd be a better person, wouldn't answer back, wouldn't keep agitating Pina, but they told me that wasn't the problem, I must never think I was the problem.

I knew differently, though. Not only had my birth opened up a rift between my too-young, party-animal parents, with me literally sleeping between them in that big, white bed, I'd interrupted my father's poetry and my mother's art with my wants, my needs, my tears, my noise, and now it was happening again. I came across pages of fuzzy scrapbook paper in Pina's erratic writing, left around the house as though she didn't care about me seeing, 'Evie … such an ungrateful little monster at the moment, completely Brian's daughter … never around, never home, says she's preparing us for when she does go but I feel like she's already gone … next time she asks if she can live with him I'll say yes, see how she likes it … what did I do to deserve this? … I need company, light, life, I gave up too much for him, her, both of them, and what do I have to show for it?'

She'd given up speaking to me, batting away my attempts to speak to her, a wounded warrior queen. 'We both love you,' Dad said awkwardly the morning he left as I sat in my pyjamas, staring at the TV, the picture of a grouchy teenager but inside, just plain terrified.

It was my fault, I knew it. Because I was queer, dark and odd. I had Brian Day's swagger, and no one would have wanted me as a daughter, not even him. It wasn't Pina – Pina was beautiful. She moved mountains. It was me.

Our Bodies Remember

I take my time getting ready. I need to avoid Kate and Cathy this morning. I do some repair work on my face, my hangover a hot pulsing mass behind my eyes, my cheeks and chin raw with stubble-rash; another new experience.

Someone knocks on the door. Probably Gray.

'Come in,' I call, bracing myself.

It's Jamie. She comes in and sits down on the bed, in her usual T-shirt and jeans, looking washed out but with some of last night's glow around her eyes.

'Hey, Evie. You all right?'

I nod, wondering if the room still has that hot, baked smell of sex. I should have opened a window. 'I'm fine. Thanks. How about you?'

'Knackered. But good.' She hands me a package. 'I know… look, I just want to say that I know this was hard for you. I didn't want to bang on about it earlier. So I got you a little present, just to say thanks.'

It's a peach silk scarf. I will never wear it and I love it completely.

The two of us hug in the still, hot room. Our bodies are clumsy. They remember each other from when we were lovers, and when we break apart, it's as if they're surprised by it, even after all these years.

Jamie has moved on to the next stage of her journey. While I'm still in flat-sharing, job-hunting limbo, she's got a life, but this morning I can't bring myself to be jealous of her. Jamie's happiness is like her – it's quiet, matter-of-fact, calm, and it can't be messed with.

'We're just about to head out, so…' she hunches a shoulder, looks at the clock. 'You nearly ready? Gray's waiting downstairs.'

'Yep. Ready to go.' I get up, pull on my jacket and grab my bag. She stands by the door, not quite letting me leave.

'Nice fella, your friend,' she says, her voice uncharacteristically blank.

Sophia Blackwell

'One in a million,' I mutter, not even sure whether I'm taking the piss.

'You know what? He told me last night he wasn't even going to charge us.'

'Really?'

'I'll give him something, of course. Just for his time. But isn't that nice?' She puts her hands in her pockets, not meeting my eyes. 'I was just wondering ... I don't know if this is me, but does he remind you of anyone?'

I think of him saying, *a brown John Lennon*, and almost smile. 'Not really, Jamie.'

'Not how he looks, I meant more like ... his personality. Single-minded, isn't he? Driven. My-way-or-the-highway.'

'What, like me? Well, yeah, I had thought about that, but ...'

'No, not you. Your dad.'

I can't think of anything to say to that.

'Don't give me that face,' she says.

'What face?'

'That oh-you-lesbians, spare-me-the-amateur-psychology face. It was just a thought.'

'You've only met him once. You only met Dad once too. And you were pissed both times.'

'You can't not drink around your Dad. All right, I barely even remember that night we all went out in college with him, there's just something I can't put my finger on ...'

'Jamie, I don't think you can really judge.'

'All right.'

'I know it's easier for you to explain it all away, but sometimes these things just happen, you know? There doesn't have to be a reason behind it.'

'But you're gay, Evie.'

'I know.' I breathe deeply and rake back my hair. 'And that hasn't changed.'

I don't want to be straight; never have. It would be like wanting to be something else entirely. A bus. A cake-stand. Since I was a teenager, I haven't even considered it, but I've spent my life fighting to be with the people I love. I can't turn that off, because of the bodies we were born in. But I appreciate the irony that I'm facing this conflict for a man.

'Then why don't you just … I don't know, get dressed up, go out on the pull? You don't look quite so insane right now, you'll be beating them off with a stick.' She puts her hand on my shoulder. 'I like who you were. Who you are. And I'm sorry. I will get off the soapbox, I promise. I just want to say one thing. I don't think this is good for anyone. You, him … any of us. I just don't feel like … like our place in the world is stable enough to mess with. You know what I mean?'

'And so, what? You want me to wait till it is?'

Jamie holds up her hands, shrugs, that ancient so-sue-me gesture. 'All right. I've said what I had to say. If it works out, you'll have my blessing too.'

'Why are you so concerned about it, anyway? You've got everything you need. Don't worry about me.'

'I'll always worry about you. I love you.'

'I love you too, Jamie. Just … go off with Susie and have a wonderful time. And when you come back, I'll have it all sorted out. I promise. Either that or I'll have emigrated.'

'Don't. I need you to talk her out of that pink bathroom when we get back from honeymoon.'

We go downstairs, Jamie hoisting one of my bags over her shoulder, old-school-butch style. At the bottom of the stairs, we embrace one more time but it's a different kind of hug, not a nod to the past but a ritual clasp, an acknowledgement that she's going on without me.

Gray is sitting on the sofa in the lobby, reading the paper. She's wearing glasses for driving. She looks vulnerable, less guarded.

She looks up at me – messy hair, smeared makeup, bags. 'Right then,' she says softly, not seeming angry with me – or cracking a smile. 'Ready to go?'

'Yeah,' I say. 'I'm ready.'

On the way back to London, we don't talk much. Gray still doesn't seem angry, though I suppose she has every right to be. After all, I left her with a room full of near-strangers so I could slope off with a boy. I feel like I'm being chastised by her silence, like the mornings when my mother used to pick me up from my dad's, but her voice is mild when she asks, 'Are you OK?'

I turn to her. 'Yeah. I'm fine.' And though I don't know when I'll see Kate or Roshan again, I am, somehow. 'Sorry I left you alone.'

'You're all right. I should be pissed off, but it turns out I got lucky.'

I feel something bite inside me. Jealousy. How odd. 'Who'd you get lucky with?'

'That blonde. You know, the dirty one. Turns out her curiosity got the better of her.'

I laugh. 'Fair play to you, Gray.'

A touch of colour rises to her cheeks. I can tell she's trying not to look too cocky. It's adorable. 'Yes, well. Nice weekend, that. A success all round, I think.'

'And we've still got some cupcakes.'

'You see?' She shakes her head, as though amazed. 'How lucky are we, Miss Day?'

The track on the CD changes – Little Jimmy Wilson, *This Is My Love*, again.

We've stopped at the lights, and Gray reaches over to skip to the next track.

'No,' I say, surprising myself. 'Leave it.'

The lights turn green. We pull forward, the road stretching out ahead of us. I start to sing softly, and after a while, she joins in.

The Fire

One of the best things about performing is the road. I need it like some girls need jewels. I need it like my Bloody Irish Poet of a dad and my smoky-haired gypsy mum.

Three festivals collide at the end of August, and I happily book myself out of my life. I spend most of the time alone, tramping barefoot over sun-caked sites, dirty hair hidden under crowns of fake flowers. I lean against stages and let their pulse kick my back. I wriggle in grass, feeling it kiss my fingers and toes. I let beer bubbles crackle on my tongue. I learn to love my sunburned shoulders, though I know they'll give me hell later. I stay up late drinking cheap wine by bonfires, I have my palm read by a woman who looks like Pina, I play to audiences of two hundred one day and ten the next, I catch up with the other singers and avoid questions about where Kate is, and what happened, and how's work …

Summer's drifting out in a bloated pumpkin-blaze of glory. In the mornings, as I lurch in pyjamas to the chemical loos, the air smells sweeter, freshened by a hint of winter. I imagine the life I want, clipping through glass-walled corridors in new boots. I promise myself I'll start job-hunting when I get back to London, but for now, I board out-of-commission Routemasters that shuttle me with the wrist-banded punters from station to site to station. I like being in transit, not having to think about where I am for a while.

Some things just still feel too raw. I'm getting good at avoiding anything that might echo in my skin. I see two girls holding hands and look away. I see an Asian man, a white woman and their serious, black-braided little girl, and just about succeed in not staring at them like a child-snatcher.

Sitting on the grass listening to a Cuban hip-hop band, I realise I'm surrounded by lovers. The two next to me, a boy and a girl, can't be more than twenty. At one point, the boy nudges up to the girl in that attention-seeking way that cats do, knocking his shoulder gently against hers. I've started noticing the way men do this, as though to say, 'I'm not gay or anything. But if you were to cuddle me right now, I could probably stand it.' It's such a Roshan-like gesture I forget to breathe, pain burning down through my chest like a swallowed sword.

On one of our days out as a sort-of couple, we went to a festival with Vi and Jack. While they treated the couples and kids with contempt, ('Shouldn't be allowed,' Vinyl muttered after a telling-off for spouting some gynaecological rap lyrics in earshot of two five-year-olds) Roshan's reaction to the children was wistful, more than anything. One morning, we saw four angelic little girls in tutus jumping up and down to a swear-filled rap track. We laughed at the surreal collision of the song and their innocence – but the way Roshan looked at them gave me the fear. Jesus, I thought, he's broody.

It was a great couple of days. Vi, sparkly and high, chattered for hours on end, grabbing my arm and steering me through the crowds, daring me to try on the craziest vintage stall outfits we could find. I remember her climbing onto Jack's shoulders as we watched a deranged French electro band and getting booed by the same people behind us who'd just realised Roshan wasn't about to get any shorter.

That night, he and I lay together in the sooty dark of the tent, waiting for dawn to find us. I was so happy that despite my spinning head I could barely sleep, and the next day while the others were washed out, I was glowing, my hair crammed under a sleek red wig. Like a child, I pointed out everything I saw to Roshan – flying paper lanterns, wild costumes, random naked people – but what I really wanted to say was, Look, look at us, aren't we something?

On the way back, the two of us stretched out in the back of a hired van, cushioned by old blankets, Jack driving and Vinyl in the passenger seat enthusiastically abusing my guitar. To block her out, Roshan got out his iPod, plugged one earbud into his ear and the other into mine, and played

Gershwin. I looked up and all I could see from the back of the van was the sky, a bowl of bruised cloud.

This will get easier, I know – like everything else. I won't always be thinking about him, or Kate, but sometimes I wonder why that's such a bad thing, why I shouldn't carry them with me. They're still good people.

Every festival has a silent disco this year. Whole tents full of people in headphones muttering. You get a choice of two tracks, so half the tent moves in a different beat to the other. Take the headphones off for a minute and you hear the others murmuring to seventies rock while you're dancing to Britpop. It never fails to make me smile. Decked with glow-sticks, I dance in a circle with my friends and watch two girls kissing, eyes on the guy they're trying to impress.

At college, my gay friends had different rules about straight women. Pulling a straight girl was a badge of honour, or taken to its political extreme, a form of colonisation. The straight girls either broke their hearts, or fell in love with them and began years of drama before either settling down for a lifetime of comfortable shoes, or running off to the home counties with the nearest Tory.

Jamie, sensible as always, washed her hands of the whole self-loathing business.

'Seriously, what's wrong with a lesbian? Not good enough for you? Do you hate yourselves enough to make a tit of yourself for some psychological torture and half-arsed fumblings with some girl who doesn't even know what she's doing?'

'Just a bit of fun,' I'd mutter defensively about some fragrant girl who was bound to make me sob embarrassingly in a toilet stall a few weeks later.

The track shifts to an overblown power ballad. I try to stop looking at another guy who reminds me of Roshan. The way he's moving like he's mildly embarrassed makes me think of a dancing bear. Stop looking at him, I tell myself. You'd never have looked twice at this man before.

Sometimes, back when we were eighteen, we'd talk about our sexualities, how we saw ourselves. What names we gave the preferences we'd created, or been born with. Strange, that I've been called so many things in my life. Dyke, poseur, careerist, bitch. Fantasist. Fat Arse. Firecracker. Babe. I don't even know what to call myself now.

One thing my friends and I all agreed on back then was just how flexible we were about our sexualities, when really we clung to them like life floats. We always pointed out that the names we'd given ourselves weren't set in stone, like vegetarians putting meat-eaters at ease by talking about the delicious smell of bacon. 'Oh yeah, well, this is just the choice I've made, but if the right man came along and I thought he was the One – then I'd be open to that too.' Then we'd nod, satisfied with our own bohemian outlooks. God, we were so enlightened, so very, very open, but we never got as far as talking about what the hell happened when you met your One.

After the last festival, I walk through the front door, which is starting to feel a little more like home. It's a beautiful, clear evening. Gray's out, the house is quiet, and I'm grateful – the silence rings tinnily in my ears after the ground-deep thump of bass.

I soak for almost an hour in the bath and then wrap myself in a towel and head back to my room. Tired, muscles and bones aching from lugging equipment around camp-sites, I lie on the floor, knees drawn up, trying to work the kinks out of my back. The sun bathes me through the window. I like to think, before it happened, I was content.

I don't even notice that I'm absently running my fingers over my body – hips, thighs, belly, the plate of my breastbone, the way I used to as a little girl, as my skin dries. I only remember the moment my fingers feel it. Right breast. Something marble-sized. I check again. I check the other and find the softness and muscle I know, but no lump.

Panic seizes me. Thick spit fills my throat and I can't swallow. I get up, wrap myself in a dressing gown and pace around the room. What to do? I can't think, so I pick up the phone and call my mother.

She sounds tired. I lie on the bed, phone clamped to my ear, cupping my breast with my other hand as though that might stop any badness spreading. I can't stop touching it. Too big, too hard. A large marble, a pearl, something else to worry about and wait for.

'See your GP,' she says, and then, 'Are you all right to do it on your own?'

Not much choice. I think about what this might do to my life, and the panic rises up a notch – my existence isn't substantial enough for this. I don't have a home of my own, a partner to drive me to appointments or cook me broccoli and pulses. I go to the doctors' alone. I have no one to hold me or tell me it's going to be all right. I have to bear this silently. Which would be the case anyway, but a partner would help to bear some of it. Even if they were rubbish, at least they'd do something, at least they'd be there, but no, I'm going to die the way I lived – watching old movies on my mother's couch.

'Evie? You've gone quiet. Have you gone down a drama-queen hole again?'

'No,' I say, unconvincingly.

'It's almost certainly nothing, you know. Just see your doctor, OK? Tomorrow.' She pauses and clears her throat. 'I love you,' she says. 'You do know that, don't you?'

After I hang up, I lie in bed, eyes wide as a china doll's. Sometimes, in the aftermath of Kate leaving, fantasies about dying cheered me up. In particularly self-pitying moments, I felt like it would be nice if I had some kind of undiscovered defect that would make my heart stop in mid-town traffic. Once, at work during a fire drill, my inner ten-year-old took over and I imagined helping my co-workers – even Amanda – out of the building before vanishing into the smoke. No one would ever know. I found myself sympathising with anyone who'd faked their own death, or used a disaster as an excuse to disappear.

Maybe someone or something has finally called time on my wallowing by reminding me I still have something left to lose. I remember standing in the street with Roshan the night we first went out with Vinyl and Jack, and thinking, if I want to get through this, I'll have to walk through fire before I'm sane again. Maybe this is the fire.

Necessary Sadness

'So,' says Vinyl, eyebrows raised at me from across the table, 'the Rage has finally hit, then.'

I glower at her. We're sitting in a cheap Indian restaurant near Soho Square and I'm dousing my food with chilli and pickles, as though to stoke the fire I feel inside. She's right. I'm not depressed any more. I'm angry. Since finding The Lump, I've had a strange feeling I couldn't identify at first, a revelation – a late revelation, but what the hell – that I am, in fact, not depressed but cataclysmically annoyed.

A month or so ago, Pina told me that depression was 'frozen anger.' I'm not sure how to describe what I'm going through now. Hot depression. That might cover it. Thawing depression, bubbling under my skin like a plastic-coated ready meal.

First thing this morning was the doctor's office, a referral, the reassurance that it's almost certainly a cyst, benign, and the prospect of waiting a month for an ultrasound. A month of not breathing. I don't know whether to tell people about it. Jamie, maybe, when she gets back from honeymoon. Vi and Gray – at the moment, anyway – no.

'I'm glad,' Vinyl says. 'It's healthy. You were probably trying to keep it in cause of the wedding and all, but it was going to happen some time.'

'How do you know I'm angry?' I ask through clenched teeth.

'Evie, it's coming off you like dodgy perfume, love. Past couple of days, you've been a total bitch to everyone. People in shops, on the street, even inanimate objects …'

'That ticket machine was asking for it!'

'Look babe, I'm not judging. I know how it is when things are all a bit too close to the surface. I feel like that all the time, to be honest with you.'

'It's quite liberating,' I admit. 'Now I know that I don't want the life I had any more. I just want a life.' I tear off some naan bread and run it around my plate. 'I want to wake up and not feel like I wish I hadn't.'

She bites her lip. 'Do you really feel like that?'

'A lot of the time, yeah. Sometimes, when I allow myself to admit that I am actually sad about what happened, it feels better than just tearing myself to shreds about how everyone's judging me and it's Not Fair, or it's All My Fault, and no one will ever love me again and that was my shot at happiness and I wasted my youth and most of my looks on her…'

'Bollocks,' says Vinyl pungently.

'I know. And I know that doesn't get me anywhere. Sometimes I get paranoid that I'll never enjoy my own company again. I can't stop thinking bad thoughts.' I give myself a break from cramming in food and lean back, hands behind my head, searching for an analogy. 'It's like being stuck in some really fucking warped, nightmarish trance track and I can't find the off switch.'

She presses her lips together tightly. 'Wow. Have you thought about, I don't know, maybe seeing someone? That's a lot to be carrying around, Evie. And if you're not working – which you're not – they reduce their rates a bit.'

'Never thought I'd hear you talking about therapy, Vi. Thought you were from the new-handbag-and-mojito school of psychology.'

She shrugs a skinny shoulder. 'I've seen a couple.'

She clearly doesn't want to talk about it, but I can't help but ask, 'When was that?'

'On and off. Since I was nineteen. I had a bit of a meltdown and ever since then I just go in every now and then to get, I don't know, re-balanced.' I can tell she's striving for nonchalance, but I can hear the strain in her voice. 'I've been on medication for a long time too. Sometimes I go off it … when I want to actually feel the world the way I used to … I miss that. It was like … the greatest lover I'd ever had, like the whole universe wanted to fuck me.'

'I think it probably still does.'

She smiles with one side of her mouth. 'All I know is, I'm single-handedly propping up the Swiss economy with all the drugs I'm on. It gets knackering. Twenty-seven years old and I'm walking around with one of them old-lady pill wheels in my bag because otherwise I can't remember whether I took the fuckers or not. Anything that knocks me off balance – a long trip where I can't sleep, being a bit naughty and taking a drug that, shall we say, wasn't prescribed for me … getting a stomach bug and not being able to keep them down – can screw me up for weeks. I'm never going to be normal. Whatever that means. But I don't beat myself up every day about not reaching some mad imaginary standard, the way you do. I know how wounded a lot of people are. I know how many of them are also off their tits on pills and living wrapped in cotton wool. You're hurting, yeah, but you're not like me. You're not ill. You're sad.'

She takes a deep gulp of lager – she loves it, even though she complains about the bloating. Strippers aren't meant to drink pints.

'I think that's one of our problems these days,' she says. 'People can't tell the difference between depression and … I don't know what you'd call it. Understandable sadness. Necessary sadness.'

I feel small and self-indulgent. 'Vi, I'm sorry for banging on. I didn't realise …'

'It's all right. Most of the time.' She smiles genuinely, looking like a little girl for a moment, her skin in the restaurant's dim light glowing like vellum. 'You know what, I know this sounds a bit mad – well, I am a bit mad – God, this isn't a great advertisement for me really, is it? … but I'm almost jealous of you. There are just times when I wish I could feel something.'

'You don't usually … ?'

She shakes her head. Motioning me closer, she pulls up her skirt and shows me a cross-hatching of faded scars at the top of her thigh.

'I've never seen those before.'

'Body make-up. A drag queen taught me to use it.'

I put my hand on them. Like trying to heal them, or maybe just saying hello.

'Careful,' she says, smiling, and then, 'Hot hands.'

'Hot everything.'

'Now you're just teasing me.'

A flower seller with an impenetrable Eastern European accent comes through the restaurant; it's that kind of joint. Everyone – the coked-up ad-men, the long-married couples – get offered a rose. I expect Vinyl to either flirt with or mock the guy with the flowers, but instead, she calmly buys a rose and offers it to me. It's not perfect – a little wilting, the petals blackened and bruised – but I love it more than the plush-petalled bouquets that Kate would buy me out of guilt. 'You're mine now,' she says.

I smile at her. 'For as long as you want me.'

After dinner, we go for a pint in one of her hole-in-the-wall pubs. As soon as we sit down, Vinyl licks froth from her lower lip and asks me abruptly, 'What have you done to Roshan?'

'What do you mean, what have I done?'

'Well, apart from the obvious.'

'What are you on about? He's the one who thinks it's not going to work.'

'Is he? All I know is that he was round to see Jack the other night and he was a right narky bastard. Never seen him like that. So I wondered. Maybe he misses you.'

'He knows where I am.'

'How did you two leave it? At the wedding?'

I remember the empty bed. 'Not … bad. Amicably. He just told me he didn't think it was going anywhere.' I gulp some beer. 'Just the latest in the long line of gits who think I'm some sort of flight risk.' It's not so much that the rejections add up – though of course they do – it's that they remind me of other, older ones. Work. Kate. My father.

'Could be that you just gave it up too easily.'

'Vi!'

'What? Come on, you didn't hold out very long.'

'Jesus, I didn't know it was a competition. Anyway, that kind of implies I … I don't know, I had a plan. Don't you only hold out if you're after something?'

'You weren't?'

'No. I didn't want to marry him. I just wanted what I got. What we had.'

'Maybe he just wasn't into the rebound thing. After all, you're still a bit mad now. God knows what you were like before.'

'Yeah, but all I wanted for him, for us, was to live in our safe little world a bit longer. I suppose it's for the best. I mean, what kind of man wants to have sex with a lesbian anyway?'

She looks incredulous. 'Er – all of them?'

We laugh.

'OK,' she says. 'If I see him, I can always tell him you're in a foul mood too. Maybe you two can team up and kick some bins over or something.'

'I miss him,' I say quietly.

'I know, love. But you're all right. You can handle it. You're strong.'

'Why are people always saying that to me? Do they think it helps?'

She shrugs. 'Maybe it helps them.'

There's a poster behind her head. Thin, cheap green paper, blocky wartime lettering. 'TAKE NOTE,' it says, in big letters – that's what caught my eye – then beneath that, in smaller writing, it reads: 'Poetry Barn Presents a Night of Music and Spoken Word. Featuring: Jack McHugh, Wendy Northgate, Blue Belle, and special guest Brian Day.'

The Bloody Irish Poet. The star – of course. Brian Day, blood full of red wine and coal. Son of a navvy, he boasted in the front of his first collection.

Left school at fourteen. Four major volumes, hundreds of commissions. Winner of the prizes Kate coveted, Writer-in-Residence, traveller on other people's money. Ladies' man. Raconteur. Dad.

'Nothing,' I say. Then I check the date on the poster. 'Vi?'

'Yeah, babe?'

'What are you up to on Thursday?'

Bedtime Stories

My dad, Brian Day, was – is – a poet. But if you ask me, and even when no one does, I'd say he was best at telling stories. Not just the ones he told my mother to keep them together a little longer, but the ones he told me before bed, on long car journeys, on cold walks home. Brian Day's stories were epic, all-singing, all-dancing productions – with all the voices, of course. One of my earliest memories is of sitting on the floor of my bedroom in my pyjamas, excited beyond all possibility of sleep and thinking, with all the objectivity of a five-year-old girl up long past her bedtime, *this is brilliant. Who else on earth has this?* I was stirred and lulled every night by his voice, rumbling from deep in his throat with faint hints of the Irish and Scouse he'd left behind ('Just a bunch of gyppos, our family, love, on both sides,' he'd say cheekily, looking at Pina, whose cut-glass accent and cheekbones suggested aristocracy even though her lineage was as muddled as his).

He could create a story out of anything – a junk-shop find, a stuffed toy, a book I'd read and found boring which he'd then turn into a punky, anarchic riff, but the story that we came back to was always about Princess Eve. Princess Eve was like me – only better. Sometimes, she ran away to sea and became a pirate; sometimes, she invented a magic medicine that saved the villagers' lives. She always solved the riddle and outsmarted the bad guys and everybody loved her. The stories always ended with the Princess saying goodbye to her adoring public and heading towards her next adventure. I had a red coat, which Pina had put together from scratch, and wore long after it was too tight. The last line of his stories was always, 'And Princess Eve put on her red coat, and she walked out into the snow.'

If you need any reason why I went into showbiz, why I sing my heart out in damp tents and on pub stages, this is it. He taught me what words could do, and how it felt to have that kind of power – even when it was all made up.

As I got older, the stories got longer, more fantastical, and much darker. Looking back, it was probably a reflection of how he was feeling as his relationship with Pina wavered and died, but I also saw it as a sign of my maturity, that he could talk to me about these things. He would send his heroes and heroines on long, dangerous quests that had nothing to do with the business of day-to-day life – the sound of the TV downstairs as Mum tried to relax after a hard day's work, whatever awaited me at school tomorrow.

When I was about seven, I was sitting on the bed in my parents' room as he braided my hair – he was always, strangely, better at that than Mum – and told me a story about a rabbit that ran away. The rabbit found a field of lettuces, and ate until he couldn't eat any more. 'And they were the best lettuces he ever tasted,' Dad told me. 'Do you know why?'

I thought. I thought hard. I wanted so badly to be right. 'Because … I don't know, because the field had … a really good farmer?'

'No,' he said, his hands full of my hair. 'Because he knew he shouldn't.' Ladies and Gentlemen, my Dad.

After he left, Pina tried, but she was just no good at stories. We compromised on other things; she could draw in a way that he never could. She made clothes for my dolls and school play costumes so elaborate they almost embarrassed me, decked in fake fur and charity-shop beads while the other kids skulked in their mums' cast-offs. Something about my love of fine things came from her, but my love of words was from him. 'The gift of the gab,' my mother would mutter when she got off the phone with him, flushed and shamefaced. 'Your father, Evie, he's incorrigible.' And though she'd been flint-sharp at the start of the call, she'd lower her head to hide a smile.

Having a poet for a father meant that I always had a window into his soul. He laid it bare for anyone who'd listen. A troubadour. Born in the wrong time, he said. Born under a bad sign, said my mother. My father had no secrets. The slim, expensive volumes tucked away in the backs of bookstores filled in the gaps for me. He wrote about a shallow night's sleep on the floor of his mother's hospital room, about London espresso bars and New York dive bars, about road trips – probably on some chintzy University-sponsored tour with a couple of other poets, but he brushed over that in favour of the unravelling road, the turning leaves. I could have lived without the sleazy poem about two Japanese schoolgirls outside Farringdon Tube, but that was my Dad – you took him, all of him, at face value.

When I was a teenager, he'd told me – though I kind of wish he hadn't – just how intense things had been with my mother. Dad was prone to exaggeration, but I knew that what he said was true – they'd wrestled, had blazing rows, ran around the house pushing each other up against walls. Pina had never raised a hand to me, but she'd slapped him silly in moments of desire and rage, dug her nails into his skin. He'd written poems about it, of course – about the big, white, bed laced with a net of her dark hairs ('Of course,' she'd snarl when I brought that poem up, 'I *trapped* him.') He wrote poems about Pina's creamy skin, the curtains of her hair, the smell and taste of her; like pine resin, he'd written, sticky, dripping sap, the damp forest floor. Most teenagers could have lived without detailed descriptions of their mother's genitals, but I learned to love the poems. Not everyone has such a beautiful record of how they happened.

Then, of course, there were the poems about me. *My Daughter's New Dress. We Play With The Stars.* In his poems, as I got older, I could see myself fade out, surfacing once or twice like an accidental reflection – a glimpse of dark hair, another woman's reproachful eyes.

Jamie wasn't the first person to ask me if I was, maybe, looking for Daddy. It's textbook, isn't it, for gay girls and boys? We've all heard the half-baked theories. Absent or distant father, overbearing mum, that's how it's supposed to work. However, Jamie's dad is a cake-baking sweetheart who's tracked every minute of his beloved daughter's life in a series of brown-tinged photos of Jamie in various outfits on high holy days that, if you sit still long enough, he'll find an excuse to show you. Kate's dad was an outdoorsy, alpha-male type who was forever building complicated things in the garden or sailing on Dun Laoghaire – he ate a lot of red meat and watched ex-SAS men surviving in the wilds on TV, suggesting to anyone who would listen that they were all a bunch of nancy boys. We didn't get on.

Superficially, yes, Dad and Roshan were similar. Tall, dark, dragged-through-a-hedge hair, raised by houses full of matriarchs and single-mindedly hooked on their art. But it stopped there. There was a bedrock of calm in Roshan that my father never had. In some ways, it's not Roshan that reminds me of him, so much as Vinyl. She has that wildness, that disproportionate worship of all things beautiful, that hint of self-destruction that clung to Brian Day like stale wine breath.

When I was seventeen and Pina and I were driving each other crazy, I went to stay with my Dad – well, rolled up on his doorstep smeared in mascara and demanding entry. He was teaching poetry at a university near us and it was strange and wonderful having him in my life again. I was roaring out of the closet at the time, and in my first band – an alt-rock outfit called Relapse. In my fishnet tights and stranger's face-paint, I was loud-mouthed, manic, and ready to party. My energy came from a pit as bottomless as Brian's capacity for long, surreal shaggy-dog pub stories, as deep as my nameless need.

I loved going to his place on Friday nights; his mate's rented flat above a stonemason's workshop, with tasteless memorial stones in the windows, which we'd point and laugh at shamelessly. It was a total bachelor pad, a boy's fantasy of a home. Ring-bound notebooks and other poets' breathlessly signed pamphlets covered every surface. Dirty dishes nestled in each other. There were stacks of old movies on VHS tapes- he still had the tape recorder – each one lettered with biro hieroglyphs and the little alphabet stickers you got with the tapes, making a language only he could understand. The purple shirts he wore for readings hung from coat-hangers in front of the windows, airing out like sails.

He tried. I'll give him that. But he wasn't ready for me, and I wasn't ready for a life like his. I'd wonder what I was doing, sitting in small, polite audiences every night, watching girls as young as me flirt with my father, what I was doing being quietly sick in the loos of a twenty-four-hour coffee house as his friends argued over desserts, what I was doing spending my nights gently pulling away from mad-haired men who looked at me and lovingly rolled out the words – Ah, Evie, if I was twenty years younger, I tell you …

I could have lived with them. I could have lived with the late nights and late breakfasts, and even the women. After a while, though, I started to see that something was wrong. There were days when he wouldn't leave the tiny flat, wouldn't get out of bed, and I'd go hungry as I got bored of the endless books he picked out for me, breathing the cigarette smoke that seeped from under his door and thickened the air like fog. I'd get restless, wanting to go out, go to the Turkish place for bread, go round the markets, something … I waited, I listened, I tried to be good, but by the time he was ready to drag me through a flea market of broken trash we didn't need, I was hysterical and he … well, he was just trying to struggle out from under the weight of what haunted him.

Depression runs in families. On the flip-side of the pub joker, the flashes of genius in his lines, there was a boy who came from a place of hunger, whose marriage had died, whose daughter called him Brian. I didn't doubt that he loved me, but trying to pretend everything was all right just felt like another secret I couldn't keep.

On Sunday nights, I'd climb back into Pina's car after a weekend of bachelor living, all poetry and pub quizzes and cheap magic tricks to impress tired-looking women in bars, and breathe a quiet sigh of relief while she told me I smelled like an ashtray and asked what he'd given me for dinner. Once or twice, I'd cry without knowing why and snap at her when she asked. By Friday, I was always raring to go again, having bragged to my school friends about the adventures I had with Dad – the famous writers we met, the dives we graced with our presence – but one Friday morning, she laid down the law. Pina told me that she didn't think this was good for me, that she couldn't stand seeing me tearing myself to shreds every Sunday night. She said she'd talked to Brian about it, and they'd agreed we needed a break.

'I hate you!' I'd screamed. Rabid before breakfast, that's teenagers for you.

'Yeah, you know what, Evie?' Her pale, angular face was tight. 'I can live with that.'

Mothers. We never do give them any credit for saving our lives.

Around this time, Pina was working as an art therapist. She was more alive than she'd been in years. She'd come home, trailing war-stories and the smells of turpentine and hospitals. Something about the tales she heard every day fired her up, so we spent these years in a hormonal haze, Mum going through an early menopause and me just plain mad in the way that only semi-closeted gay adolescents in dodgy pub bands can be.

One of her projects involved working with terminally ill patients. They were all so different, she told me, in their attitudes to death. Some were matter-of-fact, some mildly cheated, some burning with rage. My mother was particularly fascinated with two of the women; one of them hadn't had anything to do with her husband when he told her he'd been having an affair, cut him out of her life and her daughter's, but when she got the diagnosis ten years later, he was the one she called. Slowly, they were repairing the tear in their lives. Pina loved that story – it reminded her that, no matter what she thought in her own dark moments, sometimes the good things didn't come too late.

Since finding The Lump, I'd wondered what I'd say to my father if I knew we only had a short time together – if I'd dwell on the anger, the feeling of having a crack in my surface where others were whole, or whether we'd magically manage to sidestep that and just sit for hours on a veranda holding hands, gazing into a lowering sun (it all got a bit vague and Hollywood at this point). I wonder if he'd hold my mother's hand too.

You're not dying, I tell myself. This is not happening to you.

There was another woman my mother couldn't let go of. She worried away at this woman's life like a dog with a fragile bone. She was dying, and despite her prognosis not being the worst, she was slipping away faster, jerkily rushing towards the end. It turned out that this woman's mother had rejected her – never wanted her. She'd spent years trying to get over that, and suddenly here it was, underlining what she'd suspected. She wasn't meant to be here. Life, like everything else, had turned her down.

My God, Pina was upset by that. She rarely let me see when anything disturbed her – in fact, this was one of the few times she'd opened up about anything, and it made me feel grown up. 'God, Evie,' she'd say, over the black morning coffee I was still learning to like, 'the others are bad, the ones who've spent their lives grafting and are being cheated out of their retirement, and this one French woman? – so young, you'd want to cry. But this one, the one who feels like life doesn't want her…' Her face burned with evangelical zeal. 'Jesus, you know, I'd do anything if I could convince her that's not true. She's not going to be here long. I just want to take that weight from her.' But, indomitable though my mother is, I don't think she did.

So this is where I come from. Gyppos, hippies, geniuses in their own strange ways. Still, emotionally I was more his child than my mother's, with a dark, silted-up vein flowing sluggishly beneath the surface. Some of what I felt was understandable sadness, frustration, whatever – but the other stuff, the spewing, moody, irrational stuff that made my palms burn and my brain freeze, that was all Dad. Even when I'd been happy, I'd known those kinks and dark spots in me would have to come out, and now, without the safety net of contentment, they're running wild.

I felt like that woman – that my whole life until now had been some kind of mistake. My card was marked from the start. It's hard not to think of The Lump as the result of all this choked-back badness, a symptom of all I'd tried to suppress.

I'd thought that the sadness I felt made sense – that it was a rational response to what had happened. But I wasn't entirely convinced. Lying awake at four in the morning, my fingers for the hundredth time searching out The Lump, I knew what I was going through and where it came from – an older, deeper darkness.

Learning the Words

'You look amazing!' Vinyl says when she sees me. 'How was your interview?'

'Fine. Actually pretty good, I think.'

She jumps up and down on the spot, then pulls me to her in a clumsy cross between a hug and a head-butt.

I do look good – at least, I hope I do. I'm wearing a structured black pin-stripe suit with a pencil skirt that cinches my knees together, teamed with needle-sharp heels. My interview blouse is scrunched up in the plastic bag dangling at my side – after the afternoon in the offices of Willow PR, I ducked into a pub toilet and swapped it for a black satin camisole top with a hint of cream lace. Even in my frightened, unemployed state, I know I do a good impression of Glamorous London Professional, and that's exactly how I want to look tonight. It reminds me of the good old days, when I'd charge out of work across town for a gig, when I felt in control and on top of the world. I can have that again, I tell myself. It went well this afternoon – Victoria Walker, the Head of Communications, a tiny, mousy-haired woman with a mind like a steel trap, clearly took a shine to me. For a couple of hours I forgot about Kate, Roshan, the Lump – but I'd be lying if I said I'd forgotten about tonight.

Vinyl's dressed down for once, as though she knows I want the spotlight, but as I walk down the street by her side, I start to wonder if that's all it is. She's usually coiffed to within an inch of her life, but tonight there's something tired about her plimsolls and faded jeans, a limp fake flower pinned like an afterthought in her hair.

'D'you fancy a quick drink first?' she asks, not meeting my eyes. 'Sit down, have a chat before we throw ourselves in there?'

I feel the panic, which I'd managed to keep in check so far, rising up again. 'I don't think so, Vi. We're already cutting it a bit fine. I'll buy you a drink when we get there. All the drinks you want. After all, you're doing me a favour and …'

She puts her spare, bony little hand on my arm and squeezes. 'Fine. Breathe. Just thought you might need a bit of Dutch courage.'

She looks harder at me, and then reaches out and touches cold fingertips to my breastbone. 'What's that?'

I don't even have to look. Since I was a kid, I've broken out in rashes when I was stressed. The neck and chest are the worst, blossoming into red-wine blotches that look like love-bites. Right now, I feel as though I'm covered in hives. 'Nothing.'

She nods slowly. 'All right. Forget I asked.' She reaches up and brushes some hair out of my face. 'Don't worry,' she says. 'You're perfect.'

I don't see him right away. I thought I would – I imagined walking in while he was in mid-flow and as I made my dramatic entrance, he'd struggle to keep his eyes off me. Of course, that doesn't happen, especially as we're early – well, on time, which for most gigs is the same thing. Even after eight years of performing, I'd never got into the habit of showing up at the real starting time. I was always paranoid that one of these days, they'd stick to the time on the flyer and start without me.

'Which one is he?' Vinyl hisses in my ear as we stand at the bottom of the stairs. I'm in front of her, unable to move.

'Excuse me, could you please move down … ?' murmurs a middle-aged woman behind us. Vinyl turns around and gives her an evil look, then taps me on the shoulder. I feel like her bony little finger's going to drive right through my skin.

It smells simultaneously damp and burnt down here. If coldness had a smell, this would be it. I put one foot in front of the other, my skin flaring like a fever. I shouldn't be subjecting her to this – even if I feel like she's the only one who'll really understand it. Girls like Vi are used to life's chaos, and I know that no matter how weird tonight is, she'll take it in her stride.

For a disloyal moment, though, I wish it was someone else who didn't know that chaos, who just wanted to hold my hand and nod as I talked in circles afterwards. It would have been Kate, back when my world was richer and smaller. I'd fantasised that it would be Roshan – someone who my father could look at with respect rather than the distracted flirtation he treated my girlfriends to. Then it hits me – I don't want him either. I don't know why, but I want Gray.

'Your Dad,' Vinyl is murmuring on high-speed, a string of playground insults under her burnt-smelling breath, 'Your Dad Your Dad Your Dad … ah.' She's seen him. After all, he looks like me. Big, shambolic, a touch of the fairground Gypsy, the tattooed guy you'd see at the Waltzers who'd grab the sides of your car and, ignoring your screams, hurl you into the epicentre like a pissed-off god.

He looks at me for a fraction of a second, his face worryingly blank. I tell myself that maybe his eyesight's just failing, that I've lost – or gained – weight since he saw me last, that he isn't sure it's me. But he is – I know it. He's just figuring out how to react. As he looks me up and down, I do the same. Shoulder-length Samson hair, slightly thinning, a thick tweed jacket, worn slick in places like a pub carpet, over a black T-shirt and jeans – Poet uniform, circa the eighties.

Brian Day teaches Creative Writing at. Brian Day left school at fourteen and. Brian Day, youngest of six, started writing poetry in. Your Dad.

'Evie!' he bellows, his voice echoing in the basement. People turn, lazily, to look. 'My God! How are you, my darling?'

Where do I start? 'Good,' I say, aware that I'm raising my voice to match his. 'I'm good. This is Vi.'

'Vinyl,' she elaborates, shaking his hand in a strenuous, businesslike way that looks like she's going to pump it right off.

'Great name, love.' Even though she's not looking her best today, I see him thinking how pretty she is. 'Where'd you get it?'

'Bradford Market.'

'Good on you there.' He treats her to a hint of the Irish brogue and, though I can tell she came in trying to be all ice queen on my behalf, I can see her melt a little.

I'm used to women fancying him. Two of them are standing near him, so quiet – not bothering to talk to each other – that I can tell they're my father's acolytes. One of them's fair, in a concoction of ruffles and tulle – the other's thinner, with dark hair and nervous hands. He doesn't discriminate, my Dad, from what I remember. Whichever one goes home with him will just be the one that stayed.

'Drink!' He declares. 'We must have drink.'

He turns to the barman, who's been pretending he isn't watching Dad at work. Even middle-aged, with stained, knackered-looking teeth and thick veins standing out on his hands, Brian's still got it. I think if he put a bit more effort in, this anaemic, surprised-looking young man would probably shag him too.

As we try to talk, other people keep swirling in and out of our orbit. Vi – for once – is the only one sticking to the script, talking to him in a high, crackling loop about how pretty, how talented I am, as though maybe he'll suddenly look at me and agree.

I start getting annoyed with the short-haired, right-on women in black cheesecloth, the young girls glowing with the beginnings of desire, the hippy kids and the gangly fan-boy poets who swish past him, trying to look cool and jumping into gaps in the conversation. I feel like a sulky, pancake-and-kohl-faced teenager again, too old and cool to tug at his sleeve – 'Dad, Dad, look at me …' but still longing to do just that.

After a while, I start to realise that even when they're not trying to talk to us, he's pulling them in – showing them off to me, and me to them, while we stare at each other in mutual incomprehension, all the poets clearly seeing me as an irrelevance. 'Look,' he keeps saying. Like Vi, he can't keep still, eyes always darting around, looking for the next thing. I feel my skin prickle with heat and try not to scratch my arms.

'Look, Ian, Pat, look at this – it's my beautiful daughter! This is Evie. Isn't she something?'

We drink quickly, and I try to swallow down that first moment when I saw him look at me, appraising me, wondering what to do. Always the performer. There was no spontaneity in that moment. I suppose it would be strange if there was, but I still hadn't expected that blankness.

We sit patiently through the other poets' sets. Vinyl's being astonishingly well-behaved – without her usual flaky, fidgety demeanour she sits, beautiful and blank, through great swathes of unasked-for intimacies. After a break, some more cheap wine and one more poet – Blue Belle, a sex-obsessed diva with hair like electric candyfloss – it's my father's turn. I feel aware of myself, my body. My belly pushes against the waistband of my skirt, my hips feel like they're swelling. I'm too much. I wish I was a girl again, pale and blameless.

While the book he's got is already lined and thickened with Post-It notes and dog-eared pages, I can tell within a couple of poems that tonight's set list is for me. I want to bounce in my chair, all self-consciousness forgotten, and poke Vi in the arm as he reads, but I stay still. He reads *We Play with the Stars*, about the two of us lying on our backs in the garden, inventing constellations – The Fat Cuckoo, The Earwig, Elvis's Cousin. He reads about my mother – his cool-skinned Biblical princess. Finally, looking at me all the way through, he reads the poem about picking me up at night.

> *Before I hear her cry, I feel her stir,*
> *And then they're rising, those ascending notes,*
> *I move like a half-drowned man, groping the walls,*
> *Staggering down the hall, and go to her…*

I know he's saying, this is it – this is all I can give you, that like me, he's more himself in front of an audience, behind a microphone, than he could ever be with another human being. If it was just the two of us, he'd struggle to find words.

This way, he can revel in his own love and contrition. He can roll the words out as though they're enough. Not that this is a bad thing. They almost are.

Voices

Finally, I manage to get him alone, cornering him outside the Gents upstairs and dragging him outside under the pretext of having a cigarette. I don't light one, though. For all Brian Day's vices, he doesn't smoke, and I feel too self-conscious to light up in front of him.

'So,' he says. 'How are you, my darling?'

'All right.'

He picks up on the hesitance in my voice. 'You don't sound all right.'

'It's just been a weird couple of months.' I clear my throat. 'Kate and I broke up. It was … messy. I had to move. Live with someone I don't really know. She's lovely, but … then I lost my job.' I don't tell him about the Lump – it's just too much. 'I had an interview. Today. I think it went well, but I don't know. I … I worry.' I say that, knowing it's one of my biggest understatements to date, to describe the dark roiling and churning in me that way.

'You always did,' he says. Awkwardly, he reaches out and rubs my head. 'I'm sorry to hear that, love. About Kate. I always quite liked her.'

'Me too.'

'Do you think you'll ever be friends? I think I've managed it all right with your mother. We have our moments sometimes, but …'

A sudden memory pops into my head; I was seventeen, coming home from school, bag heavy on my shoulder and Walkman blaring dirty nineties pop into my ears. I'd started to dread coming home because since he'd left, Pina hadn't been doing much but sitting at the kitchen table, looking dishevelled and lost. I'd started reading nightmare true-life stories in thin glossy magazines about women who never got out of bed.

That day, though, was different. When I came through the door, she looked up at me and said frankly, 'Fuck me, Evie. This isn't much fun, is it?' Then, without another word, she got up and went into the kitchen to make dinner.

That was my mother, I want to tell him. But I'm not like her, I'm like you. Moody, irrational, tender. Endlessly picking over the same old bones.

'Are you all right for money?' he asks.

'What, have you got some?'

He smiles thinly. 'I don't enjoy the teaching, you know. Not any more. Ah, it's all right, but there's only so much shite poetry one man should have to put up with in a lifetime. If it wasn't for putting a bit by, for yourself and your mother, I'd be on the road all the time. Free as a bird. Like you.' His smile softens. 'Ah, I know you probably think I'm too old for that sort of thing. And sometimes I see the young ones there and I think, Jesus, they're half my daughter's age … but that's the way we are, isn't it? We love to write, love to be the centre of attention, love the road.'

I nod eagerly. I don't tell him about the other things I want, scared that he'll think me too conventional, that all those stories and adventures were for nothing – that I'm not his fearless Princess Eve or the spit of his fiery young bride, but just an ordinary girl. The truth is, part of me wants to be a good wife. A good mother. I think about lifting my child from its cot at night, the way he lifted me. I want to feel that lightness, a cheek soft as breath against mine. I can't tell him I dream about this, or that I'm scared it might never happen.

'Dad, can I tell you something?'

He nods warily, and I see him thinking – drugs? Debt? Pregnancy, for all he knows, though chance would be a fine thing.

'Those songs. My songs. The ones you listen to, I didn't write them. Kate did. Now she's gone and … I can't write any new songs. I don't know where to start.'

'Ah,' he says, seeming to understand me for the first time all night. 'You've lost your voice.'

'I don't know whether I ever had one.'

'Course you did. You've just mislaid it, love. Happened to me a couple of times. Couldn't write a word for two years, once.'

'Once, Dad. At least you knew you could.'

'I didn't know that, no. I've never been sure of that.'

'Dad … I was wondering. If there's any, you know, bits, any lines you aren't using …'

He blinks. 'I'm not sure I follow you, love.'

'I don't want your money. I don't want a house. I just want some words. I'm too stressed to write, even if I could, and I can't … I'm not like you, or Mum, I'm not even creative. I'm window-dressing.'

He pauses for a moment. 'Right. First, I never, ever want to hear you say that again. And second, Evie, I can't do that. You're my daughter, and …'

'So what? It's not like anyone really knows.'

'Course they do. Aren't I bragging about you all the time?'

'I don't know. Are you?'

He reaches in his pocket for his wallet and pulls out a folded magazine page. 'I found it in some shite bar round the corner a couple of months ago.'

It's me, sitting on the windowsill in the pub, green shoes dangling, staring seriously into the camera. I hear Roshan saying, 'Don't smile.'

'I collect them,' he says.

'I'm not asking for much, Dad.'

'No, you're not, Evie, in fairness. It's not how much you're asking for, though, darling, it's what. Believe me, there's not much I wouldn't give you. My name, my blood, my flat … you can even have one of my kidneys, though God knows it wouldn't be much use to you. But you need your own voice.'

Karaoke Queens

We're drunk. Front page, young-women-binge-drinking, couldn't-make-it-up drunk. We're sitting on a fire escape in Dean Street, confusing media types and homeless people who aren't sure which tribe we belong to. Vinyl, hungry as always, is polishing off a vile-looking tray of chicken and chips and being offensive to the men who ask her how much sex might be.

Leaning with my cheek against the dirty metal, I've adopted my old favourite avoidance tactic – silence. The men try to talk to me, but they can't reach me. Even my hands, with their nervous rash dying down, don't feel like mine.

'Where's your jacket?' she asks me abruptly, crumpling up the polystyrene tray and lobbing it into the gutter.

'I don't know. Did I have one?'

'For fuck's sake, Day, could you come back to earth for a second? Yes you did. You had a jacket and you're going to be cold without it.'

'I'm not going back in there.'

'He's gone.'

'Course he is. They're closed now, anyway.'

'We could go back.' She stifles a burp. 'We could.'

'Forget it.' I hoist myself upright. 'I'm wearing my beer coat.'

'Where are we going?'

'Home.'

''Nother drink?'

I think about it. I'm still too conscious to go home. 'Maybe.'

'Here,' shouts a toothless Irish guy in a Fair Isle sweater, 'are youse two sisters?'

Vinyl looks at me, and smiles. She nods. 'Yeah, what of it?'

'I knew it. I knew you was sisters. Ah, you're beautiful.' She nods, in a yeah-I-know way. 'Spare some change, love?'

She palms him a couple of coins and sweeps me past him. Vi can be a total bitch, but she always gives when she's asked, and tips generously. Before Jack and his wallet came along, she worked too many waitress jobs not to.

'That didn't go too badly, I thought,' she says, as we shuffle unsteadily down the street. 'He's a good writer. I see where you get it from.'

'I didn't write my songs.'

'Are you sure?'

'Yes, Vi, I would have noticed.'

She steers me down another flight of black metal stairs, into what's blatantly a strip club. She exchanges some nods and gossip with the guys on the door, and then we're in. It smells of dry ice and cheap, glittery body lotion and it's very, very dark.

'Learnt my trade here,' she says, eyes darting around the swirling darkness like fish in a tank. 'What are you drinking?'

'Something strong.'

'Probably for the best. They water it down when they can get away with it.' She hiccups and lurches off to the bar. 'So long as it's not that bloody sweet champagne we used to have to get the punters to buy. Melt your fillings, that.'

She comes back with two rum and Cokes – not my favourite, but needs must and, even if she knows the beautiful Asian girl at the bar, I'm sure they still cost a bomb. We clink glasses and down them like medicine. As she tilts back her head to knock back a hefty mouthful, a strobe swoops over her and something on the fourth finger of her left hand glows like a chunk of neon.

'What …' I reach over and grab her wrist. Her pulse stutters against my fingers.

She looks at me. Her gaze and voice are level, her eyes dark. 'Yeah. Gray was right. Living together for two months, and now this.'

'Wow. You look … I don't know.' With her hair loose and lipstick chewed off, she could be a ten-year-old girl in this light, instead of the high-gloss femme fatale I know. 'Freaked out, to be honest.'

'I am. I mean, I'm over the moon, at least I was when he asked me. I said yes right away. He took me to a restaurant in the country and he was in a really weird mood all the way down, I thought he was mad at me ...' she rattles off the words. I can see her telling her mum, her friends, getting bored of her own happy ending. 'But he was just scared. Now he's fine, of course. I'm the one who's shitting myself.'

'Why? I mean, you know he loves you.'

'Do I? I don't know. I don't feel like much of a catch at the moment.' She loops a ribbon of her hair around her finger, tugging at it. 'My head's been a bit wrong at the moment. I think I'm about to go down ... y'know, just plummet down in flames. I'm not that good at seeing when it's going to happen. Jack's better at it. He tells me I'm not this time, but ... I'm not so sure. And then there's you ...' she takes another gulp of her rum and coke. 'Fuck it, I know there's no point in telling you, but I have to say it. You did something to me.'

Idiotically, I say, 'Should you be drinking that?'

She looks at me evenly. 'No. Not really. It just takes the edge off, straightens me out a bit.' She smiles humourlessly. 'Now there's irony for you. If there's one thing I need right now, it's straightening out.'

I can't tell her the brutal truth, that beautiful though she is, I've barely even thought of her when she's not with me. I've been saturated in painful, delicious memories of Roshan. The ghost of his smell on the men I pass on Underground platforms, the thought of his hands.

Of all the people who dominate my thoughts, the most beautiful – and attentive – is way down the list. Why can't I care for her more than the people who bruise me?

'You're just panicking,' I say softly.

'Don't tell me what I'm doing, will you, Day?'

'OK. You're right. I'm sorry.'

We sit together for a while, watching the girls bump and grind. 'That one on the left's dreadful,' Vinyl murmurs. 'Dances like she's made of bloody lead.'

'So … what?' I ask, my tongue thick in my mouth and my head spinning. 'What do you want me to do?'

She leans back, avoiding my eyes, still looking at the stage. 'I thought you might give us a chance.'

'What, cause you're the pretty, straight princess and I'm the desperate lesbian, you thought I'd be hanging on your phone for weeks? Well, sorry. I've got more pride than that.'

'Oh yeah. That must be why you shagged your mate and let him disappear on you.'

I take a deep breath. 'What the hell is it with you and control, anyway? Make them hold on, make them wait for it … I don't even know how to do that. I couldn't if I wanted to. And you know what, you can't either. That's why this is getting to you. You think all you have to do is flutter your eyelashes and I'll come running.'

'You'd come running for him.' She leans forward, pointy chin propped on her hand. 'If he called now, you'd be off like that. You'd just forget about everything else until tomorrow when he wouldn't call you again.'

'So what if I would? It's nobody's business but ours.'

'There is no "ours." No "us." He's not coming back for you, you know.'

I can't think of anything to say so I look around at the crowd. I was expecting just sleazy guys, but it's mixed – some couples, some senior citizens who look like they've just got off the wrong tour bus, hipsters wearing sunglasses even in the blackness, a gang of drum-bellied bikers. Vi catches the eye of one of the girls, raises her finger imperceptibly and gets a nod from the waitress, who turns back to the bar. If I live to be a hundred – and God willing, I will – I'll never be able to do that.

'This isn't as bad as I thought it was going to be,' I say. 'The bar, that is. The other stuff's pretty shit.'

The girl puts our drinks down in front of us. Vinyl peels off some notes – her own ill-gotten gains, legitimate money or courtesy of Jack? – and the waitress smiles and turns back into the darkness. 'Sorry, Evie,' she says, sounding like a tired child. 'That was a bit mean.'

'It's true, though.'

'He's a nice guy. A good man. I think he was willing to give it a go.' She shrugs. 'It was just too much.'

'I'm just too much.'

'Not for everyone,' she says gently. 'Not for me.'

'I am. I want things too badly. I want to be alive too much. I'm always flitting from one thing to the other, living in a dream world. I'm always desperate. I'm always hungry.'

'Some people just manage to hide it better,' she says. 'Sometimes I do. But there are times when I don't, and … they're great. Nightmarish, but great at the same time. I feel like that too, honest, I really do. Like I'm always looking.'

'You've got someone,' I say drunkenly. I hear myself, a bitter old harridan. 'You're marrying some git with his own Canary Wharf flat and a miserable life and you're the only thing that sets him on fire. Well, good luck with that, because I know what it's like to be that for someone and it doesn't even matter how much you love him, you're never going to be enough. He doesn't really see you. He just wants to take you and put you in some big breezeblock tower and tell his mates you used to be a stripper, you used to be a model, you used to be bisexual and then he came along and fucking cured you.'

She stares at me impassively for so long I wonder if she's just about to pass out. Then she says dryly, 'And didn't you want that? Not even a little bit?'

After a painful few seconds, I nod. 'For a moment, yes. And before you start, it wasn't because he was a man. I just felt safe with him.'

'Fuck safety.' She stands up and grabs her cigarettes. 'Let's go.'

'But I haven't …' I gesture to my half-empty glass.

'Leave it. I've got an idea.'

'Karaoke?' I ask, swaying lightly outside the door of the Star Room. I've only ever seen tourists going in here. 'Is that the best you can do?'

Vinyl laughs, finishing off the last of her fag. 'It was either that or screaming in an underpass.'

The bored Chinese staff let us in and usher us to a table while a plump girl in sequins murders a ballad. I flip through a laminated phone-book of songs while Vi rifles through my makeup bag and paints on her usual face.

'Are you going to marry him?' I ask, flicking through the pages.

She stares at herself in the mirror. 'I'm not going to find anyone else who gets me like he does. The moods, the dodgy past …'

'You should be proud of those things. They make you who you are.'

'Yeah, like you're so proud.' She exhales deeply. 'Let's not talk about this again. We're here to sing.'

And we do. We hog the stage, and they love us. Vi tucks her vest in her bra like a nineties pop star's crop-top, and prowls around the front of the stage while I let rip, going for it until my throat's raw. We do vocoder impressions, Vinyl rapping in her smoke-and-helium voice. We do cock-rock and uncontrollable air guitar. No chick songs. Nothing about love or loss. By the time we stagger off stage, I'm laughing, brimming with joy.

'Look at you!' Cavorting under the spotlight seems to have sobered Vi up. 'You're … God, you're glowing.'

'I'm sweating.'

'Yeah, but … you look happy.' She claps me on the back. 'See? Aren't I a genius?'

'You are, babe. Come on, it's stupid o'clock. Let's go.'

We start to walk home. Somehow, I know she's coming with me, that she probably would be even if she could get back to Canary Wharf in time.

'You could do that,' she says. 'You know. Professionally.'

'It's not that easy. I'm not as good as half my friends. Besides, there's not that much of a business any more ... I just do it for fun, really.'

She stops and turns her pale little face to mine. The night has bleached the colour from her. 'When are you going to listen to people when they tell you how amazing you are? You drive me mad, sometimes, you know that? I know you've been going through a lot, Evie, but it's time you stopped sitting on your arse going oh-poor-me all the time. Your life ...' she raises her little fist to my chest, and knocks on my breastbone, where my heart might be. 'Your life is knocking at your door. I know you can feel it. Maybe that's why things haven't been working out for you – maybe they were just the wrong bloody things.' She knocks again. 'This is your life, Evie. And some day, it's going to have to come in.'

Just another Gig in Camden

In my dream, we're teenagers again, me and Roshan, doing what we always did – sitting in the cold outside the only independent café in our part of town. The chain coffee-houses, in our opinion, are for posh kids, label-hounds, and sheep. We're probably both extremely punchable, but we think we're great.

We spend our afternoons looking for obscure comic books and deconstructing the lyrics of Bob Dylan and The Sex Pistols with the gravity of Talmud scholars. Theories unspool in the air around us with the smoke from my cheap roll-ups. We look the same as we do now, from a distance, but my hair's darker, a plummy light-reflecting black, my face pasted into a smooth matt mask. I'm wearing my red patent boots that come up to mid-calf, like a wrestler's. God, I loved them. Where did they go?

He's talking to me, but I can't understand a word he's saying. I crane in, listen harder. I see him raise an eyebrow, his eyes wide and questioning. He leans back, waiting for me to answer him. I want to say, *This can't be it. I didn't come all this way for this. These are not our last words.*

I hear bells, and turn towards the source of the noise; Vinyl's phone. She compounds the effect of the alarm by turning over, her arm slung over her eyes like a sleeping cat's, then lets the arm drop heavily and smack me in the head. Finally, I dredge my voice back, and celebrate by swearing at her. 'Sorry,' she mutters, groping her way over me, all hot, damp skin and heady perfume. She's wearing one of my old T-shirts, her red hair gathered back in a ponytail. With her face scrubbed clean, she looks skinned and raw.

She picks up the phone, turns off the alarm and checks her messages, then her voicemails. I watch her raise an eyebrow, a corner of her mouth pulled down in a telltale, 'oh fuck,' fashion. Jack, I imagine. By the time we'd finished our odyssey of poetry, strip bars and karaoke, it had been so late that she'd had to stay here. The two of us had slept innocently side by side, but before we'd fallen asleep, she'd leant over and given me a small, damp kiss on the ear. Somehow, that touched me deeply. I'd wanted to reach out and pull her close, but I'd resisted – things were confusing enough.

'Good to be back,' she says, sprawling on her back and holding the phone up in front of her face, peering at it like a compass.

'Hey, you. I wouldn't be getting too comfortable. It's my bed now.'

'Yeah, yeah …' she rolls over and snuggles into me. 'Forgot where I was at the moment. It was quite nice.'

'You've got a bed. And a flat. And a fiancé. And some wanky recessed lighting.'

'Grass is always greener, though, isn't it?' she says.

I point vaguely at her phone. 'Heard from Jack?'

She nods, guiltily licking her lips. Without paint for once, they're pale and cracked.

'Is he mad at you?'

She shrugs. 'So long as I'm OK, he knows it could be worse. He might sulk a bit, but if I come home in one piece …' she pauses, drawing her knees up to her chest. I look again at the faded cross-hatching of scars on her thigh.

'He does love me, you know,' she says quietly. 'I do the best I can. But it's not easy having to answer to someone all the time.' She undoes her hair and lets it fall loose. On her un-powdered face, I see a smattering of freckles like careless flecks of paint. 'Sometimes it feels like he's got my whole life planned out for me. And all I have to do is show up.'

'I felt like that once,' I say.

She isn't really listening, resting her fist against her cheek, her lips slightly pouted as though she's dreaming.

'I knew that girl was your ex,' she says.

'What girl?'

She plucks the duvet between her fingers. 'I'd seen you before we even met. Just another gig in Camden. You were with her. You were singing … I wasn't dressed up or anything, I think I was going through a bit of a bad patch, so I didn't talk to you in case I said anything weird … but I wanted to. When you walked into that class, I couldn't believe it. It felt like a sign. I wasn't ready to be with you … I'm still not, to be honest. But when I saw her in that bar, a couple of weeks down the line, I couldn't help myself. Started chatting her up a bit. She liked that. Sorry.' She grimaces at me. 'I told her I knew you. She looked more alive then, y'know? Proper lit up. For what it's worth, I think she did love you. She knew you were hurting and she was worried someone was going to take advantage of you. Like Roshan.'

'So how did he find out, you know, that I said he'd been paying me a bit too much attention?'

'I think, 'stalking,' was the word she used,' says Vinyl.

'The word *she* used, yes.'

'Not very nice of either of you.'

'I was just trying to make her feel better,' I say.

Vinyl looks at me incredulously. 'Why the fuck were you trying to do that?'

'I don't know!' I take a deep breath. 'How did he even find out?'

'I think Jack told him.'

'And … you told Jack.'

She nods.

'Why'd you do that, Vi?' My voice is soft, conciliatory. I'm actually curious.

'I don't know. I like Roshan, from what I know of him. I wanted him to know if he was making a fool of himself.'

'Are you really that unhappy, you want everybody else to be miserable too?'

'Honestly… I didn't think. I didn't set out to hurt either of you. Sometimes …' she looks down, 'I can't help myself. I just do these things to see what'll happen. And I'm always surprised when something does.'

I get up from the bed. 'You're going to be late for work.'

She stares down at her bare, sculpted knees. 'Do you hate me?'

I sigh. 'No, Vi, I don't hate you. I don't understand you. Just do me a favour, OK? Next time you want a bit of excitement in your life, don't start playing around with mine.'

'Evie?' Gray knocks on the door. 'Sorry to interrupt, but you left your phone downstairs and it won't stop ringing. Thought it might be an emergency or …'

Without thinking, I open the door and watch as Gray, freshly showered and crisp in her black business suit, looks around the room; me in my bathrobe and Vi sitting up in bed, hugging her knees. Too late, I realise how this looks.

She stares at both of us for a long minute, before shaking her head, handing me my bag, and heading downstairs.

'Thanks,' I say, weakly, to nobody.

'Oh no,' says Vi behind me, like a little girl. 'No, no, no.'

'What?' I turn on her. 'What's your problem now?' Suddenly, I'm sick of her. Her brightness, her fragility. 'And can you get out of *my bed*?'

She blinks, twists her hair around her finger and then nods. Slowly and silently, she gets up and starts to put on last night's clothes.

I check the number on my phone. My recruitment agency. Shit. My heart starts to twitch and hammer in my throat. Please let it work out this time.

I leave the room and sit on the stairs – between my two girls, Vi dressing upstairs and Gray fussing in the kitchen. The smell of the strong black coffee she loves starts to drift up the stairs, making my mouth water, as I call the agency back.

'Evie!' It's my agent, Suzanne, who dresses like a reluctantly off-duty rock chick. I quite fancy her. 'Right, well, thanks for calling back.' My heart sinks. I swallow hard. 'Good news. Willow PR want to offer you the executive job.'

'…What?'

'They like you. Which is good, because they haven't liked anyone so far. One girl got a proper dressing-down. Ms Walker also wants to tell you she can't stand Rebel's music either.' I hear a smile in her voice. 'Try not to mess this one up.'

As we talk about dates, salaries and references – Amanda had said she'd give me something inoffensive if I got off the premises quietly – Vi gets dressed. She's moving more slowly than usual, her movements small and studied as a geisha's. I expect a hug when I put the phone down – one of those clumsy, rugby-tackle jobs of hers. Instead, she just sits on the bed, looking lost.

'I got the job,' I say.

She nods. 'I know. I know, it's great. Well done.'

'Are you all right, Vi?' I ask.

She bites her lip. 'Just a bit … wobbly. I don't know.' She gets up. 'You're right. I am going to be late.'

'You don't have to go. Sit down for a minute.'

She shakes her head. 'No. I think you and Gray are best off without me. And Jack. And pretty much everyone.' Her eyes look like I've never seen them before, soft and wet with tears. They're like fresh wounds.

'Vi, that's not true. It really isn't.'

She moves back towards me, wraps her skinny arms around my waist, and presses her face into my shoulder.

'You're going to be fine,' I tell her.

She shakes her head. She's so hot, so narrow against me.

'You are. You're wonderful.'

She lets me hold her for a while, before tapping me lightly on the hip twice – like, *enough now*. With an unconvincing smile, she clatters down the stairs.

Retail Therapy

Gray's standing at the kitchen counter, staring out of the window. It's a beautiful autumn morning. The kitchen smells of coffee and the first hint of frost. She doesn't acknowledge me.

'That was my agency,' I say, wondering why my voice sounds so weak. 'I got the job.'

I expect some sort of reaction. Instead, she just breathes deeply, like she's trying to contain anger, and turns around to face me. 'Yeah. Vi said.'

I feel anxiety creeping up on me again. 'Are you all right?'

'Look. I don't care what you do on your own time. Whether it's girls or boys or God knows what. But if you're going to mess around with Vi, can you not do it under my roof?'

I stare back at her. 'OK. First of all, we weren't doing anything. Second, I didn't just club her over the head and drag her back here. I don't know what you two did together, but I can tell you're not wild about her moving out. That's fine, I don't want to know what went on. Just don't take it out on me.'

'You really expect me to believe you weren't doing anything up there?' she asks. 'The way you two look at each other? I come home, night after night, find you giggling in the kitchen … you must think I'm blind, the pair of you. Or stupid.'

The tiled floor is cold against my bare feet. I'm suddenly very conscious I'm just wearing a T-shirt and knickers under my bathrobe, that I'm wearing no makeup, that my hair must look like it's recently exploded. Everything seems plain, and small, and ugly today.

'Look, Gray, let's not get into this now. I just wanted to tell you about the job. So I'll be out of your hair now, maybe in a couple of months I'll get a place of my own. Or do you have something to say about that too?'

She stares at me. Finally, her pointed chin quakes a little, like she's trying

295

to hold back laughter. 'You're funny when you're mad. And no, I don't want you to go. Kind of got used to you, to be honest.'

I think of Vinyl last night, her face glowing under the streetlamps, her little fist knocking on my heart. Like that woman outside the pub, telling me I could go anywhere. Knocking and knocking, like, *anyone alive in there? Hello?*

Never apologise, never explain. That's what they say. Though who actually says that? Pricks, probably. Either way, it seems like I do little else these days.

Gray steps towards me, neat and self-contained in her suit, her skin glowing from her shower and the remains of anger. I feel sweaty, stale, uncontrolled. 'I just want you to watch yourself, that's all. She doesn't mean any harm, but sometimes things get a bit chaotic when she's around. Part of her charm, but I don't think you need it right now.'

'Thanks for your concern.' I sound clipped, empress-like, like Pina. 'But I think I can decide that for myself.'

She moves back slightly, shrugging in a suit-yourself way.

'Besides, you're not really one to talk, are you? Why would I listen to you about this when you blatantly still fancy her?'

'I don't. All right, I did, everyone does, but she's like my kid sister these days …' For once, she's looking self-conscious.

'Please. Why else would you be like this?'

She blinks twice, slowly, leans back against the cupboards and looks me up and down. 'God,' she says. 'Vi was right. You really don't live on the same planet as the rest of us, do you?'

Then she walks past me, leaving me standing in our empty kitchen.

I spend the day doing the one thing I know I'm good at. Shopping. I take all the comfortable couch-potato clothes from my Kate years, bung them into plastic bags, and deposit them in charity shops on Holloway Road.

Then I head into Camden, a seething consumer wrecking-ball desperate to distract myself by buying more things; lipstick, hand-tooled cowboy boots, a glittery Lucite handbag. Accompanied by several strong cappuccinos, the high I get from possession hits me like a muffled explosion, but, as soon as the sun goes down, I find myself exhausted, standing in the middle of Camden High Street, dripping with bags of overpriced tat I don't need.

I look at the bags in my hands and wonder what I really need, what's going to heal me. Then I take a deep breath and reach in my pocket for my phone. I find the last texts we sent each other. I write, 'Hello, stranger.'

Roshan meets me in The Dog and Monkey, a bar full of Camden hipsters we're on the verge of outgrowing. We've spent long nights here before, chatting to the local deadbeats, discussing the relative merits of nineties punk bands – the things friends do. Still, sitting by the window, my hands start to shake and I can't focus. I watch all the other men walk in, thinking how puny they are in comparison to him, with their gelled lesbian hair and skinny jeans, but when I get a glimpse of six-foot-something of hair and black denim and terrible posture I have a moment where I just think – Oh my Christ, what have I done? – and there, finally, there he is.

We look at each other for a moment before I jump into his arms and he lifts me up, the way he did back in January, hoisting me up while the bar staff watch impassively, clearly thinking what a strange couple we are. We sit down and eat each other up with our eyes, our words tumbling over each other's. He's so familiar – messy black hair constantly pushed back with a huge hand, a tired work-shirt straining a little at the arms and shoulders, that crammed, slightly crooked-toothed smile that mirrors mine. But still, there are some things I've forgotten – those dry, crackling flashes of humour, his verbal quickness, the sweet openness of his face. I inhale his smell as greedily as nicotine, drink it up like expensive wine. Its associations are so powerful they stop me from thinking – not just cinnamon, cream and the soft breath of his skin but the feeling of lying naked and wrapped in his arms, cuddles on the couch, the salt of sex and fresh sweat, the smell of home.

We last about three hours before we kiss, but the minute he reaches for my hands, we ruin the whole terribly painful Brief Encounter vibe by lunging for each other other like a pair of libidinous teenagers. The bar staff at this point heave an almost visible sigh of relief, clearly wishing these two freaks would go away and have sex somewhere they don't have to watch. It's messy, it's adolescent, there are tongues and teeth and spit and hungry moaning sounds that are me, him, the two of us. Still, I don't feel as ridiculous as I should. He has been on my mind for so long it feels like he's always been my story, always all my heart.

Waking up is a strange thing to do. I do it a little more every day.

Sometimes I'm newer, more awake, than I've ever been – sometimes I'm still picking over the past, searching for scars and tearing them open in stinging little shreds. Sometimes I'm the person I was before any of this happened. Twenty-five, waiting to go onstage at GreenFest to the biggest crowd of sweaty, roaring, drugged-up hippies I'd ever encountered. Twenty-three, striding through the Grand Café in a backless gown. Twelve. Eight. It's like reaching out for someone and realising you're in front of a mirror.

We lie, a little warm island on another grey London day, the whirr of his fan sounding like rain outside, making us desperate to lie together for hours, safe and untouchable.

I know this is the last time and I can live with that. I'm late for the rest of my life. I have more adventures to go to now. I have my new job and my new friends and my new, narky, strangely attractive flatmate. It's not like this little slice of him is all I have. It was once, but not now.

'I was talking to Vinyl yesterday,' I tell him. No need to mention that she was in my bed at the time. 'She said she was sorry for telling Jack that whole thing about you stalking me. I was just talking to my ex, still a bit emotional. It came out wrong.'

'To be honest, that wasn't why I stopped seeing you,' he says. 'It was just good timing. Well, if you could call that good …'

'What are you talking about?' I ask him. 'What else did I do?'

'Well.' He leans up on the pillows, absently stroking my hair. 'You remember that festival we went to, right? When we were coming back, and you fell asleep on me in the back of the van?'

'Not really. I remember you playing Gershwin …'

'Yes. And you crashed out on me. I don't blame you, though, you'd been up for nearly two days. You and Vinyl tearing around the place. Me and Jack were struggling to keep up with you.' He turns his head away from me and looks out of the window into the milky morning light. 'You weren't asleep for long. But when we pulled in here and I tried to wake you, I believe your exact words were, 'Piss off, Kate.'

I wince. 'Sorry.'

'No need to be sorry. I just couldn't handle spending my life being called a girl's name …'

'I was asleep! For God's sake. Anyone could have done it.'

'Anyone in your situation, yes.' He looks back at me. 'You're still with her. It's been, what, almost a year now? Fine, if that's not enough time for you. But you're still hers. I can't change that and I'm not about to drive myself mad trying.'

I sigh. 'You always were a lazy bastard, Rosh.'

'Evie. I'm not serious with you very often. So just listen to me for the next two seconds. If I thought this was what you really wanted, things would be different.'

I know he's right. If we tried, if we put everything we had into this, we could turn it around, but I never thought love should work like that.

Still, it's hard to shake the sadness that settles between us, and when I finally get up and put my clothes on, it feels as though I'm going off to war.

'Are you going to be all right?' he asks, as he helps me into my coat.

'What … you mean, in general?'

He smiles ruefully. 'No, but, since you ask, are you?'

I think so, babe. How about you?'

He thinks for a moment, and then nods.

Are you going to get pissed and stand on my lawn?' I ask him.

'Probably not. How about you?'

'Yeah … don't think so.'

'Poor effort,' he says.

'Poor.'

He holds me so tight I can't breathe, but then, too quickly, lets me go.

Out in the street, I realise how little I've told him. Since we got together, I've stopped being honest with him. He doesn't know about me losing my job, or The Lump, or seeing my dad. I wonder why I'm sparing him, what I'm trying to be for him, and then I realise that I don't think I ever saw this as a relationship either. I just wanted him to be a luxury, a little sweetness, the one purely good, uncomplicated thing in my life – a hit of mango juice, the chocolate you know you shouldn't take. More than anything, I had wanted to be his friend. It still makes me sad, knowing that it couldn't stay this simple, that in the end we had so little time.

When I get back, it's mid-morning and the sky is the dense violet-blue of autumn. The house is silent. I stand in the darkened front room, take my shoes off, flex my toes against the carpet.

I admit to myself that I like it here. I like my starlet's room, the slanting ceiling that makes me feel cosy and enclosed, the tattered net canopy over the bed. I like the sound of Gray's old movies with their endless overtures drifting up the stairs, hearing her muttering lovingly at the orchestras, 'Come on, lads, what's this got to do with anything?' I like hearing her in the shower when I'm still sleepy in the mornings, watching her take off her jacket when she gets in from work, I like the sound of her laughter. I like her sweetness, always so reluctantly revealed.

Upstairs in my room, there are two letters lying on the bed, but they're not what catches my eye. It's what's sitting between them like a beautiful paperweight. The snow globe from that little boutique in Brighton. I pick it up, solid, heavy and cool in my hands. It's more beautiful than anything I've bought to reward myself for surviving in this lovely brutal city a little longer, and without knowing it, it's the only gift I've been waiting for.

There's a note with it.

Evie,

I'm sorry about this morning. I thought I was going to be here when you got back. Turns out I got called out of town for the night with work, they're paying me double-time, so, well, I'm not here. Obviously. I thought I'd leave you this and ask if you want to have dinner somewhere when I get back.

(Don't worry, I'm not asking you out. I don't know if it's possible to ask out the woman who lives in the room next to you. I think that gives me some sort of immunity).

Don't go. Unless you really want to. You know far too much about strange old movies for me to lose you this easily. I put up a fight when things matter to me. You might have noticed.

G.

PS. I'm not magic or anything. I bought this in Brighton when you weren't looking. You're not very observant when you're stressed.

I smile. I sit down on the bed and clutch the snow globe to my chest.

Then, without knowing why, I press my lips to its cool, curved side as I look at the letters – both indistinguishable at first sight, but then the one on the right gives me a strange sense of déjà vu.

I remember them. I stuffed enough envelopes that looked just like that in Medical Records, before I even knew Kate, back when all that mattered to me was paying the rent. It's been a long time since I was that carefree girl, but sitting on my bed, my bare feet tucked under me, the snow globe cupped in my palms like a miniature crystal ball, I realise that I'm closer to being that girl now than I've been in years. *You can go anywhere.* I repeat that middle-aged woman's mantra to myself, adding my own postscript. Please, God, whoever. Let me still go anywhere. Please.

Medical Records. You got to a stage when you could tell how sick, or litigious, someone was by the thickness of their files. It was grim, but there wasn't much to hold your interest unless it was idle speculation about the lives of the people whose files you held. Lots of babies, routine checks with the ink on their names barely dry, but then there were the old people, daredevils, criminals, rape victims, brides, refugees, nuns, children with paperwork from Make-A-Wish charity foundations in their files – I saw the lot.

I remember boxing up the files of the dead ones. The last one was a guy two years younger than me. I sat on the floor of the office and thought – I need to get out of this job.

I open that one first. Yes, familiar, very familiar. 'Dear MISS DAY (*Ms*, please), We would like to invite you to the BREAST SCREENING UNIT on …' God, that's in two days. I clutch the snow-globe tighter.

Benign. Almost certainly benign.

I'm alive. I repeat those two words again and again – a moronic chorus, a bridge. I want to stay that way. I think about all the things I love. Long, dreamy afternoons in the underwater light of pubs. Fabric-shop windows with bolts of gauze and winking sequins. The velvety blackness of cinemas. Duvet days. Jazz. Sitting in Vinyl's rough below-street joints with bin-end celebrities, movie marathons with Gray, dancing at Jamie's wedding, lying in bed with Roshan and breathing him in, wishing the clock would stop.

It's not perfect, God knows, but it's mine.

The other letter says what I expect it to – that they'd like to offer me the job. I put down the snow globe, place it between my knees as though I'm praying and hold one letter in each hand, as though one could cancel the other out. My insides and outsides. My past and my future.

In my head, that morbid old voice is hissing, of course you're sick. You're so twisted inside, how could you not be?

I pick up my phone and call my mother. First, I tell her the good news, and then about the screening. I don't remember exactly what I say, but in my head I hear Gray saying, 'You can't keep pushing people away. You do it to me, you do it to Vi, maybe you even do it to your mum.' Well, maybe I do. But I can always stop.

'I can't do this alone,' I say, as she's talking. I hear her stop and breathe.

'Evie,' she says eventually. 'When are you going to realise you don't have to?'

Revelations

'Mum, can you not look?' I'm topless on a slab with two women circling around me like I'm some sort of sacrifice. The younger one is swabbing my right breast with a chilly antiseptic solution. In the darkened room, I look at my breasts, rising in front of me, fragile and moon-skinned. They don't seem to want to be here either.

Pina, sitting at the side knitting something unidentifiable, raises her head briefly. 'Whatever you want, darling. But I wish mine still looked like that.'

I look up apologetically at the doctor. 'I bet you don't often see this,' I say, tilting my head towards my mother.

She smiles. 'You'd be surprised, Miss Day. Now can you try to relax, please.'

'Do you want me over there?' my mother asks softly.

My eyes sting. 'No, I'm all right.'

'I hate needles,' she mutters to no one.

'A lot of people do.' The doctor presses down lightly on my skin. 'And you're all right with them, are you, Miss Day?'

I nod. 'Well, I'm not in love with them. But no, I'm not going to faint or anything.'

'Good girl.' The doctor reminds me of one of my old teachers, the ones who used to tell me off for wearing gold-flecked lipstick in gym class. They always made me feel safe somehow. Tough, salt-and-pepper-haired, no-nonsense old birds. The kind of women you need in moments like this.

'They did explain to you that the results will take a couple of hours?' says the doctor, as the younger woman hands her a sharp implement I don't want to look at. I think of those teary faces on the children's medical charts.

'We'll just wait,' says my mother calmly. 'We're in no hurry.'

It seems ungracious to point out that we've already been waiting for hours. The waiting room is full of couples – no one is doing this alone. It's one of the quietest places on earth, and all human life is there – Muslim women in the hijab, young women with expensive handbags, older women with dandelion hair, nearly all of them gripping their partner's hands. I'm the only one who decided to bring a middle-aged woman with a knitting bag and a voice like a loudhailer, but I know I couldn't do this without her.

It's been a long, dull afternoon with me reading and Pina pointing out things that she thinks might make me laugh. We've seen a doctor, who took my blood pressure, wrote some things on her chart and asked me about my intake of cigarettes, alcohol and caffeine – a few of my favourite things.

'Now this is it, isn't it?' The doctor's fingers find The Lump. 'Could you try to relax a bit more for me, please?'

'She doesn't really relax,' Pina says. 'I'm not sure she's going to start.'

'Close to the surface,' the doctor murmurs. She raises her voice. 'It's very mobile, though. I'm having a little trouble getting the sample. Evie, can you tell me a bit about yourself, please, I need you to think about something else. When's your birthday?'

'September eighteenth.'

'Virgo,' Pina supplies. 'That's why she's a bit uptight.' I hear anxiety creep into her voice. 'You're not hurting her?'

My own voice sounds like it's coming from underwater. I'm outside myself. 'They're not hurting me, Mum.'

'We're getting there,' says the doctor. 'Now, Evie, tell me a bit about work. What do you do?'

'PR stuff. It's … you know, fun.' I hear the brittleness in my voice. 'I've actually been out of work for a while. I'm going to start a new job soon, though. Next week …'

I wonder if I've jinxed myself by saying that – like in old war movies, where the young man who's about to get blasted into a million pieces is showing the others photographs of his sweetheart.

'That's good,' says the doctor. 'Not easy at the moment out there, is it? And you like what you do?'

'Well, it's all right, but …' Suddenly, I feel something rush through me. It's like that dark big-mouthed angel who touched my cheek when I was twelve. That anarchy, that power. The words pour out of me.

'It's all right and everything I mean it pays the bills and it's sort of glamorous and I know loads of other girls would like to be in my shoes … but what I am is a singer, that's what I do, that's what I've always done … and I try to do it, I try, but I let everything else get in the way, work, relationships just plain old laziness, rather be shopping in Camden Lock than practising or writing, I'm scared that I can't write my own songs, that I have nothing left to sing about, I'm scared I'm going to be crap and that gets in the way, it gets in the way of everything but I know I can't be happy if I don't do it, it's the only thing I came here to do …'

After that burst of words, the silence seems very loud.

'Thank you,' says the doctor. 'We're in now.'

'What just happened?' I ask, staring up at the dark, faraway ceiling.

My mother's voice is dry and calm. 'I think they call it a revelation.'

We're the last two people in the waiting room. We sit together silently, my mother's knitting pooled, forgotten, in her lap. My book is open, but I haven't turned the pages in a while. We try not to stare too hard at the women as they walk out. We pray that they'll look relieved. Seeing one of them crying would be too much like bad luck.

It's like a strange audition, an identity parade. The fleshy girl with the tracksuit and tight ponytail, the bobbed middle-aged woman in a pencil skirt, the one in tweeds and an amethyst brooch who could be a grandmother or music teacher or both. What do we have in common? We're mortal. We're hurting. We're afraid.

A young couple walk out, beaming, relieved. We wait for a while longer.

'What is it with you and lateness?' my mother asks lightly.

'This isn't exactly up to me, Mum.'

'You were late for your own birth, darling.'

I've heard this story a million times, but I want to hear it again. I could be five years old, crawling into her arms on the couch, asking – tell me again how I was born. I'm almost thirty, but she's still my Mum. She starts to tell it again.

'I was so big, and so tired, I could barely walk. Your father had been tying my shoes for me for months and my hands were swollen up like boxing gloves, darling. I always had such pretty hands. The doctor said that if you didn't come along in a couple of days, they'd do a C-section, but you showed no sign of wanting to come out. I remember crying in the car on the way back from the doctor's and your Dad began to talk to you, you know, to the bump. He was telling you how wonderful it is out here.' There is no bitterness in her voice. She smiles, her face soft, as though remembering a visit to another country. 'And as soon as I got out of the car, ready to go back upstairs and just, I don't know, lie on the bed and cry some more ... well, you know what happened.'

'Your waters broke,' I say quietly. The room is now empty except for us.

'You always did listen to him,' she says, without rancour.

The nurse pops her head round the corner. 'Evie Day? Sorry for the wait. The doctor's ready to see you now.'

My mother gets up along with me, but I motion for her to sit back down. 'Mum, is it all right if I do this bit alone?'

She nods. I follow the nurse down what feels like miles of corridors. I sit in the little room with the doctor who asked me how many cups of coffee I drank a day. She offers some pleasantries which I can't listen to and then, at some point during the stream of words, in between asking if it's nice to have my mother around and giving me some pastel-coloured leaflets, she tells me I'm all right.

'Sorry?' I ask.

She smiles. 'Nothing is one hundred per cent, Miss Day, but there aren't any signs of malignancy. You can have the lump removed, if you want. There is a chance that it might cause you problems down the line, but it's a very slim chance and frankly, if you can live with it, I wouldn't go down the surgical route. I'd like you to keep checking your breasts and come back in a year for a check-up, but what you've got is really quite normal.' She smiles at me. 'Don't take that the wrong way.'

'I won't,' I say, getting up. 'Thank you.'

The corridors seem a lot shorter on the way out. Mum is all packed up now and standing in the middle of the empty waiting room. Her face drawn and anxious, under the fluorescent lights, she suddenly looks her age. When she sees me smiling, her eyes clench shut and she mutters a wordless prayer to whatever New Age deity she's channelling this week before opening them again and asking me, 'What did she say?'

'She says I'm OK.'

I bury my face in her shoulder and we drink each other in. Two single ladies with the same wild dark hair, royal bossiness and huge pride.

He was right. She was right. It is wonderful out here.

An Intelligent Man

'I can't remember the last time I had ice cream.' Pina looks dubiously at her spoon piled with sugars and additives as if it's going to poison her or report her to the hippy police.

'It just felt right.' I pick up my teddy bear wafer and lick ice cream off its feet.

'I suppose this is what we'd do when you were little. After I'd taken you to the dentist or something.' She looks around. 'I used to come here when I was a model. Did I ever tell you about that?'

'Only a few hundred times, Mum.'

She smiles. 'I didn't eat for about two years. I'd come here, have black coffee, watch some of the other girls shovelling in these massive ice-creams. I was so jealous.' She takes a spoonful of whipped cream. 'Well, my turn now.'

'Yeah, I don't know what it is about this place. This is always where I come when important things happen.' I take another bite. 'I was meant to have a photo-shoot here once. We ended up doing it in a pub instead. I didn't keep the picture. Dad's got it, though.'

'I thought for sure you'd want to go to the pub.'

I laugh, light-headed. 'I haven't ruled that out. Maybe later. No, we'll have dinner somewhere … there's a nice Italian place on the Archway Road. Been meaning to try it out.'

'You saw your Dad, then.'

I nod. I hadn't meant to drop that into the conversation.

'It's all right,' she says. 'I knew anyway. He called me the other day.'

'Did he?'

'He does sometimes, Evie. Mainly to see how you are.' She gestures vaguely at my breasts. 'I didn't go into details about this. Just said that you were having a rough time. He said you were worried you couldn't write your own songs. You do know that's basically bollocks, right?'

'Part of me does. Maybe I can. I thought he'd get it.'

She nods slowly and takes another spoonful. 'Yes. He does. He didn't write anything for two years once. That was a bad time.'

'Yeah, well …' I look down into my sundae glass. 'Guilty as charged.'

'What are you talking about, Evie? It didn't have anything to do with you.'

'Come on. I came along, disrupted everything …'

'Babies do that, darling. We were very young, but I knew it would be like that.'

The ice cream parlour's almost deserted. It's getting dark earlier these days. We sit in an island of dim gold light, surrounded by darkness, perched on our long stools like barflies at an all-night diner.

'Is that what you think?' she says. 'That you, I don't know, ruined things for us?'

I swallow hard. 'You might still be together if I hadn't come along.'

'On the contrary,' she says. 'You gave us another couple of years. It's hard to explain what happened. But it had just run its course. It wasn't your fault.'

'Even though I was a total bloody nightmare?'

'You weren't! Where are you getting this?' The colour's back in her cheeks now and she looks like her old self – an angry, tangle-haired queen. 'I certainly never said anything like that. And as far as I know, neither did your dad. Yes, he's got his demons, and a lot of them were there before I even met him. But he adores you. He's not perfect. Neither of us are. We might be a couple of mad old hippy bastards, but we still love each other, in our own imperfect way, and we will always love you. Whatever you are. Whoever you sleep with. Whatever you do.'

I sit there, silently, taking that all in. Another weight lifted. She's been saying this to me for a long time. It's just that this time I choose to believe it.

'He wants to see you,' she says. 'He'd like you to call him.'

I turn to her. 'Do you think I should?'

'Not my call, darling. But yes, if it was up to me, I'd give it a go.' She takes one last mouthful of ice cream. 'He's an intelligent man, after all. And like I said, you always did listen to him.' She pushes the glass away. 'Right. Italian, did you say?'

When we get back to the house, Mum busies herself in the kitchen. Thankfully, despite her no-nonsense demeanour, Gray is enough of a lesbian to have herbal tea. I can tell she's in from her keys on the table by the door, so I do something I've never done in the past six months – I knock on her door. She opens the door, smiling warily, her hair slightly messy and her face softened as if she's been taking a nap.

Suddenly, I'm shy. I don't believe it. The one thing that never happens to me. I'm the girl who got groped in a short, frothy skirt in a Soho burlesque house, who monopolised the stage in a karaoke bar last week accompanied by a stripper, dancing in a way that, in a different part of town, might have got us both arrested. I'm the girl who chases her parents' old hippy dreams through the countryside, guitar slung over her shoulder, staggering over the hills in high heels into this weekend's nirvana. And now, in my own home, with the girl who regularly sees me in my pyjamas, I'm shy.

'Thanks for the snowstorm,' I say.

She smiles, playing politely along. 'You're welcome. I was looking for the right moment. I hope that was it.' She blinks and looks at me more closely. 'You look great. Bit of colour in your cheeks for once.'

'It's cold outside.'

'Ah, that would be it, then.'

We stand, smiling at each other. It feels like that moment. Out in the street, outside the Boudoir Café with its green-tea walls, Kate holding the door for me, waiting. A moment beyond words, where you can only laugh.

'Not packing your bags then, are you?' she asks.

'Actually, I've got something to ask you.'

'Go on.'

'Grace Miller,' I say, using her full name, because after all, this is serious, 'Do you want to meet my Mum?'

In the restaurant, the handsome Italian waiters flirt with my mother and bring us little snacks that reminds her of the workers' cafes in Rome and Venice that she and my Dad used to love; tiny pizzas layered with black-edged aubergine discs and striped with fennel, discs of polenta, tomato slices rich as red velvet. Pina, looking beautiful again in the candlelight, raises a glass of red wine in a toast.

'To life,' she says. 'Which goes on. Scary, isn't it?'

If I was more than I think I am, more than the sum of the things that happened to me, who would I be? The three of us clink glasses. My life, apparently, is going to go on a while longer. I'm terrified. In a good way.

We walk Pina to the Tube station, and walk back together. It really is getting cold. Beneath us, the street is spangled with tiny crystals of frost like sequins on soft dark gauze.

'Thanks for that,' says Gray, her breath making thin white vapour in the air. 'I liked meeting your Mum. She's a laugh.'

'Yeah. Very beautiful, too, isn't she?'

Gray shrugs. 'A fine-looking woman for her age, yeah, but not a patch on you.'

It's the first time she's said anything like that.

'She was, when she was younger. I always wanted to be skinny like her. Elegant.'

'You're gorgeous, Evie,' she says, almost crossly.

As we turn into our street, she takes my hand, holding it like it's a glass slipper, something unbearably precious and unique. I give her fingers a squeeze, my icy breath catching in my throat.

'Is this okay?' she asks, her voice hushed.

'It's very okay.' Moving a little bit faster, we walk up to the front door.

Morning breaks over us. I turn over and see Gray opening her eyes. 'Hey,' she says.

'Hey.'

'I think this is a lesbian record,' she says. 'You moved in before you slept with me. Most of them at least wait for the second date.'

I laugh. 'You don't think this was a mistake, do you?'

'Actually, Evie, surprisingly, no.' She looks at the clock radio next to the bed. 'Ah, the joys of flexi-time. You don't have to be anywhere, do you?'

'Not till this afternoon.'

'Good.' She kisses her way down my neck, halting slightly when she reaches the blue plaster on my breast. She presses her lips to it gently. 'Does it hurt?'

'No,' I tell her. 'Not any more.'

Angeletti's is one of the last, best coffee-houses in Soho. It's cold as I clack up to the door in my new cowboy boots – which hurt like hell but I'm determined to break them in. I've just walked past the offices of Willow PR, imagining myself there. It's good to be back. It's good to be in Soho, at the centre of things again with the confused tourists and the plastic pants and bras in the windows, the cakes like jewels in Maison Bertaux, the slopping, overpriced pints of coffee, the junkies, the whores, the actors outside the French House with their broken veins and laughable hats ... but I know that, no matter how much I love the so-called glamour of it all, there are more important things.

I see him before he sees me, sitting at a table in the window. He's come prepared. Next to him on the table there's a stack of slim, battered books – none of them, thankfully, his own – and something that makes me smile, an equally tired-looking rhyming dictionary. So he doesn't just pluck those words out of the ether, then.

Next to the books, there's a small, round portable CD player – the kind that went out of style a couple of years ago, or maybe never really came in – and a neat pile of CD cases. All the women that lazy reviewers have ever compared me to, and a couple of others I don't recognise. He looks older today than he did last week, somehow, as he raises his eyes to me under those wild black brows.

He doesn't bother with, 'Hello.'

'You know something,' he said. 'I always wanted to be a rock star. But, I'm a poet. A good poet, or so they tell me, but some days I still wish I'd been a rock star.' He smiles as I sit down. 'Let's see what we can do for you.'

'Dad …' I begin, but I don't know what to say, what to tell him first.

'No. Give me a minute.'

He looks at me steadily.

'I think about you all the time,' he says.

I bring out the notebook I've been scribbling disjointed lines in all year.

It's the coldest day of the year. Getting over you will happen eventually. Getting over hope is hard.

'I thought … if we wanted to have something of me in there … it might be a start?'

'Oh, I think we definitely want something of you.' The waiter brings us coffee, and we settle in for the afternoon. He smiles at me with my eyes.

'Right,' he says, picking up a book. 'Are you familiar with Pablo Neruda?'

Epilogue

Advent

'Great boots,' she says. I recognise her voice; of course I do.

I turn around. 'All right?' I ask her.

'Yeah.' She nods. As though she hadn't been sure until now. 'You?'

I smile at Kate. A real, unforced smile.

'I'm great. How'd you know I'd be here?'

'Well, you are on the posters,' she says.

I look around. This isn't my gig – but over on the far wall, there's a huge black and white picture of me. Bare shoulders, smudged eyes, wrapped in white like a recently fallen angel. It's a great picture, the pain in my eyes contrasting with my softened post-coital smile.

He did ask my permission, of course, in one of the shortest and most awkward phone conversations I'd had in a while, but even though he'd warned me, it was still a shock seeing my own face, blown up to twenty times its size, staring at me from the side of an underground platform.

Kate looks good. She's no longer got that car-crash look.

'Bastard,' I say, gesturing to Roshan's photographs. No brides, this time, but there are some I recognise. A tulip, its tired petals swirling like a ball gown; a terrier chasing pigeons in Trafalgar Square. The earrings I left at his place, nestled like little moons in his big, dry palm. A vase full of dead irises. 'He made it before me. I always told him.'

'Have you said hello to him yet?'

'Can't get near him. But I will.'

I've got my cowboy boots to protect me from the cold, and an old fake fur, but under that I'm wearing a gauzy red dress and sheer stockings, a green tasselled boa around my neck. I suppose I must look like Miss Claus, but after all, I am looking forward to Christmas this year. Even this oh-so-hip gallery's serving mulled wine as well as champagne, and the air is charged with celebration – not just for Roshan and his fellow Young British Artists, but for all of us, for making it through another year.

'You'll make it too,' says Kate. 'I've got no doubt about that.'

'How's Cathy?' I try to say it without malice. I'm not sure it works.

'She's all right.' She looks sober, but not anxious. 'We're getting on better now.'

'That's good.' I look back at the picture of myself on the far wall.

'How about you and Gray? Jamie tells me she's never seen you so happy.'

'We're fine. Both of us have our last days at work tomorrow, which is great. We've been busy as hell, but we're nearly all set for Christmas. So, yeah, it's good.'

Gray is at home with Vinyl, who's staying with us after she decided she wasn't having a psychotic break, she just really didn't want to marry Jack. She gave him back the ring and moved back into her old room; I'm in Gray's room all the time now, and we could use the little extra she gives us for the rent. I like it, waking up on chilly mornings, hearing Vi stirring – she's a light sleeper – in the dusky pink satin sheets that always suited her better than me. She's thrown herself properly into Christmas, making glittery decorations of hearts and candy-canes, and she's promised me my own hat this Christmas, to wear on stage when I finally start doing burlesque with her. I'm thinking about it, but right now, I'm busy just practising my songs so they're ready to record in the New Year.

Last Sunday night, I was in the kitchen, cooking. Gray had just opened a bottle of wine. Vi was sitting in the living room, taking a break from her endless Christmas decorations to read aloud from one of her celebrity gossip magazines, 'Daisy Jones says, 'I don't want to be seen as a sex kitten,' – well, don't worry, love, you're not.' I'd just put some bittersweet blues on the CD player and the onions were simmering to themselves, the dark windows clouding with steam. Gray's fingers lightly traced the small of my back, then touched my neck where I'd pulled my hair out of the way.

'It's all right, this,' she said, 'isn't it?'

It is.

'I've got to go in a minute,' Kate says. 'I just wanted to see you.'

'She doesn't know you're here, does she?'

She smiles ruefully and shrugs. 'I don't see any point in complicating things. Hard enough for her that the gallery's put my ex's face on the back of a bus.'

'I don't know. I'd say that was a comedy goldmine.'

She laughs, and we hold each other close. We know this may not be our last ending. We know we didn't always manage to be kind to each other, that we let things slide, that we weren't always good at love.

Once she's gone, I think about the day that I'll forgive her. It hasn't happened yet, but it will. I'll wake up and I won't feel it any more and maybe I'll let her know and maybe I won't, and either way, it'll be all right.

I stand alone for a while, until I'm sure she's gone, holding a glass of mulled wine that's growing cold and bitter. Suddenly, I feel ridiculous. I came here feeling like the star, his muse, but all I am is that mascara-smeared girl on the wall. I decide I've waited for him long enough.

I'm half-way down the stairs when I hear him call my name. I turn – I can't help it. Something about him will always do this to me.

'You're leaving?' he asks. 'You can't just go without saying goodbye.'

'Yeah. Imagine that.' I know it's a cheap shot, but he deserves it.

We stand at the bottom of the stairs, looking at each other.

'Outside,' he says. 'Come on.'

'It's freezing.'

'I know. But it's beautiful. Come on.' His hand is already on the door.

We stand in the cold and look at each other. At least I've got my coat. He doesn't. He's wearing a new shirt – a rich dark purple – and his hair's brushed back in a way that looks almost neat. There's a new, professional gloss there I hadn't seen before. He looks smart. He looks grown up. And there's something different about his face.

'You got glasses. Finally.'

He shrugs. 'Yeah, well, getting on a bit, you know.'

'They suit you.' I point up at the lit windows. 'Check you out. You've arrived.'

'Hell of a year.'

'It has been, hasn't it?'

'I miss you,' he says.

I reach for his cold hands.

'I know,' I say, because I do.

He shivers – it could be pleasure at having me touch him, or he could just be freezing. 'You're so warm,' he says. 'I'll always remember that.'

I lean into him and rest my head against his chest, listening for the steady pendulum of his heart. I look up into the black sky.

'Cold enough for snow,' he says.

'Coldest day of the year. Or so they're saying. You should get back inside.'

'Evie, can I see you some time?'

'Some time. Yeah. Not for a while, though.'

'OK.' He nods. 'That makes sense.'

He pauses in the doorway for a while. 'We'll always have Doris,' he says.

I laugh. I can't help it. 'Doris Day, I presume? Rosh, that was terrible.'

'I know.'

'Can I ask you something?'

'Sure.'

'Do you regret it?'

'No. Never. How about you?'

I think about it for a moment, and shake my head.

He goes back inside, but I can feel him watching me until I turn away and set off down the street. I huddle into my fur coat, eager to get home.

It takes me a while to realise what was so special about him. It wasn't so much that I'd loved a man, but even in my twisted state I'd taken that leap of faith. He would always be the one who reminded me I wasn't broken.

I cross the road into Piccadilly. It has, indeed, been a hell of a year. I began it with one life, which I thought was perfect, and ended it with another – which isn't, but it's a relief not to be seeking perfection any more, to have stepped out of my snow-globe.

I'm open now, with all the dangers that brings, and all the joys. I've got a lover, a home, a pair of cowboy boots, and ten new songs with all the pain and fear tempered with beauty, the words that my father guided me towards on cold afternoons in a coffee shop, the way we once searched the night sky, giving names to the stars.

The centre of town is full of light, even in the winter darkness, the electric banners of Piccadilly Circus blinking on and off, screens glowing, fading, glowing again.

And Princess Eve put on her red coat, and she walked out into the snow. No snow yet, but I can smell it. People rush past me, teeth glinting in the dark as they turn to their friends, faces framed with hoods, all of us in the grip of a communal, childlike excitement. Fragments of conversation flood the air.

God, it's cold!

That bloke chatting you up, I bet he was loaded!… did you get his number?

Oh my days…

Right, where next? Where are we going?

I smile to myself. The lights change. I step off the pavement and into the battered, lit-up heart of the city. I move on.

ACKNOWLEDGEMENTS

I want to thank everyone at Limehouse Books, particularly my publisher, Bobby Nayyar, Emily Foster for her invaluable design work, Rukhsana Yasmin for editing the text, and Kerry Hyndman for creating the perfect cover.

Much appreciation to the following artists and impresarios for their support over the years: Paul Burston, Helen Sandler, Stella Duffy, V.G. Lee, Jen Roberts, Salena Godden, Russell Thompson, Sarah Ellis, Kat Francois, Roddy Lumsden and Tim Wells.

Love and thanks to: Elizabeth Geary, Ella Genty, Catherine Godfrey, Helen Higginbottom, Simon Hughes, David Will Holloway, Aimee Kleinman, Liz Langstaff, Caz Marshall, Nancy and Kerry-Anne Mendoza, and Carey Wood-Duffy, my Security.

Most of all, I want to thank my parents Christina and David for all their love and support.

ABOUT LIMEHOUSE BOOKS

Limehouse Books is an independent publisher of quality fiction and non-fiction. Founded in October 2009 – originally under the name Glasshouse Books – we have grown to publish eight print titles, with two more to come in 2012, as well as one iPhone app.

Uniquely we commission every title we publish and obtain World English Language rights in both print and digital. Our aim is to be a small, focussed publishing house with a global reach. We have an eclectic list of titles, all of them with one unifying characteristic:

Books that are beautifully designed and produced, printed to respect the environment and published for me, you, everyone.

A LIMEHOUSE BOOKS PUBLICATION

Written by Sophia Blackwell
Cover illustration by Kerry Hyndman
Design by Emily Foster
Managed by Bobby Nayyar
Typeset in Arno Pro and Apex New
First published 8.03.2012

ISBN 978-1-907536-29-8

Limehouse Books
58 Glasshouse Fields
Flat 30, London E1W 3AB
limehousebooks.co.uk

Printed and bound in Great Britain by TJ International Ltd, Padstow, Cornwall

LIMEHOUSE BOOKS 2012 TITLES

AFTER MY OWN HEART

THE RULES OF POKER

INTO TEMPTATION
PUBLISHED BY TOLLINGTON PRESS

Into Temptation is the debut collection of poems from Sophia Blackwell, a regular on the UK poetry scene who has been holding crowds spellbound in bars, nightclubs and festival tents.

Sophia takes us through love in all its guises – burning obsession, one-night stands that last too long, domestic bliss, and the insecurities in even the most loving relationships. Here also is a series of elegies for the everyday – the quiet, mysterious pleasures of Tube journeys, cats, and spaghetti sauce.

Into Temptation is all lipstick, corsets and hedonistic jazz-fuelled rhythms, raging against and revelling in life.

'Blackwell's poems deliver what poetry usually only promises … astonishingly intricate, precise, witty, self-aware and formally complete.'
Will Holloway

'Her brilliant rhymes turn me on and make me laugh simultaneously. Her "f*** it" attitude is infectious – you can't help but like her.'
Spoonfed London

'Some of Sophia Blackwell's poems read like Nico should be singing them to John Cale's viola, some as if Shakespeare's slut sister taught him all he knew, while others are as new as the next dawn. Dirty, juicy, knowing and open – works for me.'
Stella Duffy

Available from online retailers.

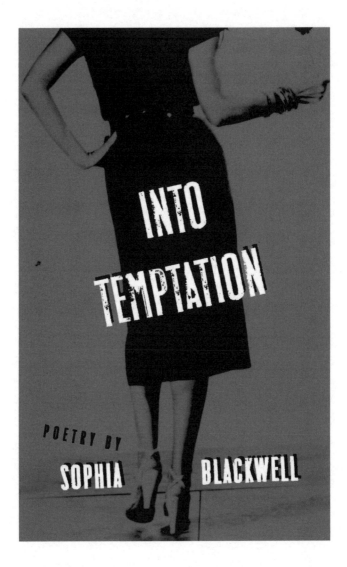

INTO
TEMPTATION

POETRY BY

SOPHIA   BLACKWELL

Me. You. Everyone.

limehousebooks.co.uk

P